HALFWAY HOUSE

SELECT NOVELS BY ELLERY QUEEN

The Roman Hat Mystery

The French Powder Mystery

The Dutch Shoe Mystery

The Greek Coffin Mystery

The Egyptian Cross Mystery

The American Gun Mystery

The Siamese Twin Mystery

The Chinese Orange Mystery

The Spanish Cape Mystery

*Halfway House**

*The Door Between**

*The Devil To Pay**

*The Four of Hearts**

The Dragon's Teeth

Calamity Town

*There Was an Old Woman**

*The Murderer Is a Fox**

Ten Days' Wonder

Cat of Many Tails

Double, Double

The Origin of Evil

The King Is Dead

*The Scarlet Letters**

The Glass Village

Inspector Queen's Own Case
    (November Song)

*The Finishing Stroke**

The Player on the Other Side

And On the Eighth Day

The Fourth Side of the Triangle

A Study in Terror: Sherlock Holmes
    versus Jack the Ripper

*Face to Face**

*Available as a JABberwocky Edition

ELLERY QUEEN

HALFWAY HOUSE

Published by JABberwocky Literary Agency, Inc.

DRAMATIS PERSONAE

THE NEW YORKERS

Borden, Jasper
Finch, Grosvenor
Frueh, Senator Simon
Gimball, Andrea
Gimball, Jessica Borden
Gimball, Joseph Kent
Jones, Burke

THE PHILADELPHIANS

Angell, William
Wilson, Joseph
Wilson, Lucy

THE TRENTONIANS

Amity, Ella
De Jong, (Chief) Ira
Pollinger, (Prosecutor) Paul

I

THE TRAGEDY

"... the play is the tragedy, 'Man',
And its hero the Conqueror Worm."

TRENTON IS THE capital of New Jersey. According to the census of 1930 it has a population—man, woman, and child—of 123,356. Originally it was called Trent's Town, after William Trent the royal magistrate. (Did you know that, Mr. Kloppenheimer?) On the Delaware, of course. Most beautiful damned river in the whole United States."

The dried-up little man nodded cautiously.

"Delaware? Say, this is the place where George Washington licked the daylights out of those, now, Hessians. Christmas of 1776, it was," continued the large fat man, burying his proboscis in the clay tankard, "in a terrible storm. Old George got his boys into boats and sneaked across the Delaware and caught those Hessian baby-killers with their pants off. Didn't lose a man—that's history. And where was this? Trenton, Mr. Kloppenheimer, Trenton!"

Mr. Kloppenheimer rubbed his dry little jaw and mumbled something placative.

"Why," said the fat man, smacking the tankard down, "do you know what? Trenton was once almost the site of the national capital! Fact. Congress met right here in this little old burg in '84, Mr. Kloppenheimer, and voted to lay out a Federal city on either side of the river!"

"But," pointed out Mr. Kloppenheimer timidly, "the Capitol's in Washington."

The fat man jeered. "Politics, Mr. Kloppenheimer. Why…"

The large person, who looked eerily like Herbert Hoover, had been singing the glory that was Trenton into the desiccated ears of Mr. Kloppenheimer for some time. Fascinated, the spare young man in pince-nez glasses at the next table had divided his energies between the pig's knuckle and sauerkraut before him and the monologue beside him. It took no Poesque power of ratiocination to conclude that the fat man was selling something to the timid man; but what? The city of Trenton? It seemed improbable…. Then he heard Mr. Kloppenheimer utter the word "hops" and again the word "barley" in reverent breaths, and the mist lifted. Mr. Kloppenheimer clearly represented brewing interests, and the fat man no doubt was spokesman for the local Chamber of Commerce. "Ideal location for a brewery," beamed the fat man. "Ah, there, Senator! Now, look here, Mr. Kloppenheimer…"

The mystery solved, the spare young man stopped listening. Notwithstanding the knuckle and stein before him, puzzles were his meat and drink; and there was no riddle too lean for his appetite. And the fat man had helped while away a half hour. For despite the male crowd in the small taproom of the Stacy-Trent, with its horsy red-and-white cloths and its clink of glassware behind the wooden screen, he felt a stranger in a strange land. In the shadow of the gilt-domed Capitol on West State Street, the Stacy-Trent was frequented by men who spoke another language; the air crackled with legislative talk—and he did not know a bloc from a caucus! The spare young man sighed. He signaled the waiter, ordered deep-dish apple pie and coffee, and consulted his wristwatch. Eight forty-two. Not bad. He—"

"Ellery Queen, you old ferret!"

Startled, he looked up to find a man as tall and spare and young as himself chuckling down at him, hand outstretched. "Why, Bill Angell," said Ellery, with delight in his voice. "I trust these failing eyes of mine aren't playing tricks. Bill! Sit down, sit down. Where the deuce have you sprung from? Waiter, another stein! How on earth—"

"One at a time," laughed the young man, dropping into a chair. "Still as quick on the trigger as ever, I see. I poked my head in here to spot some one I knew, and it took me a full minute to recognize you, you ugly Hibernian. How've you been?"

"This way and that. I thought you lived in Philadelphia."

"So I do. I'm down here on a private matter. Still sleuthing?"

"The fox changes his skin," quoth Ellery, "but not his habits. Or would you prefer it in Latin? My classics used to irritate you."

"The same old Ellery. What are you doing in Trenton?"

"Passing through. I've been down Baltimore way on a case. Well, well, Bill Angell. It's been a long time."

"Damned near eleven years. At that, the fox hasn't changed much." Angell's black eyes were steady and controlled; but Ellery fancied that the pleasure on their surface covered a certain lurking worry. "How about me?"

"Wrinkles at the corners of the eyes," said Ellery critically. "A mastiff set to the jaw that wasn't there, and a pinch to those very sensitive nostrils. Hair microscopically thinner at the temples. A pocket bursting with sharpened pencils—that denotes at least a receptivity to labor; clothes are careless, unpressed, and well-cut as ever; an air of self-confidence mixed with what might be termed a quivering qui vive… Bill, you've grown older."

"There," said Angell, "is a deduction."

"But you're essentially the same. Still the little boy smarting at the injustices of the world and lashing back. And a very handsome dog. Bill, I've been reading things about you."

Angell flushed and picked up his stein. "The usual tripe. They never stop dishing it out. That Curry will case was a lucky break."

"Lucky your foot! I followed it closely. Sampson—the DA in New York County—tells me it was the most brilliant piece of legal research in a year. He predicts a future for you."

The young man calmly drank some beer. "Not in this rich man's world. Future?" He shrugged. "I'll probably finish behind the eight-ball, pleading small-claims cases before some liverish old goat with halitosis."

"Always on the defensive. I recall you used to have the most chronic inferiority complex on the campus."

"The poor man hasn't a—" Angell showed his small white teeth in a grin. "Lay off, you mug. You're baiting me. How's the Inspector? I loved that old bird."

"He's very well, thanks. Married, Bill?"

"No, thank you. All the poor wenches I know think I'm screwy; and you've no idea what I think of the wealthy ones."

"I've known some that were passable," sighed Ellery. "And how is that charming sister of yours?"

"Lucy's doing nicely. She's married, of course. To a traveling man—Joe Wilson. Very decent chap; doesn't drink, smoke, gamble, or beat his wife. You'd like him." Angell looked at his watch. "I suppose you don't remember Lucy very well."

"Don't I! I recall how smitten my poor adolescent heart used to be. Botticelli would have gone into fits over her."

"She's still a stunner. Lives over in Fairmont Park in a modest little private house. Joe's done pretty well—for a bourgeois."

"Now, now," said Ellery chidingly. "What line is he in?"

"Cheap jewelry. Trinkets. Gewgaws." Bill's voice was bitter. "I'm afraid I gave you the wrong impression. To tell the truth, Lucy's husband is on his own, and he's little more than an itinerant peddler. Oh, he deserves credit; he has no family and he's pulled himself up by his non-existent bootstraps. One of our self-made men. But I always thought my sister would do better than…" He scowled.

"What on earth's wrong about a man who makes his living going from place to place selling honest merchandise? You damned snob!"

"Oh, it's honest enough. And I suppose I am a fool. He's madly in love with Lu, and she with him; and he's always provided for her very handsomely. The trouble with me is that lean and hungry look Caesar mentioned."

"You have a case."

"Lord love you! I've a guilty conscience, that's all. My apartment's in the heart of town and I don't get out to see Lucy very often. I've been beastly about it; Joe's on the road most of the time, and she must get lonesome as the devil."

"Oh," said Ellery. "Then it's woman trouble you suspect?"

Bill Angell studied his hands. "My dear old friend, I see it's still futile trying to keep anything from you; you always were a magician in these matters. The trouble is that he's away so much. Four, five days a week. It's been that way for ten years—ever since they got married. He has a car, of course, and I've no reason except my own blasted suspicious nature to believe that he stays away on anything but business…" He looked at his watch again. "Look here, Ellery, I've got to be going. I've an appointment with my brother-in-law not far from here for nine, and it's ten to now. When are you pushing on to New York?"

"As soon as I can breathe life into old Duesey again."

"The Duesenberg! Lord, have you still got that ancient chariot? I thought you'd donated it to the Smithsonian long ago. How would you like a companion on your trip back to the city?"

"Bill! That's handsome of you."

"Can you wait an hour or so?"

"All night, if you say so."

Bill rose and said slowly: "Joe shouldn't take long." He paused. When he continued it was in a casual tone. "I was intending to run down to New York tonight anyway; tomorrow's Sunday, and I've a New York client who can't be seen at any other time. I'll leave my car in Trenton. Where will you be?"

"In the lobby yonder. You'll stay over with Dad and me tonight?"

"Love to. See you in an hour."

Mr. Ellery Queen relaxed, watching the wedge-like back of his friend vanish past the coatroom girl. Poor Bill! He had always shifted to his own broad shoulders the burdens of others… Ellery wondered for a moment what lay behind Bill's appointment with his brother-in-law. Then, shrugging, he told himself that it was very clearly none of his business, and he ordered another cup of coffee. In the dumps or out of it, he reflected as he waited, Bill would be a tonic; and in the young man's company the ninety-minute drive to the Holland Tunnel would doubtless dwindle to nothing.

And that, strangely enough, was its fate. For, although Mr. Ellery Queen was at the moment unaware of it, neither he nor Mr. William Angell, young Philadelphia attorney, was destined to leave Trenton at all that mild Saturday night, the first of June.

Bill Angell's aged Pontiac coupé puffed along the deserted Lamberton Road, which paralleled the eastern shore of the Delaware River. It was a narrow road, and his dimmers shimmered on the puddles in the black and rubbly macadam. A warm rain had fallen in the afternoon and, although it had stopped just before seven o'clock, the road and the bleak stretches of dump and field on his left were still muddy. A few lights blinked pallidly on the river to the west, where Moon Island lay; to the east the uneven terrain was gray and flat, like paint.

Bill slowed down as he passed a long bulky mass of buildings on the riverside, the Marine Terminal. It was not far from here, he thought. According to Joe's instructions… He knew the road well;

he had often taken it in traveling by automobile from Philadelphia to Trenton by way of the Camden bridge. In the vicinity of the Marine Terminal there was nothing but dreary dumping-ground; the Sewage Disposal Plant on the east had effectively spoiled the section for housing development, and there were no dwellings in the neighborhood. The directions had been specific: a few hundred yards past the Marine Terminal, reckoning from Trenton....

He trod on his brake. To the right, toward the river, on the narrow shore between Lamberton Road and the water polished to sullen steel by the quarterlight of deep dusk, stood a building with dimly glowing windows.

The Pontiac snuffled and stopped. Bill examined the scene with fixity. The structure, black against the river, was little more than a shack—a random, dilapidated affair of weather-beaten clapboards, with a sagging roof half-denuded of its shingles and a crumbling chimney. It was set well back, approached in rather grotesque grandeur by a semicircular driveway which led from Lamberton Road past the house in an arc and back to the road. In the shadows of near night, there was something repellent about the place. An empty roadster of huge dimensions stood directly before the closed door of the shack, almost on its stone step. The snout of the silent monster faced him. Bill twisted about like a suspicious animal, searching the thick dark blue murk for other details. That car... Lucy ran a small car; she'd always had a runabout for herself—Joe was considerate enough, and he seemed to realize how much alone she was; and Joe himself ran an ancient but serviceable Packard. But this was overpowering, a magnificent sixteen-cylinder Cadillac with, he thought, a special body. Oddly, for all its bulk, there was something feminine in its appearance; it seemed in the murk to be the color of cream, and he could just make out its multiplicity of chromium gadgets. A rich woman's sporting car...

Then Bill spied his brother-in-law's Packard drawn up to face the side of the shack nearer him; and for the first time he noticed a second driveway, this one an unkempt dirt lane, branching off Lamberton Road a few feet in front of his car. The lane, a welter of mud, did not touch the exit of the semicircular drive, but skirted it and curved slightly inwards to lead to a second door in the side of the house. Two drives, two doors, two cars…

Bill Angell sat very still. The night was pacific, its silence accentuated by the sawing of crickets, the faint chug of a motor on the river, the hum of his own engine. Except for the Marine Terminal and a small watchman's house facing it Bill had passed no dwelling since leaving the outskirts of Trenton; and as far as he could see beyond the shack stretched flat deserted country. This was the meeting-place.

How long he sat there he did not know; but suddenly the evening quiet exploded, touched off by a horrible sound. Bill's heart convulsed in warning before his senses became conscious of the nature of the cry. It had been a scream, and it had been torn from a woman's throat: a single protest of outraged vocal chords released from the paralysis of fear all at once, like a plucked string let go. It was short and sharp, and it died away as unexpectedly as it had been born. It came to Bill Angell, sitting in the Pontiac frozen to the wheel, that it was the first time he had ever heard a woman scream. Something inside him responded with a quiver, and he felt it with a sensation of pure astonishment. At the same moment, and for no conscious reason, his eyes went to the watch on his wrist and he read the time in the light of his dashboard. It was eight minutes after nine.

But he glanced up quickly; the light before him had subtly changed. The front door had flown open; he heard the bang as it struck against the inner wall of the shack. A prism of light bathed the side of the roadster before the stone step. Then it was partially blotted out by a figure. Bill half-rose behind his wheel, straining to see. The figure was a woman's, and her hands were before her face as if to shut out the sight of something obscene. She stood there for only an instant, a silhouette the details of which were indistinguishable. With the light behind her and her figure in darkness, she might have been young or old; there was a slenderness about her that was ambiguous. He could make out no details of her dress. This woman had screamed. And she had fled from the shack as if sick and blind with loathing.

Then she saw the Pontiac, and sprang toward the big roadster, clawing at the door. She was in the car in a flash. The Cadillac roared forward toward him. It swept along the curve of the semicircular drive; it was only when it was almost upon him that his muscles came to life. He jerked the Pontiac into first speed and twisted the wheel to the right. The Pontiac plunged into the muddy lane leading to the side of the house.

Their hubs rasped against each other. The Cadillac swung out, careening on two wheels. For the sheer instant that the two drivers were side by side Bill saw that the woman's gloved right hand was clutching a handkerchief, and that the handkerchief covered her face. Her eyes were wild and wide above the fabric. Then she and the roadster were gone, roaring down Lamberton Road toward Trenton and in a twinkling swallowed by the darkness. It would be futile, Bill knew, to follow her.

Dazed, he drove the Pontiac along the muddy side-lane and brought it to rest beside his brother-in-law's old Packard, conscious that his hands were clammy with sweat. He shut off his motor and stepped from the running-board to a small wooden-floored porch at the side of the shack. The door was slightly ajar. He braced himself and pushed it open.

Blinking in the light, he made out only the general features of the interior. He stood in a low-ceilinged room with discolored walls from which the plaster had in many places dropped off. He became aware of an old-fashioned telescopic clothes-rack on the opposite wall, draped with men's suits, of a dingy iron sink in a corner, of a naked and crypt-like old fireplace, of a round central table with an electric lamp on it from which the only light in the room emanated. There was no bed, no bunk, no stove, no closet. A few decrepit chairs and one overstuffed armchair which sagged badly… Bill stiffened.

A man was lying on the floor behind the table. He could see two trousered legs, crooked at the knees. There was something about those two legs that suggested death.

Bill Angell stood still where he was, just inside the side door, slowly thinking things out. His mouth was hard. It was very quiet in the shack. He felt the overwhelming loneliness of his position. People who breathed were far away, and laughter was a remote and inconceivable luxury. The curtains at the windows rustled a little in the breeze from the Delaware… One of the legs moved. Bill watched it move with a dull and impersonal surprise. He found himself moving, too, across the carpeted floor of the shack to the table and beyond.

The man was lying on his back, glassy eyes staring up at the ceiling. His hands, peculiarly gray, scratched at the carpet like talons in a slow and patient digital exercise. His tan sack-coat was open and the white shirt above his heart was almost gaily splashed with blood. Bill dropped to his knees and with the same surprise heard his voice, which sounded unfamiliar to his ears, say: "Joe. For God's sake, Joe." He did not touch his brother-in-law's body.

The glaze was drowned in the man's eyes. They crept sidewise in a stealthy manner until they came to rest.

"Bill."

"Water—?"

The gray fingers scratched more quickly. "No. Too… Bill, I'm dying."

"Joe, who—"

"Woman. Woman." The broken voice stopped, but the mouth continued to move, lips curling and closing, tongue rising and falling. Then the voice succeeded again: "Woman."

"What woman, Joe? Joe, for God's sake!"

"Woman. Veil. Heavy veil—face. Couldn't see. Knifed me… Bill, Bill."

"Who in the name of hell—"

"Love—Lucy. Bill, take care of Lu…."

"Joe!"

The mouth stopped moving, the lips uncurled, the tongue trembled and was still. The glaze returned to the eyes, which continued to stare at Bill with the same savage wonder and agony. Then Bill was conscious that the fingers had stopped scratching. He got stiffly to his feet and walked out of the shack.

*

Mr. Ellery Queen was sprawled comfortably under a palm in the lobby of the Stacy-Trent, eyes closed over his fuming brier, when he heard a voice bellowing his name. He opened his eyes in astonishment to find a boy in the forest-green and maroon livery of the hotel shuffling past. "Boy! Here."

The lobby was jammed, and a peacock's tail of eyes regarded him with curiosity. His name had rung through the verdant room, and he beckoned the attendant in some annoyance. "Mistuh Queen? Telephone."

Ellery tossed the boy a coin and made his way, frowning, to the desk. Among the heads that had jerked up at the attendant's bawl was that of a red-haired young woman in a brown tweed suit. With a queer quirk of the lips she rose and quickly followed Ellery. Her long legs flashed noiselessly over the marble floor.

Ellery picked up the telephone. The young woman took up a position a few feet behind him, turned her back, opened her handbag, extracted a lipstick, and began to paint her painted mouth.

"Bill?"

"Thank God."

"Bill! What's the matter?"

"Ellery… I can't go back to New York with you tonight. I—Could you possibly—?"

"Bill, something's happened."

"God, yes." The lawyer paused for a moment, and Ellery heard him clear his throat three times. "Ellery, it's simply—it's a nightmare. It can't have happened. My brother-in-law… He's been—he's dead."

"Good Lord!"

"Murdered. Stuck in the chest like a—like a damned pig."

"Murdered!" Ellery blinked. The young woman behind him stiffened as if she had received an electric shock. Then she hunched her shoulders and applied her lipstick furiously. "Bill… Where are you? When did this happen?"

"Don't know. Not long ago. He was still alive when I got there. He said… Then he died. Ellery… these things just don't happen to your own people. How am I going to break it to Lucy?"

"Bill," said Ellery insistently, "stop wool-gathering. Listen to me. Have you notified the police?"

"No…. No."

"Where are you?"

"In the watchman's house across the road from the Marine Terminal. Ellery, you've got to help us!"

"Of course, Bill. How far from the Stacy-Trent is this place?"

"Three miles. You'll come? Ellery, you'll come?"

"At once. Tell me how to get there. Shortest way. Clearly now, Bill. You've got to get a grip on yourself."

"I'm all right. I'm all right." Over the wire came the sound of his breath, a shuddering inhalation like the lung-filling gasp of a newborn infant. "Easiest way… Yes. You're on the East State and South Willow now. Where are you parked?"

"In a garage behind the hotel. Front Street, I think."

"Drive east on Front for two squares. You'll hit South Broad. Turn right, go past the courthouse, right again into Center Street one square south of the courthouse. Two on Center and turn right into Ferry. One on Ferry brings you to Lamberton. Turn left there and keep going south on Lamberton until you hit the Marine Terminal. You can't miss it. The shack… is a couple of hundred yards beyond."

"Front to South Broad, to Center, to Ferry, and into Lamberton. Right turns all the way except into Lamberton, which is left. I'll be there in fifteen minutes. Wait at the watchman's place for me. Bill, don't go back. Do you hear me?"

"I won't."

"Call the Trenton police. I'm on my way." Ellery dropped the telephone, jammed on his hat, and ran like a fireman. The red-haired young woman stared after him with a light in her hazel eyes that was almost lustful. Then she snapped her bag shut.

It was twenty minutes to ten when Ellery slammed his brake on before the watchman's house opposite the Marine Terminal. Bill Angell was sitting on the running-board of his Pontiac, head between his hands, staring at the damp road. A knot of curious men thronged the doorway of the house. The two men gazed briefly into each other's eyes. "It's rotten," choked Bill. "Rotten!"

"I know, Bill, I know. You've called the police?"

"They'll be coming along soon. I—I've called Lucy, too." A spark of desperation glittered in Bill's eyes. "She's not home."

"Where is she?"

"I'd forgotten. She's always downtown seeing a movie on Saturday nights when Joe… when he's away. No answer. I've sent a wire telling her to come, that Joe'd had an… accident. The wire will get there before she will. We—there's no sense in not facing facts. Is there?"

"Certainly not, Bill."

Bill took his hands out of his pockets and looked at them. Then he raised his head to the black sky. It was the night of the new moon, and only the stars were visible, small and brilliant after their wash in the rain. "Let's go," he said grimly, and they climbed into the Pontiac. He turned his car around and retraced its trail south.

"Slowly," said Ellery after a moment. His eyes were on the shimmering cones of the headlights. "Tell me all you know."

Bill told him. At mention of the woman in the Cadillac roadster, Ellery glanced at his companion's face. It was dark and dangerous.

"Veiled woman," murmured Ellery. "That was fortunate, Bill; I mean poor Wilson's living long enough to tell you. Was this woman wearing a veil?"

"I don't know. It wasn't over her face when she passed me. But she might have slipped it up over her hat. I don't know… When Joe— when he died I went out to the car, backed it out of the side-lane into the road, and drove to the Terminal. Then I called you. That's all."

The shack loomed ahead. Bill began wearily to turn the wheel. "No!" said Ellery sharply. "Stop here. Have you a flashlight?"

"In the door-pocket."

Ellery got out of the Pontiac and nosed the flash about. In a few sweeps of the beam he fixed the scene indelibly in his mind; the silent shack, the muddy lane leading to the side, the semicircular drive before the front door, the weed-grown segments of ground bordering the drives. He turned the light on the mud of the side-lane, crouching a little. So far as he could see there were no man-made marks in the soggy earth except tire tracks, of which there seemed to be several sets. He scrutinized these closely for a moment and then returned to the Pontiac. "Bill! We'll walk from here."

"Yes."

"Or better still, turn your car about to block the road. We don't want anyone running cars up these drives. I don't see any footprints in the mud here, and that may be important. The tire marks which already exist should naturally be preserved. The rain this afternoon was an act of God… Bill! Are you listening?"

"Yes. Yes, of course."

Ellery said gently, "Then do as I say." He ran forward to the point where the semicircular drive began. He stopped at the edge of Lamberton Road, careful not to set foot on the driveway. There were ruts in the mushy earth in which were clearly stamped the treads of tires. He eyed them for a moment and strode back.

"I was right. Bill, perhaps you had better remain out here and guard the drives. Warn the police when they come. Don't let anyone walk on either driveway; they can reach the house by skirting them and walking on those weedy borders... Bill!"

"I'm all right, Ellery," muttered Bill. He was fumbling with a cigaret and shivering. "I understand."

As he stood in the middle of the main road leaning against his car, there was something in his eyes that made Ellery turn away. Then, on impulse, he turned back. Bill smiled; a ghastly smile. Ellery patted his shoulder rather helplessly and, raising his flashlight, hurried back to the dirt lane. He vaulted over to the weeds on the river side, played the flash, and made his way cautiously toward the side door of the shack.

Fifteen feet from the porch, he stopped; the weeds ended there, and between the last clump and the porch was bare earth. He gave the old Packard to the side only a passing glance; it was ground around and beyond it that held his attention. For some time he swept the flash about and with a vaguely sensed satisfaction convinced himself that no human foot had trodden anywhere within range. Then he set his own feet down in the muck.

The wooden porch was tiny, a square platform of rotting boards raised a few inches from the mud. For the moment he ignored the half open side door and the quiet leg which he could see protruding from beyond the round table inside; instead, he crossed to the farther edge of the porch and stabbed the ground with his torch. His brows went up. A narrow path led from the porch toward the river. In the mud of this walk there were two sets of male footprints, one going and one coming. Those which pointed toward the porch were for the most part superimposed upon those which pointed toward the river. Even on superficial examination it was evident that they were all impressions of the same feet.

Ellery sent the beam dancing down the path. It led straight to a small, staggering structure perched on the very edge of the Delaware River, some forty feet away. This second shack was even more woebegone in appearance than the house. "Garage or boathouse," he thought, peering at it. Then he quickly snapped off his flash and stepped to the threshold of the shack; for a roaring sound was growing on Lamberton Road, coming from Trenton, and it sounded like a high-powered motor car.

His panoramic survey of the room was hasty; but Mr. Ellery Queen had a genius for rapid and accurate observation, and he missed nothing in that first glance… The carpet was a curious note in this seedy hovel: it was well-worn but of superb quality—silky, deep-piled, without design, and a warm fawn in color. It had no borders and had obviously been cut to fit a room of larger size, for it was doubled under where the floor met the walls.

"Made for some woman's modern bedroom, I'll wager," muttered Ellery. "What the devil is it doing here?" Then, noting that the rug was spotless, he scraped the soles of his muddy shoes on the sill of the side door—someone else had done the same thing before him, he saw—and gingerly walked into the room.

Joseph Wilson's eyes were still open and twisted sidewise; but now they had the appearance of steamed glass. His breast had bled copiously; the shirt was saturated; but the nature of the wound was evident enough: there was a thin incision over the heart in the very vortex of the blood-welter, a wound which could only have been inflicted by a narrow-bladed cutting instrument. The approaching motor was thunderous now.

He swiftly examined the table, illuminated by the cheap lamp. A chipped crockery plate lay in the glow, its surface covered with the burnt stubs of many small yellow paper matches; otherwise it was perfectly clean. Near the plate lay a bronze-hafted paper-knife, its long wicked blade bathed to the hilt in dry blood. Something was impaled on the point—a tiny truncated cone of some indeterminate substance, for its surface was concealed under a layer of soot. Whatever it was, it had been thoroughly charred by fire. His eyes went back to the dead man.

There was something about Wilson's contorted face, he realized with a sensation of annoyance, that had piqued him from the very first glance. Disregarding the distortion of death, it was a rather striking face, crisp-featured and interesting and in a subtle way handsome. Wilson had been in the prime of life—between thirty-five and forty, Ellery judged. The forehead was high and mild, the mouth almost feminine, the nose short, the chin faintly cleft. The curly chestnut hair at the temples was thin, but it was vigorous still. What it was that bothered him Ellery could not decide. Perhaps it was the overcast of delicate intelligence, a certain refinement, the mark of good blood…

"Who the devil," said a cool bass voice, "are you?"

"Ah, the police," said Ellery. "Come in, gentlemen, come in." He flipped something negligently on the table. "Wipe your shoes off before you walk on this rug."

The side door was crowded with men, at the head of whom stood a tall broad man with flinty eyes. The two men regarded each other for a moment; then the tall man said curtly, "Clean your shoes, boys," and scraped his own soles on the sill. He glanced from the fawn rug to Ellery and strode in to pick up what Ellery had thrown on the table. "Oh," he said, handing it back. "Glad to have you, Mr. Queen. This man Angell outside didn't mention your name. I've met your dad once or twice. I'm De Jong, chief of police in Trenton."

Ellery nodded. "I've just been poking about. I hope you haven't been tramping all over the driveways?"

"Angell told us what you said; good hunch. I'm having the drives boarded over. Let's see this stiff."

The room dwindled. Men scuffed about, packing it. De Jong went down on his knees beside the dead man. A fatherly-looking old gentleman with a black bag pushed him aside. Flash lamps burst silently. Bill Angell stood in a corner out of the way and watched with stones in his eyes. "Tell me everything that's happened, Mr. Queen," said a wheedling woman's voice from behind Ellery.

He turned from his puzzled scrutiny of the dead man's face to find a tall young woman with red hair and vivid lips, pencil poised over a notebook, smiling at him. Her hat, which looked like a large discus, was pushed dowdily back on her head and a red curl drooped over one bright eye.

"And why," asked Ellery, "should I?"

"Because," said the young woman, "I am the voice and conscience of the pee-pul. I represent public opinion and some damn' captious advertisers. Give, Mr. Queen."

Ellery lit his pipe and carefully dropped the match-stub into his pocket. "It seems to me," he said, "that I've seen you somewhere before."

"Mister Queen! That line had whiskers when Cleo suckled the asp. I was sitting only a few feet away in the lobby of the Stacy-Trent when your boy-friend called you up. Good work, Sherlock; you're living up to your reputation. Who's the pretty lad on the floor?"

"Now you and I," said Ellery patiently, "haven't been formally introduced."

"Rats! I'm Ella Amity, feature-writer for the Trenton Times. Come on now, sport. I've got the jump on everybody, but it won't last long. Open up!"

"Sorry. You'll have to see De Jong."

"Stuck-up," said Miss Amity, and she scowled. Then she burrowed in between the old gentleman with the bag and Chief De Jong, and began scribbling like mad in her notebook. De Jong winked at Ellery and slapped her round rump. She giggled, lunged at Bill Angell, hurled questions at him, scribbled some more, threw him a kiss, and darted out of the shack. Ellery heard her screaming: "Where in hell's the nearest telephone?" and a man's gruff: "Hey, you, walk on the weeds." A moment later he heard the sound of a motor retreating toward the Marine Terminal.

De Jong said, "Angell," in a friendly voice. The men stepped aside to let Bill pass. Ellery slipped into the group standing over the body.

"Let's have it," said the tall man. "Murphy, notes. You said outside this man was your brother-in-law. His name?"

"Joseph Wilson." The dazed look had gone out of Bill's eyes; his chin was forward. He mentioned an address in the Fairmont Park section of Philadelphia.

"What's he doing here?"

"I don't know."

"And where do you come in on this, Mr. Queen?"

Ellery related the story of his meeting with the young lawyer in Trenton and, before either man could interrupt, the tale Bill had told him about his first journey to the shack.

"Veiled, Wilson said, eh?" De Jong frowned. "Do you think you'd recognize this dame who beat it in the Cadillac, Angell?"

"All I saw were her eyes, and they were distorted with fright. I'd know the car, though." He described it.

"Who owns this dump?"

Bill muttered, "I haven't the faintest idea. This is the first time I've been here."

"One hell of a hole," grunted De Jong. "I remember now. It used to be a squatter's shack. They were kicked out years ago. I didn't know anyone was living here; land belongs to the city… Where's your sister, Angell?"

Bill stiffened. Ellery murmured, "Bill's tried to get her on the 'phone, but she's out. He's sent her a wire."

De Jong nodded coldly and went away. When he came back he demanded, "What business was this Wilson in?" Bill told him. "Hmn. Well, this whole thing begins to smell. What's the verdict, Doc?"

The old gentleman struggled to his feet. "A knife through the heart. Deep wound, De Jong; very neat job. It's a miracle he didn't die instantly."

"Particularly," said Ellery, "since the weapon was removed from the wound soon after the attack."

The chief looked at him sharply, and then at the blood-crusted paper-knife on the table. "That is funny. And what the hell's that thingamabob doing on the tip? What is it, anyway?"

"On consideration," said Ellery, "I believe you'll find it to be a cork."

"Cork!"

"Yes, the kind that's often stuck on the tip of a letter-opener when it's bought."

"Hmn. It's a cinch this lad wasn't skewered with that on it. Somebody put it on the tip of the knife after the kill." De Jong studied the burnt match-stubs on the plate with irritation. "And charred the cork good and plenty. In the name of hell, why?"

"That," said Ellery, puffing at his pipe, "is technically an epic question. Most pertinent. By the way, it might be wise not to drop any matches about. I'm an intolerant believer in leaving things as they are on the scene of a crime."

"Nobody's smoking but you," said De Jong in a surly way. "I'm not much on this fancy business, Mr. Queen. Let's get down to brass tacks. You say you had an appointment with your brother-in-law, Angell? Let's have the whole story."

Bill did not move for a moment; and then he put his hand in his pocket and produced a crumpled yellow envelope. "I suppose I may as well," he said harshly. "Joe came home from one of his trips last Wednesday. He left again this morning—"

"How d'ye know that?" snapped the chief, eyes on the envelope.

"He called at my office Friday afternoon—yesterday—to see me about something, and he told me he was going away the next morning—that is, today. That's how I know." Bill's eyes flickered. "About noon today I received this wire at my office. Read it, and you'll know as much about this ghastly business as I do."

De Jong opened the envelope and extracted a telegram. Ellery read it over the big man's shoulder.

IMPORTANT I SEE YOU TONIGHT WITHOUT FAIL STOP PLEASE KEEP SECRET FROM EVERYONE THIS MEANS A GREAT DEAL TO ME STOP I WILL BE AT AN OLD HOUSE ON DELAWARE THREE MILES SOUTH OF TRENTON ON LAMBERTON ROAD SEVERAL HUNDRED YARDS SOUTH OF MARINE TERMINAL STOP IT IS ONLY HOUSE OF ITS KIND IN VICINITY YOU CANNOT MISS IT STOP HAS A HALF CIRCLE DRIVEWAY AND A BOATHOUSE IN REAR STOP MEET ME THERE AT NINE PM SHARP STOP VERY URGENT AM IN GREAT TROUBLE AND NEED YOUR ADVICE STOP NINE PM TONIGHT DO NOT FAIL ME... JOE

"Queer, all right," muttered De Jong. "Sent from downtown Manhattan, too. Was he supposed to go to New York, Angell, on this last business trip of his?"

"I don't know," said Bill shortly. His eyes were fixed on the corpse.

"What did he want to talk to you about?"

"I don't know, I tell you. This wasn't the last I heard from him. He 'phoned me from New York at two-thirty this afternoon at my office."

"Well? Well?"

The words came slowly. "I couldn't make out what he was driving at. He sounded horribly depressed and in great earnest. He wanted to make sure, he said, that I'd received his wire and was coming. He repeated how important it was to him, and of course I said I'd be there. When I asked him about the house..." Bill rubbed his forehead. "He said that was part of his secret, that no one he knew was aware of its existence, and that it was the best place for our talk for reasons he couldn't divulge. He was growing excited and rather incoherent. I didn't press him, and he hung up."

"No one knew," murmured Ellery. "Not even Lucy, Bill?"

"That's what he said."

"Well, it sure must have been important," drawled De Jong, "because somebody shut his mouth tight before he could spill it. At that, he wasn't telling the truth. Somebody did know about this house."

"I did, for one," said Bill coldly. "I knew when I received the telegram. Is that what you're driving at?"

"Now, now, Bill," said Ellery. "You're naturally unstrung. By the way, you said that Wilson had visited your office in Philadelphia yesterday. Anything important?"

"Perhaps, perhaps not. He left a bulky envelope in my keeping."

"What's in it?" snapped De Jong.

"I don't know. It's sealed, and he didn't tell me."

"Well, for cripes sake, didn't he say anything about it?"

"Just that I was to keep it for him temporarily."

"Where is it now?"

"In my safe," said Bill grimly, "where it's going to stay."

De Jong grunted. "I forgot you're a lawyer. Well, Angel I, we'll see about that. Doc, is there any way of telling exactly when this man was knifed? We know he died at ten after nine. But when was the knife stuck into him?"

The coroner shook his head. "I couldn't say. Certainly not long before. The man must have held on to life with remarkable tenacity. I could hazard a guess—eight-thirty, perhaps. But don't bank on it. Shall I send for the wagon?"

"Yes. No," said De Jong, showing his teeth. "No, we'll keep him here for a while. I'll call for the wagon when I want it. G o on home, Doc; you can do the autopsy for us in the morning. You're sure it was the knife did the job?"

"Positive. But if there was anything else, I'll find it."

"Doctor," said Ellery slowly. "Have you found—on the hands or anywhere else—any burns?"

The old gentleman stared. "Burns? Burns? Certainly not!"

"Would you mind keeping a weather-eye out for burns when you're doing the autopsy? Particularly on the extremities."

"Damned fool thing. Very well, very well!" And in something of a huff the coroner stamped out.

De Jong's mouth was open, ready to ask a question, when a fat detective with a scarred mouth shambled up and engaged him in conversation. Bill strolled about in aimless fashion. After a while the detective waddled away. "Mess of fingerprints all over the place, my man says," grunted De Jong, "but most of 'em seem to be Wilson's... Now what are you doing on that rug, Mr. Queen? You look like a frog."

Ellery rose from his knees. He had been crawling about the room for the past few minutes scrutinizing the surface of the fawn rug as if his life depended upon it. Bill was planted by the main door, a peculiar glitter in his eye. "Oh, I revert to the animal once in a while," smiled Ellery. "Does a body good. Remarkably clean rug, De Jong. Not a speck of mud or anything else anywhere on it."

De Jong looked puzzled. Ellery puffed placidly on his pipe and strolled toward the wooden clothes-rack on the Well. Out of the corner of his eye he watched his friend at the door. Bill looked down at his feet suddenly, grimaced, and stooped to fumble with the lace of his left shoe. It took him some time to get it tied to his complete satisfaction. When he rose his face was red from his exertions, and his right hand was buried in his pocket. Ellery sighed. He felt sure, as he glanced at the others, that they had not seen Bill pick up something from the one spot on the rug which he himself had not examined.

De Jong strode out, flinging a glance of warning at his man Murphy. They heard him shouting orders on the wooden porch. Bill dropped into a chair and propped his elbow on his knee, staring down at the dead man with the oddest look of bitter inquiry.

"I grow more and more fascinated by this extraordinary brother-in-law of yours," growled Ellery, standing before the rack.

"Eh?"

"These suits, now. Where did Wilson buy his duds?"

"Philadelphia department stores. He often picked things up at Wanamaker's clearance sales."

"Really?" Ellery flipped back one of the coats and exposed a label. "That's strange. Because, if you'll accept the evidence of this label, he patronized the most exclusive tailor on Fifth Avenue in New York!"

Bill's head jerked around. "Nonsense."

"And the cut, general swank, the material of the garment don't give the label the lie, either. Let's see… Yes, yes. There are four suits here, and they all purport to come from the same Fifth Avenue source."

"That's utterly incredible!"

"Of course," observed Ellery, "there's always the explanation that neither the shack nor what's in it belonged to him."

Bill was glaring at the rack with a sort of horror. He said eagerly: "Certainly. That's it, that's it. Why, Joe never spent more than thirty-five dollars for a suit in his life!"

"On the other hand," frowned Ellery, picking up something from the floor beneath the rack, "there are two pairs of shoes here that come from Abercrombie & Fitch. And," he added, reaching for the single hat on one of the pegs, "an Italian fedora that set somebody back twenty dollars, if I'm any judge of what the well-dressed man is soaked for his headgear."

"They can't be his!" cried Bill, springing to his feet. He brushed the gaping detective out of his way and knelt by his brother-in-law's body. "Here, you see? Wanamaker's label!"

Ellery replaced the hat on the peg. "All right, Bill," he said gently. "All right. Now sit down and cool off. All this confusion will right itself in time."

"Yes," said Bill. "I suppose so." And he went back to his chair and sat down, closing his eyes.

Ellery continued his deliberate saunter about the room, touching nothing and missing nothing. Occasionally he glanced at his friend; and then he would frown and quicken his pace a little, as if at some irresistible compulsion... One thing impressed him: the shack was a single room and there was no possible corner or closet which might have served as a place of temporary concealment. He even poked into the fireplace, which was very low, and saw that the flue was much too small to admit a human body.

After a while De Jong hurried back and proceeded to squat behind the table, becoming busy with the dead man's clothing. Bill opened his eyes; he rose again and went to the table and leaned on his knuckles to stare down at the policeman's massive neck. From outside the shack came the voices of many men. They seemed to be occupied with a work of importance in the two driveways. Once the silent men inside heard the shrill voice of Ella Amity engaged in ribald banter with the detectives.

"Well, Mr. Queen," said De Jong at last in a hearty tone, without looking up from what he was doing, "any ideas?"

"None that, like Shaw's Superman, I would fight for. Why?"

"I'd always heard you were a fast worker." There was a trace of sardonic humor in the big man's voice.

Ellery chuckled and took something down from the mantel above the fireplace. "You've seen this, of course?"

"Well?"

Bill's head came about in a flash. "What the devil is it?" he asked hoarsely.

"Yeah," drawled De Jong. "What d'ye make of it, Mr. Queen?"

Ellery glanced at him briefly. Then he deposited his find, with its wrappings, on the round table. Bill gulped it down with his eyes. It was a desk-set in brown tooled leather: desk-blotter pad with

25

triangular leather corners, a bronze-based penholder with wells for two fountain pens, and a small curved bronze blotter-holder. A white card protruded from one of the corner pockets of the large pad. The card was blank except for an inscription in blue ink, written in a large neat masculine script: 'To Bill, from Lucy and Joe.'

"Your birthday soon, Angell?" asked De Jong genially, squinting at a piece of paper from the dead man's breast-pocket.

Bill turned away, his mouth working. "Tomorrow."

"Damned considerate brother-in-law," grinned the chief. "That's his fist, too, on the card, so there's no question about that. One of the boys checked it with a sample of Wilson's handwriting from his clothes. See for yourself, Mr. Queen." He tossed to the table the paper he had been holding, a meaningless and unimportant scrawl.

"Oh, I believe you." Ellery was frowning at the writing-set.

"Seems to interest you," said De Jong, piling up a number of miscellaneous articles on the table. "Lord knows why! But I'm always ready to learn a new trick. See anything there that escaped me?"

"Since I've never had the pleasure of watching you work, De Jong," murmured Ellery, "I'm scarcely in a position to gauge the extent or accuracy of your observations. But there are certain minutiæ of at least hypothetical interest."

"You don't say?" De Jong was amused.

Ellery picked up the wrappings of the package. "For one thing, this desk-set was purchased in Wanamaker's in Philadelphia. That, I confess, means little. But… it's a fact; and facts, as Ellis Parker Butler might have said, is facts."

"Now, how'd you know that?" De Jong fingered a sales slip from the pile of articles on the table. "Found it in his pocket, all crumpled. He bought it in Wanamaker's yesterday, all right. It was a cash sale."

"How? By no startling means. I recognized the Wanamaker wrapping-paper, because I bought a little gift for my father there only this afternoon in passing through Philadelphia. And of course," continued

Ellery mildly, "you've noticed the condition of the paper. The question arises: Who undid the package?"

"I don't know why it should arise," said De Jong, "but I'll bite. Who did the foul deed?"

"I should say anyone but poor Wilson. Bill, did you touch anything in this room before I got here tonight?"

"No."

"None of your men opened this package, De Jong?"

"It was found just the way you saw it, on the mantel."

"The probability is, then, that it was opened by the murderess—the 'veiled woman' Wilson told Bill about before he died. Probability only; of course it may have been done by still a second intruder. But certainly it wasn't opened by Wilson."

"Why not?"

"This writing-set was purchased as a gift—witness the card. It was wrapped as a gift—the price-tag has been removed, and the sales slip is in Wilson's pocket rather than in the package. Therefore whoever bought it did so with the preconceived idea of presenting it to Bill Angell. The chances are Wilson bought it in person; but even if he didn't and delegated someone else to buy it for him, the inspiration would have emanated from him. This being the case, Wilson could have had little reason for opening the package here."

"I don't see that," argued the big man. "Suppose he didn't write this gift-card in the store—suppose he opened the package here to get one of these pens to write the card with."

"There's no ink in either pen, as I've already ascertained," said Ellery patiently. "Of course, he would know that. But even if I grant that he might have had some other reason for opening the package here, he certainly could have had no reason, as donor of the gift, to destroy the wrappings!" Ellery flicked his thumb at the paper: it had been ruthlessly ripped from the writing-set. "Those wrappings could scarcely be used again for their original purpose; and there are no other wrapping materials on the premises. So I say, Wilson at least didn't open the package; for, if he had, he would have been careful not to tear the paper. The murderess, on the other hand, would have been deterred by no such consideration."

"So what?" said De Jong.

Ellery looked blank. "My dear De Jong, what an asinine question! At this stage I'm chiefly interested in discovering what the criminal may have done on the scene of her crime; her reasons, whether significant or not, we may worry about later... Now, that paper-knife, used as the weapon. It comes from the writing-set—unquestionably—"

"Sure, sure," growled De Jong. "That's why the woman tore open the package—to get at the knife. I could have told you long ago it was the killer who opened it."

Ellery raised his brows. "I shouldn't say that was the reason at all, you know. For one thing, since the gift was purchased only yesterday, it's highly improbable that the murderess knew there would be a sharp new letter-opener handy for her crime tonight. No, no; the use of the letter-opener as a dagger was completely fortuitous, I'm convinced. It's more likely the murderess was prowling about here before the crime and opened the package out of sheer curiosity, or from an inner necessity due to nervousness in anticipation of what she was about to do. Naturally, discovering the letter-opener, she would prefer to use it rather than the weapon she must have brought along—if this was a premeditated murder, as it seems to have been. And from time inconceivable the female of the species has found in the knife the fullest expression of her homicidal impulses."

De Jong scratched his nose and looked annoyed. Bill said in a halting way, "If she had time to prowl... It would look as if she had the place to herself for a while. Then where was Joe? Had she attacked him first? The coroner—"

"Now, now, Bill," said Ellery soothingly, "don't fret about these things. We haven't enough facts yet. You didn't know anything about this gift, Bill?"

"Not a blessed thing. It sort of… bowls me over. I've never bothered much with birthdays. Joe—" He averted his face.

"Well," shrugged De Jong, "I'll admit a croaked brother-in-law is one hell of a birthday present. What else did you find, Mr. Queen?"

"Do you want a complete résumé?" asked Ellery calmly. "You know, De Jong, the trouble with you fellows is that you can never overcome your professional contempt for the amateur. I've known amateurs to sit at the feet of professionals, but I can't say the reverse has held equally true. Murphy, if I were you I should take notes. Your local prosecutor may bless them some day."

Murphy looked embarrassed, but De Jong nodded with a grim smile.

"A general description of the shack and its contents," said Ellery, puffing thoughtfully on his brier, "leads to a rather curious conclusion. In this one-room shack we find neither bed nor cot—no sleeping equipment of any kind. There is a fire-place but no firewood—in fact, no débris or ashes, and the hearth is remarkably clean. The fireplace obviously hasn't been used for months. What else? A broken-down old coal-stove, eaten away by rust and entirely useless for cooking or heating purposes—no doubt a relic of the days when this shack was occupied by squatters In this connection, observe that there are no candles, no oil-lamps, no gas connections, no matches of any description—"

"True enough," admitted De Jong. "Didn't this bird smoke, Angell?"

"No." Bill was staring out the front window.

"In fact," continued Ellery, "the only means of illumination here is the electric lamp on the table. There's a power-house—?" De Jong nodded. "It's immaterial whether the occupant of this place had the electricity installed or found it here; probably the latter. In any event, note the bare fact. And, to complete the picture, there is only a handful of chipped crockery, not a trace of foodstuffs, and not even the most ordinary first-aid equipment kept by the poorest for medical emergencies."

29

De Jong chuckled. "Got all that, Murph? That's dandy, Mr. Queen; couldn't have put it better myself. But when it's all added up, what the devil have you got?"

"More," retorted Ellery, "than you apparently realize. You have a house in which the occupant neither slept nor ate—a place with extraordinarily few of the characteristics of a dwelling and all the indications of... a transient shelter, a wayside convenience, the merest stopover. Moreover, from various signs you can deduce the quality of the occupant. This fawn rug is the only one of the accouterments here which doesn't date from the squatter era—much too regal and costly. I should say whoever has been using this place picked it up somewhere second-hand at a respectable price. A concession to sheer luxury in taste—that's significant, don't you think? This tendency to Sybaritism is borne out by the clothes on that rack, by the curtains on the windows—rich stuffs, but badly hung... the masculine touch, of course. Finally, the interior is almost meticulously clean; there isn't a speck of dirt or ashes anywhere on the rug, the fireplace is clean as the proverbial whistle, no dust visible to the prying eye. What kind of man does all this paint?"

Bill turned from the window; his eyes were rimmed with red. "It doesn't paint Joe Wilson," he said harshly.

"No," said Ellery. "It certainly does not."

De Jong's smile faded. "But that doesn't jibe with what Wilson told Angell over the 'phone today—that nobody but himself knew about this place!"

"Nevertheless," said Ellery in a queer tone, "I think that another man entirely is involved."

The voices were loud outside. De Jong scrubbed his chin and looked thoughtful. He said: "That sounds like the goddamned press," and went away.

"Now let's see," said Ellery softly, "what friend De Jong has found in poor Wilson's pockets."

The pile on the table was composed of the usual assortment of odds and ends a man carries about with him: a bunch of keys; a worn wallet which contained two hundred and thirty-six dollars in bills—Ellery glanced at Bill, who still stared out the window; a number of miscellaneous scraps of paper; several registered-letter receipts; a driver's license in Wilson's name; and two snapshots of a very pretty woman standing before an unpretentious little frame house. Ellery recognized her as Bill's sister Lucy, more buxom than he remembered her, but still the warm and vivid creature he had known in his university days. There was a receipted bill from a Philadelphia gas company; a fountain pen; and a few empty old envelopes addressed to Wilson on the backs of which were various numerical computations. Ellery picked up a bankbook and opened it; it had been issued by a leading Philadelphia savings bank and it indicated a balance of a little over four thousand dollars.

"The saving sort, I see," he remarked to Bill's motionless back. "There hasn't been a withdrawal in years. And although the deposits are modest, they're quite steady."

"Yes," said Bill without turning, "he saved his money. I think he had some money in the Postal Savings, too. Lucy really hasn't lacked anything for a woman married to a man in Joe's position."

"Did he own any bonds or stocks?"

"My dear Ellery, you forget we're the lower middle class in the fifth year of the Depression."

"My error. How about a checking account? I don't see a checkbook."

"No. No, he didn't have one." Bill paused. "He always said he didn't need one in his business."

"How very odd," said Ellery in a tone touched with astonishment. "It's—"Then he stopped and looked over the pile of articles again. But there was nothing more.

He picked up the fountain-pen, unscrewed its cap, and tried to write on one of the papers. "Hmm. Pen's run dry. Clarifies that business of where the gift card was written. Certainly not here. No pencils on him, pen's empty, and I'm sure from my little reconnaissance that there's neither writing equipment nor ink anywhere in the shack. That seems to suggest…"

Ellery circled the table and knelt by the dead man, fixed to his patch of rug as if pinned there. And he went about a curious business: he turned Wilson's empty pockets inside out and examined with the glare of a jeweler the detritus in the seams. When he rose he went to the rack and repeated his examination in the empty pockets of the four suits hanging there. And he nodded with a satisfaction that held the merest suggestion of puzzlement. He returned to the body and lifted the dead hands, intently studying the rigid fingers. Then he set himself, grimaced, and with difficulty parted the dead lips to reveal the fiercely clenched teeth behind. He rose and nodded again to himself.

Ellery was sitting on the table frowning down at Joseph Wilson's distorted face when De Jong stamped in, followed by several detectives. "Well, that takes care of the Fourth Estate for a while," said the Chief briskly. "Been enjoying yourself some more, Mr. Queen? I guess you'd like to hear what we've found out."

"Thanks. Very kind of you."

Bill turned from the window. "I suppose you realize, De Jong, that while you've been waltzing around here that woman in the Cadillac's got clean away?"

De Jong winked at Ellery. "Just a small-town cop, eh? Now, Angell, keep your pants on. I sent an alarm out five minutes after I got here. No reports yet, but the whole State Police force is combing the highways. Colonel Merry of the Troopers is in charge himself."

"She's probably in New York already," said Ellery dryly. "It's getting late, De Jong. Well, what have you found?"

"Plenty. On those two driveways outside."

"Ah, the tire marks," said Ellery.

"Meet Sergeant Hannigan." A cow-faced man bobbed his head. "Hannigan's made a sort of private study of automobile tracks. Spill it, Hannigan."

"Well, sir," said the Sergeant, addressing Ellery, "this main driveway in front of the house—the curved one, where Mr. Angell saw the Cadillac parked—there are three sets of tire marks in the mud."

"Three?" croaked Bill. "I saw only that Cadillac and I didn't run my own car onto the front driveway at all."

"Three sets o' marks," repeated Hannigan firmly. "Not three cars. Matter of fact, there were two cars. Two of the sets were made by the same boat, the Cadillac. Distinctive treads—that was a big Caddy, all right, Mr. Angell. The third set was made by peewee Firestones. I wouldn't say for sure, but they prob'ly came from a Ford. Tires are marked up and kind of worn, so it's prob'ly a '31 or '32 Ford. But don't bank on that."

"I shan't," said Ellery. "How do you know that the 'two sets' of Cadillac marks aren't really one?"

"Well, it's an easy figure," said the Sergeant. "First there's the tracks of the Caddy, see? Over some of the Caddy marks there's the marks of the Firestones. That shows the Caddy was there first. But over the marks of the Firestones there's the tracks of the Caddy again in some places. That means the Caddy was there and went away, then the Ford came and went away; then the Caddy came back."

"I see," said Ellery. "Quite ingenious. But how do you know the two sets of big-car marks were made by the same car? Mightn't the first set have been made by another car using the same kind of tires?"

"Not a chance, sir. Those tires left fingerprints." The Sergeant coughed at his fancy phrase. "There's a gash across one of the treads that shows up the same on both sets. Same car, all right."

"How about the directions involved?"

"Right smart question, sir. The Caddy came from Trenton way the first time, stopped by the stone step and later drove on around the curve and went off in the direction of Camden. The Ford came from the Camden side, stopped by the stone step, kept on around the drive and made a sharp turn onto Lamberton Road to go back to Camden, the way it'd come. Then the Cadillac came back from Camden, stopped by the stone step—and Mr. Angell saw it drive off past him toward Trenton again."

Ellery removed his pince-nez and tapped them against the cleft in his chin. "Splendid, Sergeant; that's a graphic story. How about this dirt driveway to the side of the shack?"

"Nothin' special there. The old Packard Mr. Angell says belonged to Wilson drove in from the direction of Trenton. Wet marks in the mud, so I'd say the Packard got here after the rain started."

"More probably after the rain stopped," murmured Ellery. "Otherwise the tracks would have been washed out."

"That's right, sir. And that goes for the other ones, too. The rain stopped a little before seven this evening, so I guess we can say all the cars came here startin' with seven o'clock… Only other marks in the side driveway are from Mr. Angell's Pontiac—once driving in and once backing out. And that's the story."

"And a good one, Sergeant. Any footprints approaching the house?"

"Nary one, except yours on that fifteen-foot stretch," said De Jong. "We boarded that over, too, coming in here. All right, Hannigan, see that those tire marks are cast up." The Sergeant saluted and left. "Not a footprint anywhere around the house or on the two drives. Both of 'em lead right to the little porches and I suppose whoever came here tonight hopped from their cars to the porches without stepping on the ground."

"And the footprints in that lane leading to the boathouse?"

De Jong glanced down at a detective who was crouched behind the table fussing with the dead man's feet. "Well, Johnny?"

The man looked up. "Stiff made 'em, all right, Chief. Must 'a' scraped his shoes off on the side porch before comin' in here. But his shoes made those prints outside, like we figured."

"Ah," said Ellery. "Then it was Wilson who walked down to the river. And returned to his death. What's in that shack down there, De Jong? It is a boathouse, isn't it?"

The big policeman frowned down at Wilson's still face. "Yeah." His cold eyes were puzzled. "And it sure looks like you were right about another man using this shack. There's a small sailboat down there with an outboard motor—pretty expensive toy, looks to me. Motor's still warm. One of the men at the Marine Terminal's come forward to testify that he saw a man answering Wilson's description sailing the boat out of the landing below at a quarter after seven tonight."

"Joe? Joe sailing a boat?" muttered Bill.

"That's the ticket. This man also saw Wilson coming back—says it was around half past eight, and he had his motor going on the trip in. He was just sailing on the trip out. Wind died around seven-thirty, you'll remember."

Ellery rubbed the back of his neck. "Odd... Wilson was alone?"

"That's what this Terminal man says. It's a small craft with no cabin, so he couldn't be wrong."

"Out for a sail. Hmm." Ellery looked at the dead face. "An appointment with his brother-in-law on a matter of extreme urgency for nine—he goes out for a sail two hours before... nervous, the need for reflection, solitude... I see, I see. Of course, De Jong," he added strangely, not looking at Bill, "you realize that his use of the boat doesn't mean it belonged to him."

"Sure, sure. Only"—De Jong's eyes flickered—"this man says he's seen Wilson out sailing on a number of occasions in the past. And always alone. Fact, he seems to regard Wilson as a sort of fixture around here."

"Joe's been here before?" cried Bill.

"For years."

Somebody outside laughed.

"I don't believe it," said Bill. "There's a devilish mistake somewhere. It can't possibly be true—"

35

"And not only that," continued De Jong without changing expression, "but in the shed back there there's another car."

Ellery said mercifully, "Another car? What do you mean?" Bill's cheeks turned the color of dirty clay.

"Lincoln sports roadster, latest model. Key in the ignition. But the motor's dead cold, and there's a swanky tarpaulin over the car. No owner's license inside, but it's going to be pie tracing the serial number, gents, just apple pie." De Jong grinned at them. "That car must belong to this fawn-rug guy who's been using the shack. Looks like a real live lead. Yes, sir… And there's something more. Pinetti!"

"Good Lord," said Bill in a strangled voice, "what next?"

One of the silent men behind De Jong stepped forward and handed his superior a small flattish suitcase. De Jong opened it. It was untidily packed with cards displaying cheap jewelry—necklaces, rings, bracelets, cuff-links, fraternal emblems. "That's Joe's." Bill licked his lips. "Samples. Stock."

De Jong grunted. "Came from his Packard; that's not what I meant. Pinetti, that other thing."

The detective produced a metal object. De Jong held it up, turning it over in his fingers with a false preoccupation. Then his cold eyes shot up to the level of Bill's face.

"Ever see this before, Angell?" He slammed it into Bill's hand.

It was very curious. As if De Jong's question had been composed of oil, Bill's manner altered, smoothing out to a blank and glassy stillness. Ellery was astonished, and De Jong's eyes narrowed. They could actually see the metamorphosis as Bill's bare fingers gripped the thing: features settling back into normal lines, the frown vanishing from the forehead, leaving it calm and inscrutable, eyes hardening into marbles.

"Of course," he smiled. "On hundreds of cars." And he turned the object slowly over in his hands. It was part of the radiator-cap of an automobile—the rust-flecked figurine of a running naked woman, metal hair and arms streaming behind her. The figure had been broken off at the ankles, leaving two rusty jagged ends of metal where the tiny feet had been attached to the threaded plug.

De Jong snorted and snatched the figurine away. "That's a clue, gentlemen. It was found in the main driveway right in front of the house, half-buried where—Hannigan says—the Ford ran over it. I'm not saying it mightn't have been lying there for a month. But then again," his lips curled away from his mouth in a leer, "it mightn't have. See what I mean?"

Bill said coolly: "You've put your finger on the weak spot of that exhibit as evidence, De Jong. Your prosecutor would have a sweet time proving that that was broken off the cap of a car on the evening of June first, even if you found the car it came from."

"Oh, sure," said De Jong. "I know you lawyers."

Ellery glanced absently from the little naked woman to Bill's face, blinked, and walked around the table. He stooped over the dead man, his eyes riveted to Wilson's fingers, caught by death as they clawed the rug... No rings. No rings. That, he thought, was good. He remained in his stooped position, unmoving except for his eyes, which went to Wilson's chill face for the twentieth time that evening and with the same faint expression of annoyance. De Jong was saying with exultation, "So I'm getting after the car this came from right away, get me? And when I find it..."

Ellery slowly straightened up. Across the body of Joseph Wilson he looked at his friend, and for an instant teetered on the thin edge of a mad impulse. Then he looked down at the dead man again, and this time both the uncertainty and annoyance were gone from his face, leaving wonder, conviction, and pity behind. "Excuse me," he said in a flat voice. "I'm going out for a breath of air. This stuffy room..."

De Jong, Bill stared at him. He smiled faintly and hastened out of the shack as if it had become intolerable to him. The sky was shiny black, like jet damp under an indirect light, and flecked with polka-dot stars; the air felt cool and bracing against his perspiring cheeks.

Detectives stood aside to let him pass. He hurried down the muddy side-lane over the loose protecting boards with long strides.

It was hard, he thought, damned hard. And yet it was bound to come out. If it were in his power alone… As he turned into Lamberton Road a group of dark figures smoking in the shadows of the many cars now parked there fell on him, pressing forward, chattering questions. "I'm sorry, boys. I can't talk now."

He managed finally to shake them off. He fancied that he had seen Ella Amity's tall figure seated on a man's lap in one of the parked cars, and that she had calmly smiled at him as he passed. When he reached the little frame house across the road from the Marine Terminal he went inside, said something to the old man there, pressed a bill into his hand, and picked up the telephone. The old man stared at him with curiosity. He called Information, gave her a name in New York City; and while he waited he looked impatiently at his wristwatch. It was ten minutes past eleven.

It was a quarter of twelve when he returned to the shack in his Duesenberg, which he had parked near the Marine Terminal. Something seemed to have happened inside the tumbledown house, for the newspapermen were storming it, held back with curses by police and detectives. The Amity woman clutched imploringly at his arm as he slipped through the cordon, but he shook her off and quickened his pace.

Nothing had changed in the shack except the people who had invaded it. The detectives were gone. De Jong was still there, coldly and rather cynically pleased, talking in low tones to a short nondescript man with a brown face. Bill was there and Lucy Wilson, née Angell.

Ellery recognized her instantly, after almost eleven years. She did not see him as he watched from the doorway; she was standing by the table, one slim hand on Bill's shoulder, staring down at the floor with an expression of glazed horror. Her plain black-and-white dress was crawling with wrinkles, as strained as her face. A light coat was hung crazily over the overstuffed armchair. Her shoes were a little muddy…

She was still the handsome, vigorous creature he had known—almost as tall as her brother, with the same sound chin and black eyes, and a body as strong and pliant as a spring. Her figure had burgeoned with the years; it had grace and sap in it, and sexual beauty. Mr. Ellery Queen was no sentimentalist where women were concerned, but he felt now—as he had always felt in the past when in her presence—the pull of her sheer animal attractiveness. She had always been a woman, he recalled, who drew men to her with an easy unconscious lure that refreshed even as it eluded the grasp. There was nothing small or wantonly delicate about her; her charm was the charm of moist and generous white skin, sweet lips and eyes, and a large and undulant grace of movement…. It was all fixed now, tapered to the horror in her eyes as she looked at the cold body of her husband. The contour of her breast as she leaned on Bill's shoulder was unsteady, like a round pool shivered by a stone.

Ellery said in a low troubled voice, "Lucy Angell."

Her head came about slowly, and for a moment her black eyes reflected nothing but the dreadful reality of the thing on the floor. Then suddenly they flashed. "Ellery Queen. I'm so glad." She extended her free hand and he went to her and took it.

"There's nothing I can say, of course—"

"I'm so glad you're here. It's so horribly, horribly… unexpected." A tremor shook her. "My Joe dead—in this awful place. Ellery, how can that be?"

"It can't, but it is. You must learn to face that."

"Bill told me how you happen to be here. Ellery—stay." He pressed her hand. She managed the ghost of a smile. Then she turned back to look down again.

Bill said coldly, "De Jong played a dirty trick. He knew I'd sent Lucy a wire. Yet he sneaked this detective of his off in a department car to Philly to wait for her, and when she got home from the movies had her hauled back here as if—as if—"

"Bill," said Lucy gently. Ellery felt her hand warm in his own, the plain thin gold wedding-band on her fourth finger strong and unyielding against his palm. The hand on Bill's shoulder was white with pain and as unadorned as a pine crucifix.

"I know my job, Angell," said De Jong without rancor. "I see you're acquainted with Mrs. Wilson, Mr. Queen. Old friends, eh?" Ellery flushed and released the warm hand. "I suppose you want to know what she says?"

Bill growled deep in his throat. But Lucy said in a steady voice without turning, "I want him to know. There's nothing, Ellery, no explanation I can give... I've answered all this man's questions. Perhaps you can convince him that I've told the truth."

"My dear woman," said De Jong, "don't get me wrong. I know my job." He seemed offended. "All right, Sellers; good work. Stick around." A glance of secret understanding passed between him and the short brown man; the detective nodded without expression and went out. "Here's the story. Mrs. Wilson says her husband left their house this morning in his Packard on one of his regular business trips. That's the last, she says, that she saw or heard of him. He seemed all right, she says; maybe a little absent-minded, but she put it down to some business worry or other. Is that right, Mrs. Wilson?"

"Yes," Her eyes refused to leave the dead man's face.

"She left her house in Fairmount Park about seven tonight, just after the rain stopped—she'd had dinner at home alone—took a trolley into town, and went to the Fox to see a movie. Then she trolleyed home. My man was waiting for her, and brought her out."

"You forgot to explain," said Bill in a dangerous voice, "that my sister always goes to a movie on Saturday night when her husband is away."

"That's right," said De Jong. "So I did. Got that, Mr. Queen? Now as to the crime." He tapped his points off on his fingers. "She never heard of or saw this shack before—she says. Wilson never breathed a word about it to her. I mean, she says. She's never known of any real trouble he's been in. He's always been good to her, and as far as she knows," De Jong smiled, "faithful…"

"Please," whispered Lucy. "I know what you men must think in a—in a case like this. But he was faithful to me, he was! He loved me. He loved me!"

"She doesn't know much about his business affairs, because he was kind of secretive about them and she didn't want to pry. She's thirty-one, he was thirty-eight. Married ten years this past March. No children."

"No children," muttered Ellery, and there was the most extraordinary gladness in his eyes.

De Jong continued imperturbably: "She never knew he could sail a boat, though she knows he was good with engines and things. She never knew he had rich friends; their friends—the few they have in Philly, she says—are poor people like themselves. Wilson had no vices, she says—didn't drink, smoke, gamble, or take dope. They'd go picnicking when he was home—when he was home—or drive out to Willow Grove of a Sunday, or stay home"—his eyes were mocking as he glanced at her sidewise—"making love. That right, Mrs. Wilson?"

Bill whispered, "You damned—"

Ellery seized his arm. "Now, look here, De Jong. What have you up your sleeve? I see no point in innuendo."

Lucy did not move. Her eyes were infinitely remote now, deep with tears. De Jong chuckled. He went to the door and shouted: "Let those newspaper bastards in!"

Time passed, and they were buffeted about in a sea of noise. In many ways it was nightmare: the air in the low-ceilinged cabin was soon thick and foul with cigaret smoke, blazing occasionally to the lightning of photographers' flashlamps; the walls re-echoed with laughter and shouted conversation. Every few minutes someone jerked the newspaper De Jong had placed there off the dead man's face and photographed it from a new angle… Ella Amity flew from group to group like a red-haired harpy, but she always returned to the black-eyed woman enthroned like an unwilling queen in the armchair. She hovered over Lucy in a proprietary way, whispering to her, holding her hand, smoothing her hair tenderly. Bill watched from behind, raging in silence.

Eventually the room cleared. "All right folks," said De Jong as the sound of the last departing motor died away. "That's all for tonight. You'll keep available, of course, Mrs. Wilson. We've got to take your husband's body to the morgue—"

"De Jong," said Ellery from the corner. "Wait."

"Wait? For what?"

"It's inconceivably important." Ellery's voice was grave. "Wait."

Ella Amity gurgled from the doorway: "Always play hunches. Something up your sleeve, Mr. Queen? Nobody puts anything over on Little Ella." Her red hair was wild and her teeth gleamed. She leaned against the wall, watchful as a cobra. They were still for so long that the random sounds of the river began to creep into the shack again, after hours of being drowned out.

Then De Jong said, "All right," with a peculiar irritation, and went out. Lucy sighed. And Bill shut his mouth tight. After a long time De Jong came back, accompanied by two uniformed men carrying a stretcher. They dumped it by the corpse.

"No," said Ellery. "Not yet. Let the body alone, please."

De Jong snapped, "Wait outside," and eyed him hostilely, chewing at a cigar. Eventually he stopped pacing and sat down. Nobody moved. They sat stupefied by inaction, too weary to speak or protest.

And then, at two o'clock in the morning, as if by prearrangement, a motor came roaring down Lamberton Road. Ellery flexed his arms a little. "Come outside, De Jong," he said in a flat tone, and went to the door. De Jong followed, lips drawn back. And Ella Amity's red-tipped fingers curved in triumph… Bill Angell hesitated, glanced at his sister, and quietly went out, too.

Three people stepped out of a long chauffeur-driven limousine onto the tarry road. Conducted by detectives, they walked slowly along the boards placed over the main driveway, their feet curiously reluctant. All three were of a height, tall and somehow, despite everything, poised—a middle-aged woman, a young woman, and a middle-aged man. They were in evening clothes: the older woman in a sable coat over a white sequined gown, the younger in a short ermine wrap over a flaming chiffon that swept the ground, the man carrying a silk hat in his hand. The women had been weeping; the man's stern, rugged face was set in hard and angry lines.

Ellery said soberly in the driveway, "Mrs. Gimball?"

The older woman raised eyes underscored with leaden sacs, brittle blue eyes whose self-assurance had recently been shattered. "And you, I suppose, are the gentleman who 'phoned my father. Yes. This is my daughter Andrea. And this is a very dear friend, Mr. Grosvenor Finch. Where—?"

"So what?" said De Jong softly.

Bill drifted away from the lighted doorway into a deep shadow. His eyes, narrowed a little, were on the slender fingers of the young woman's beautiful left hand. He stood so close to her that he could have touched her ermine wrap. To his ears the deep suspicious tones of De Jong, the silk-hatted man's cultured voice, the older woman's harassed quaver were blurred and half-unheard. In his shadow he hesitated, and his eyes went from the young woman's hand to her face.

Andrea Gimball, he thought. So that was her name. And he saw that her face was young and unspoiled, not at all like the faces of the young women he knew, not remotely resembling the faces of the young women who were habitually pictured on society pages. It was a good face, delicate, soft, and somehow it touched a responsive chord.

Singularly, he wanted to talk to her. A sharp corner of his brain buzzed warning, but he ignored it. He extended his hand from the shadow and touched her bare arm.

She turned her head slowly toward him, and he saw that her blue eyes were deep with alarm. Under his fingers her skin felt suddenly cold. He knew that he should not be touching her; he felt her instinctive withdrawal. And yet something made his hand tighten about her arm and draw her, quiet and only half-resisting, into his shadow.

"You—you—" she said and stopped, straining to search his face. She could only dimly make it out, but it seemed to reassure her, for her skin warmed against his fingers and the alarm became simply fatigue in her eyes. With a guilty feeling he released her. "Miss Gimball," he whispered. "I have only a moment. Please listen to me…"

"Who are you?" she asked softly.

"It doesn't matter. Bill Angell. It might have been anyone." But he knew that to be untrue as he said it. "Miss Gimball, for a moment I meant to expose you. I thought—Now, I don't know."

"Expose me?" she faltered. "What do you mean?"

He came closer in the shadow, so close that he could smell the faint aroma in her hair and skin. And he lifted her left hand suddenly and said, "Look at your ring."

From the start she gave, from the odd way in which she jerked her hand to the level of her eyes and stared, he knew he had been right. And curiously, he wished now that he had not been right. She was so different from the woman he had visualized.

"My ring," she said with difficulty. "My ring. The—the stone's gone."

The ring was on the fourth finger of her left hand, an incredibly delicate circlet of platinum with naked uplifted prongs, two of them a little bent. Where the stone had been there was a hole.

"I found the stone," whispered Bill, "in there." And he nodded in the direction of the shack. Suddenly he looked around, and she caught something of the caution in his manner, for the alarm came back into her eyes and she crept a little closer to him. "Quickly," he whispered. "Tell me the truth. You were the woman in the Cadillac?"

"Cadillac?" He could barely hear her voice. For a maddening moment her aroma filled his nostrils with increased insistence.

"Tell me the truth," he muttered. "I could have told the police. You came here earlier tonight in a Cadillac roadster. You were dressed differently—in dark clothes. You came out of this house. What were you doing here, Miss Gimball? Tell me!"

She was silent for so long that he thought she had not heard him. Then she said, "Oh, Bill Angell, I'm so frightened I—I don't know what to say. I never thought… If I could only trust you—"

Bill thought bitterly, This is what comes of weakness with a woman. Is this cleverness, or desperation? And he said in a low voice: "I haven't had time to think. I don't trust women—as a rule. But I suppose…"

He felt her slender body straining against him, and her voice floated with odd cadence into his consciousness. "I've no right at all, Bill Angell—whoever you are. But you won't say anything? You'll protect me? Oh, it would be so easy for—for them to misunderstand!" She was trembling as if she had just emerged from cold water.

"Wall," he said at last, "well… no, I won't say anything."

The glad little cry was music. For a stunned instant he felt the pressure of her arms about his neck and her lips, fumbling and then sure, against his own. Then she had slipped out of his shadow, and he felt so curiously alone that his own body shivered, and he stepped back into the shack and ugly reality.

Ellery said quietly from an adjoining shadow: "I think, De Jong, you could defer all this until later."

Her mother, the tall man, De Jong, had not missed her. They fell silent, and then De Jong led the way into the house. Lucy Wilson was sitting where they had left her. It might have been the instant before, she was so still and pale and changeless. Bill was in a corner, gazing at the floor. Something kept him from looking at the girl in the ermine wrap. Every fiber inside him demanded refreshment in this full, bold light. She must be pretty, he thought. No, beautiful. What had he done?

"Where is—" began the sabled woman, hesitating near the doorway. Her old eyes, older than they should have been, went from one face to another, uncertainly, and then settled with a slow horror on the stiff legs behind the table.

Andrea Gimball murmured, "Mother. Please. Please don't."

Then Bill looked at her. In the light of the lamp he saw grace and youth and beauty—and something else which made the unrelaxed pressure against his lips burn a little with remembrance. This was so futile, he thought, and so ill-timed. This girl represented everything he had always held in contempt. A young débutante. Society. Wealth. The snobbishness of blood. Idleness. The antithesis of what he and Lucy were and stood for. His duty was clear. There was more than duty to the law; there was something else. He glanced at his sister, so deathly still in her chair. She was beautiful, too—but in a different way. And she was his sister. How could he be thinking such thoughts at such a time… And now two things burned: his lips and fingers in his pocket closed about the diamond he had picked up from the rug.

"Mrs. Gimball," came Ellery's cool, remote voice, "will you please identify the body?"

The blood was sucked out of Lucy Wilson's face. The sight of her increasing pallor brought Bill Angell sharply to himself.

"I still don't see," said Chief De Jong in a puzzled tone, "what the devil you're driving at, Mr. Queen."

But the woman in the sable coat was floating across the fawn rug like a somnambulist. Her thin figure, erect and regal and dehydrated, was steel. The girl remained where she was, and the silk-hatted man put out a hand and steadied her. De Jong's nostrils were oscillating; he darted behind the table and snatched the newspaper from Joseph Wilson's face.

"That is—" began the woman, and she stopped. "He is—" She groped with one heavily jeweled hand for the table behind her.

"You're sure? There's no possibility of error?" asked Ellery calmly from the door.

"None… whatever. He was hurt in an automobile accident fifteen years ago. You can still see the permanent scar over his left eyebrow."

Lucy Wilson uttered an inchoate scream and leaped to her feet. Her control was gone; under the plain dress her breasts heaved wildly. She sprang forward as if she meant to tear the other woman to pieces. "What do you mean?" she cried. "What do you mean? What do you mean coming here like this? Who are you?"

The tall woman turned her head slowly. Their eyes touched—hot young black eyes and the brittle blue of age.

Mrs. Gimball drew her sable coat more closely about her in a gesture almost insulting. "And who are you?"

"I? I?" Luck shrieked. "I'm Lucy Wilson. That's Joe Wilson, of Philadelphia. That's my husband!"

For an instant the woman in evening clothes looked bewildered. Then her eyes sought Ellery's at the door and she said coldly, "What nonsense. I'm afraid I don't understand, Mr. Queen. What sort of game is this?"

"Mother," said Andrea Gimball in an anguished voice. "Please, Mother."

"Tell Mrs. Wilson," said Ellery without moving, "precisely who the man on the floor is, Mrs. Gimball."

The cold woman said, "This is Joseph Kent Gimball of Park Avenue, New York. My husband. My husband."

Ella Amity screamed "Oh, my God!" and sprang like a cat for the door.

II

THE TRAIL

"… the trail of the serpent is over them all."

IF THAT DOESN'T beat all hell," said De Jong. "Cheese!" With a brutal gesture he tore the cigar from his mouth and hurled it to the floor. And then he sprang after the Amity woman.

Lucy Wilson stood gripping her throat as if she were afraid it might burst. Her black eyes were groping from Mrs. Gimball to the man on the floor in helpless agony. Andrea Gimball was shivering and biting her lips.

"Gimball," said Bill in a shocked voice. "Good Lord, Mrs. Gimball, do you realize what you're saying?"

The society woman made an imperious gesture with her fine thin white veined hands. The jewels sparkled under the lamp. "This is insanity. Who are these people, Mr. Queen? And why am I subjected to this ridiculous scene when my husband is… lying here dead?"

Lucy's nostrils expanded like sails in a storm. "Your husband? Yours? This is Joe Wilson, I tell you. Maybe your husband just looks like my Joe. Oh, please go away, won't you?"

"I refuse to discuss my personal affairs with you," said the woman in sables haughtily. "Where is that man who's in charge? Of all the disgraceful exhibitions—"

"Jessica," said the tall middle-aged man patiently. "Perhaps you had better sit down and permit Mr. Queen and me to handle this matter. It's obvious that a shocking error's occurred, but it won't be helped by nerves or a brawl." He spoke as if he were addressing a child. The angry line between his brows had vanished. "Jessica?"

Her lips were bitter parallel lines. She sat down.

"Did I understand you to say," asked the man with the silk hat in a courteous voice, "that you are Mrs. Lucy Wilson of Fairmount Park, Philadelphia?"

"Yes. Yes!" cried Lucy.

"I see." The glance he gave her was cold, rather calculating, as if he were weighing in his deliberate way how much of her was real and how much false. "I see," he said again, and this time the line reappeared between his brows.

"I don't believe," said Bill wearily, "I caught the name."

The tall man made a wry face. "Grosvenor Finch, and I've been an intimate friend of the Borden and Gimball families for more years than I care to count. I came here tonight only because Mr. Jasper Borden, Mrs. Gimball's father, is an invalid and requested me to take his place by his daughter's side." Finch placed his silk hat carefully on the table. "I came, as I say," he continued in his quiet way, "as a friend of Mrs. Gimball's. It begins to appear that I shall have to stay in quite a different capacity."

"And what," said Bill softly, "do you mean by that?"

"May I question your right to ask, young man?"

Bill's eyes flashed. "I'm Bill Angell, attorney, of Philadelphia. Mrs. Wilson's brother."

"Mrs. Wilson's brother. I see." Finch glanced at Ellery, nodding in an interrogatory way. Ellery, who had not stirred from the door,

49

muttered something; and Finch rounded the table and stooped over the body. He did not touch it. For a moment he stared at the frozen, upturned face; then he said in a low voice: "Andrea, my dear, do you think you could bring yourself—?"

Andrea swallowed; she looked sick. But she set her smooth jaw and came forward and stood at his shoulder, forcing herself to look down. "Yes." Andrea turned away, ashen. "That's Joe. Joe, Ducky."

Finch nodded, and Andrea went to her mother's chair and stood behind it rather helplessly. "Mrs. Wilson," continued the distinguished-looking man, "you must understand you've made a horrible mistake."

"I haven't!"

"A mistake, I repeat. I sincerely hope it's that—and nothing more." Lucy's hands fluttered in protest. "I assure you once more," the tall man went on soberly, "that this gentleman on the floor is Joseph Kent Gimball of New York, the legally wedded husband of the lady in the chair, who was Jessica Borden, then Mrs. Richard Paine Monstelle, and then—after the early death of Monstelle—Mrs. Joseph Kent Gimball. The young lady is Joseph Gimball's stepdaughter Andrea, Mrs. Jessica Gimball's daughter by her first husband."

"You may spare us," remarked Ellery, "the genealogical details."

Finch's clear and honest gray eyes did not waver. "I've known Joe Gimball for over twenty years, ever since his undergraduate days at Princeton. I knew his father, old Roger Gimball of the Back Bay branch of the family; he died during the War. And his mother, who died six years ago, a Providence Kent. For generations the Gimballs have been—" he hesitated—"one of our more prominent families. Now do you see how impossible it is for this man to have been your husband, Mrs. Wilson?"

Lucy Wilson uttered a curious little sigh, like the breath of an expiring hope. "We've never been anybody. Just working people. Joe was, too. Joe couldn't have been—"

"Lucy dear," said Bill gently. Then he said, "You see, the funny part of it is that we're just as certain he's Joe Wilson, of Philadelphia, itinerant peddler who made his living selling cheap jewelry to middle-class housewives. We've got his car outside, and his peddler's stock. We have the contents of his pockets, samples of his handwriting—all evidence that he was Wilson the peddler, not Gimball the society man. Impossible, Mr. Finch? You can't really believe that."

The tall man returned his gaze; there was something reluctant and stubborn in the set of his handsome jaw.

Jessica Gimball said, "A peddler?" in a voice sick with loathing.

Andrea was staring at Bill with a horror in her eyes that had not gone away since she set foot in the shack.

"The answer," said Ellery from the doorway, "is obvious enough. Of course you've guessed it, Bill." He shrugged. "This man was both."

De Jong burst in, bug-eyed with triumph. He stopped short. "Oh, getting acquainted?" he asked, rubbing his hands. "That's the stuff; no sense getting the wind up. It's just too bad all round, just too bad." But he kept rubbing his hands. There was a continuous sound of departing motors from the road.

"We have just come to the conclusion, De Jong," said Ellery, walking slowly forward, "that this is not some fictional case of twins, or impersonation, but a sordid one of deliberately assumed double identity. More frequent than people realize. There can't be any doubt about it. You have positive identification on both sides. Everything fits."

"Does it?" said De Jong pleasantly.

"We know that, as Joseph Wilson, this man for years spent only two or three days a week in Philadelphia with Lucy Wilson; you yourself, Bill, were disturbed by this peculiarity in his behaviour. And I am sure Mrs. Gimball can tell us that her husband spent several days each week away from the Gimball home in New York."

The middle-aged eyes were haggard, red with lacquered resentment that made them glow from her bony face. "For years," she said. "Joe

51

was always… Oh, how could he have done such a thing? He used to say he had to be by himself or he would go mad. The beast, the beast!" Her voice was choked with passion.

"Mother," said Andrea. She placed her slim hands on the trembling woman's shoulders. "Joe said he had a hideaway somewhere not far from New York. He would never tell mother or anyone where, saying that a man was entitled to his privacy. We never suspected because he never liked the social life…."

"I can see now," cried Mrs. Gimball, "that it was just an excuse to get away and be with this—this woman!"

Lucy quivered as if she had been struck. Grosvenor Finch shook his head at Mrs. Gimball in disapproval and warning. But she plunged on. "And I never suspected. What a fool!" Her voice was savage. "Cheap. Cheap. To do such a cheap thing… to me."

"Cheapness is a point of view, Mrs. Gimball," said Bill coldly. "Please remember that my sister is involved. She's as good—"

"Bill," said Ellery. "We'll get nowhere with these childish recriminations. On the other hand, common sense demands a clarification of the situation. This place confirms the dual-personality theory. Here we find the two personalities intermingled. Wilson clothes and Gimball clothes, a Wilson car and a Gimball car. This was, in a manner of speaking, neutral territory. Undoubtedly he stopped here periodically on his way to Philadelphia to change into his Wilson outfit and take the Wilson Packard; and stopped again on his return journey to New York to change back into his Gimball clothes and take the Gimball Lincoln. Of course, he never did sell this cheap jewelry; he merely told Mrs. Wilson he did… And by the way, Mrs. Gimball, what makes you think your—this man was conducting a tawdry tabloid affair with Mrs. Wilson?"

The woman's lip curled. "What would a man like Joe Gimball want with a woman like this but one thing? Oh, I suppose she's attractive enough in a coarse way"—Lucy blushed to the cleft between her breasts—"but Joe was a man of breeding, of taste. It wouldn't be more than the most passing fancy. Husband! Fiddlesticks. It's a plot." Her brittle eyes examined Lucy with a corrosive hatred that melted the clothes away and left her victim naked. Lucy flinched as the acid bit; but her eyes glittered. Bill checked her with a whisper.

"Mrs. Gimball—" began Ellery frigidly.

"No! Do something about these people, Ducky, please. You can see that this woman is paid hush-money, or whatever it is they call it. Anything! I'm sure a cheque will keep her quiet; it always does."

"Jessica," said Finch angrily. "Please."

"I'm afraid it won't be as simple as that, Mrs. Gimball," snapped Ellery. "Lucy… Lucy!"

Lucy's black eyes went smoking to his face. "Yes?"

"Did you ever go through a marriage ceremony with the man you know as Joseph Wilson?"

"He married me. I'm not a—a… He married me!"

"Married you," sniffled the society woman. "A likely story!"

"Where were you married?" asked Ellery quietly.

"We got our license in the Philadelphia City Hall. We were—we were married by a minister in a midtown church."

"Have you your marriage certificate?"

"Oh, yes, yes."

Mrs. Gimball moved restlessly. "How long," she demanded, "do I have to submit to this intolerable situation? It's quite obvious this is a plot. Ducky, do something! Marriage certificate…"

"Can't you see, Mother," whispered Andrea, "that Mrs.. Wilson isn't—isn't what you said? Please, Mother. This is more serious than—Oh, you must be reasonable!"

Bill Angell asked in a strangled tone: "When did you marry Joseph Kent Gimball, madam?"

The elderly woman tossed her head, disdaining to reply. But Grosvenor Finch said in a worried voice: "They were married at St Andrew's Cathedral in New York on June tenth, 1927."

Lucy cried out, in something so much like triumph that the cold woman opposite her started. They faced each other, separated by five feet of empty space, the stark legs of the dead man beyond and between them, like rails of a fence. "Sunday. Fifth Avenue," said Lucy in a throbbing murmur. "The Cathedral. High hats, limousines, jewelry, flower girls, society reporters, the Bishop himself… Oh, my God!" She laughed. "I suppose it was cheap when Joe courted me in Philadelphia, hiding behind the name of Wilson because he was afraid, I suppose, to become involved under his right name. I suppose it was cheap when he fell in love with me and married me." She sprang to her feet, and in the shocked silence her voice rang. "For eight years the cheapness has been all on his side and yours. Cheap, am I? For eight years you've lived with that man with no more right than—than any woman of the streets!"

"What," whispered Andrea, "do you mean, Mrs. Wilson?"

Bill said slowly, "As Joseph Wilson he married my sister on February twenty-fourth, 1925. Over two years before he married your mother, Miss Gimball."

The only sounds for seconds after was the short sharp cry wrung from Jessica Gimball. Then she said, "1925? You accuse him of being a bigamist, me of—of not… You're lying, the pack of you!"

"Are you sure, Bill Angell?" whispered Andrea Gimball. "Oh, are you sure?"

Bill passed his hand over his lips. "It's true, Miss Gimball, and we can prove it. And unless you can produce a marriage certificate ante-dating February twenty-fourth, 1925, your mother is in for it. We've nothing but justice on our side, and we must protect ourselves."

"Oh, but this is infamous!" said Mrs. Gimball furiously. "There must be a mistake somewhere. There must!"

Grosvenor Finch said, "Now let's not be hasty, please. Mr. Angell, Mrs. Gimball is naturally overwrought, and of course she's sorry for what she said about your sister. Can't this be adjusted in some way? No, Jessica! Perhaps, Mr. Queen, a little influence—"

"Too late," said Ellery coldly. "You saw that red-haired young woman fly out of here. She's the press. The story is already on the wires, Finch."

"But this bigamy angle. She hasn't heard that. I'm sure—"

Bill scowled and began to pace about. "Nothing on earth will stop those bloodhounds from hunting up the marriage dates. We'll have to face it together. God knows we're all in the same mess." Lucy sat quietly, still as death.

"Very well," said Finch slowly. The muscles of his large jaw were churning. "If it's to be a battle, I've a card to play—"

"I think," said a sardonic voice from the corner, "that I've let this go just about far enough." Chief De Jong grinned at them without humor; they had forgotten him. "Now that everybody's getting ugly, I'll get tough myself. Murphy, you took it all down?" The detective in the doorway chewed his pencil, nodding. "Now, then," continued De Jong, striding forward, "let's get organized. You first, Queen. I think your actions call for an explanation."

Ellery shrugged as he put his pipe away. "This man's face bothered me all evening. I didn't know why. Then it came back to me. The irritant was a resemblance. I attended a banquet some months ago in honor of somebody or other, and I met and conversed with a man who, I saw, might have been the twin brother of the man I had been told tonight was Joe Wilson, Lucy's husband. But my tête-à-tête had been introduced to me as Joseph Kent Gimball of New York. When I recalled Joseph Wilson's habitual absence from his Philadelphia home, it seemed to me a tragic possibility that Wilson and Gimball were the same man. So I went down the road and telephoned Gimball's home in New York."

"We'd have spotted it soon enough," said De Jong grudgingly. "So?"

Ellery stared at him. "The only one in was Jasper Borden, Gimball's father-in-law. I asked a few questions, discovered that Gimball hadn't been home since the middle of last week, knew I was on the right track, and announced what had happened. Mr. Borden said his family was out, but that he'd sound the tocsin and send them out here as soon as possible."

"Borden, hey?" muttered De Jong. "Old railroad man. Why isn't your father with you, Mrs. Gimball?"

Andrea sighed. "Grandfather hasn't stirred from the house for several years. He suffered a stroke in 1930 that paralyzed his entire left side."

"Where were you people tonight? Where'd the old boy reach you?"

"Mother and I attended a charity ball at the Waldorf. We were there with a party of friends. Mr. Finch, my fiancé Mr. Burke Jones of Newport, Mrs.—"

"All together, hey?" said De Jong. "Big ball, I suppose?" For some reason not altogether clear, Bill Angell felt himself flushing. He might have known, he thought. He glanced at the girl's face, and then at her left hand. She had slipped the setting off her finger.

"If you mean," said Finch icily, "that any of us could have stolen off, driven out here, and stabbed Joe Gimball to death, I suppose you would be hypothetically correct. But if you've quite finished with this nonsense, I have something to say—"

"A good alibi never hurt anybody, see?" drawled De Jong. "Where's this boy-friend of yours, Miss Gimball? This Jones."

"We weren't sure that it was Joe who'd been…" Andrea caught herself up; she avoided Bill's gaze. "Well, I—I didn't tell Burke. Grandfather spoke to Mother on the telephone when he had located us, and we didn't believe it. But he was so insistent we felt we had to come and see. I didn't want to involve Burke in a—in a…"

"I get it, I get it," said De Jong. "Might spoil the match. Boy-friend jilts gal. Bad stuff for the papers. Nuts! Now, Mr. Finch, you've been steaming to get something off your chest. Go to it."

"Under ordinary circumstances," replied Finch in a stiff tone, "I should dislike even to bring the matter up. But we have our position to defend as well. This middle-class antagonism toward wealth, De Jong, can be damned annoying at times. Yes, I've something to reveal; and I'm afraid it's going to prove unpleasant."

Ellery stirred. "May I suggest you come to the point?"

"I suppose you do not know who I am. It wouldn't matter ordinarily, and I shouldn't bring it up; but it happens to be relevant to what I have to say. I am Executive Vice-President of the National Life Insurance Company, you see."

"Yeah?" said De Jong; he did not seem impressed, although the National was one of the largest life-insurance companies in the world.

"In the course of my connection with the company," continued Finch gently, "I've had occasion to insure many of my friends. Not as a broker, you understand—we've progressed since those days." He smiled a little. "Purely as an accommodation. My friends call me the highest-paid insurance broker in the world. Ha, ha!"

"Ha, ha," said De Jong sourly. "So?"

"Among the small number whose policies I have handled personally was Gimball. We've often jested about it. Rather remarkable policy. He came to me in '30 and asked me to insure him for a million dollars."

"A what?" gasped the policeman.

"A million dollars. It isn't the largest policy I've seen drawn, by any means, although it's the only one I've ever heard of issued to a man so young. You see, in 1930 Gimball was only thirty-three years old. The annual premium came to a mere twenty-seven thousand or so. At any rate, we managed it for him; he was in perfect health; and the policy was issued as of that year."

"All by the National?" murmured Ellery. "I've always thought some law or other forbids one insurance company assuming such a large risk."

"Quite true. The legal limit for a single company is three hundred thousand. In the case of a contract exceeding that amount the excess is underwritten by other companies; quite the usual procedure. The National took three hundred thousand, and we arranged matters so that seven other companies took up one hundred thousand each. The contract was handled as a unit, and Gimball paid his premiums through the National. Policy's in excellent condition—no loans outstanding and the premiums are paid up to date."

"A million dollars," said Bill dazedly. De Jong looked down at the still body in awe.

"Just what," asked Ellery in a patient tone, "is the point?"

The tall man looked him in the eye. "I am an officer of the National," he said dryly. "Every insurance company has occasion to question the death of some insured. We have here a case of out-and-out murder. A case of murder, moreover, in which the victim was carrying a million dollars' worth of insurance. I presume you know the law. In effect the law says that an insurance contract is automatically cancelled upon sufficient proof that the insured met his death through the instrumentality of his beneficiary."

For a moment there was silence; and then Mrs. Gimball said with a gasp, "But, Ducky—"

"Ducky!" cried Andrea. "Are you mad?"

Finch smiled. "My duty, of course, is first to the company. The merest routine would dictate that we thoroughly investigate this murder. The amount at stake is considerable. If Gimball was murdered by his beneficiary proof of that would mean that the National and the seven other companies are liable only for the money he invested, plus accumulated dividends and interests—over a period of only five years—especially when the cash-surrender value is taken into consideration, a negligible sum compared with the million-dollar face of the policy."

"By God," exclaimed De Jong, "don't tell me an outfit like the National Life can't stand paying out three hundred grand."

The tall man looked shocked. "My dear man! That's not the point at all. Under the law it is virtually impossible for any company insuring

lives to be in a precarious financial position. As for the National…
Preposterous! It's a matter of principle, that's all. If insurance companies didn't protect themselves by such investigations, it would invite
every morally unbalanced beneficiary to murder the insured."

"And who," asked Ellery, "is Gimball's beneficiary?"

The same two uniformed men who had appeared hours before with
their stretchers clumped in. They dropped the stretcher by the body.

Mrs. Gimball suddenly buried her stern face in her hands and began
to sob. From the expressions of stupefaction on the faces of Grosvenor
Finch and Andrea it was evident that the spectacle of Jessica Gimball
weeping was as rare as rain in the Sahara.

"Jessica," said Finch in a troubled voice. "Jessica! Surely you don't
think—"

"Don't touch me, you—you Judas!" sobbed the middle-aged
woman. "To accuse me of—of…"

"Mrs. Gimball is Gimball's beneficiary?" remarked Ellery. He
watched them without expression.

"Jessica, don't, please. I've been an ass… Look here, Queen, of
course I'm not accusing Jessica Gimball of the murder. That's…" He
could not find an adequate word to express the ridiculousness of the
thought. "I meant to explain than Jessica Gimball was the beneficiary
of Joe Gimball. She isn't any more."

The weeping woman stiffened. Andrea drew her slender figure to
its full height, her blue eyes sparkling with indignation. "Hasn't this
gone far enough, Ducky? We all know that Mother was Joe's beneficiary—it was Grandfather who suggested his taking the insurance in
the first place, with his old-fashioned ideas about the 'responsibilities'
of a husband. Not that Mother needs it! You can't be serious."

"But I am," said Finch miserably. "I was in no position to tell you,
Jessica, or I should have. These matters are confidential, and when I
discovered that Joe had arranged for a change of beneficiary, he swore
me to silence. What could I do?"

"Let's get this straight," said De Jong, his predatory eyes glittering. "Start from the beginning. When did he come to you?"

"He didn't come to me. About three weeks ago—it was on May tenth—I was informed by Miss Zachary, my secretary, that a request had been received in the mail from Gimball for a change-of-beneficiary form. I was surprised that Joe hadn't spoken to me about it, because I had always handled his policy—with a select few others— personally. However, it didn't make any difference, because all Gimball policy matters automatically reached my desk. Of course, the requested forms were immediately sent out, and then I telephoned Joe at his office."

"Hold it," rasped De Jong. "Hey, you guys, get that stiff out of here, will you? What the hell you rubbernecking for?" The uniformed men stopped gaping and hastily departed with their covered burden.

"Joe," faltered Lucy, staring at the closed door; and then she fell silent. Mrs. Gimball glared at the door with resentment, as if she could never forgive what the dead man had done. Her jeweled fingers were twitching.

The tall man said quickly, "I 'phoned him for a confirmation. I couldn't understand why Joe should want to change his beneficiary. Of course, strictly speaking, it was none of my affair; and I told him so at once. But Joe wasn't angry; just nervous. Yes, he said, he meant to change his beneficiary for reasons too involved to go into at the time. He did say vaguely that Jessica was independently wealthy, didn't need the protection of the policy, or some such rot; and he asked me to keep his intention a secret, at least until he could talk to me alone and explain."

"And did he?" murmured Ellery.

"Unfortunately, no. I hadn't seen or talked with him since our telephone conversation three weeks ago. I've the feeling he was avoiding me, perhaps to escape the necessity of explaining as he had promised. When I saw the name of the new beneficiary on the application it meant nothing at all to me, of course. And I'm afraid that after the first reaction of worry over the implication of a rift between Jessica and Joe I quite forgot the whole matter."

"What happened after your talk?" demanded De Jong.

"He filled out the forms and mailed them to me with the policies a few days later; it took a couple of weeks to handle the matter with the other companies, but the altered policies were returned to him last Wednesday; and that's the last of it. Until tonight." Finch frowned. "And tonight he's dead by someone's hand. It's deucedly odd."

"We seem to be arriving at the crucial point," said Ellery patiently, "by the most circuitous route. Will you please—?"

Finch stared from face to face. "You will understand," he said uneasily, "that what I am about to tell you is merely a statement of fact. I've not made up my mind, and I shouldn't care to have my position misconstrued... The significance of this change of beneficiary didn't strike me until I walked into this hovel tonight and discovered..." He paused. "When Gimball returned his applications and policies, he indicated in the proper places that his beneficiary was to be changed from Jessica Borden Gimball to... Mrs. Lucy Wilson. Mrs. Lucy Wilson, I repeat, giving a specific address in Fairmount Park, Philadelphia!"

"Me?" said Lucy faintly. "Me? A million dollars?"

"You're sure of that, Mr. Finch?" De Jong leaned forward in an eager attitude. "You're not just making that up to throw dust in my eyes?"

"I suppose," said Finch coldly, "I shouldn't bridle at anything. I assure you I have nothing against Mrs. Wilson, whom I've never even seen before tonight and who is, I feel certain, the victim of a terrible misunderstanding. On the other hand, if I am to argue the point, I should think 'making it up', as you put it, would be quite stupid of me. The National is an institution above personalities or the possibility of individual machination."

"Talk United States."

Finch stared. "Nor do I see the necessity for your insulting manner. However, to proceed, the records exist, and no one, not I nor Hathaway, President of the National, nor anyone on this earth could falsify them. Besides, you will find Joseph Kent Gimball's application, in his verifiable handwriting, both in our photostatic files and in his own policies, wherever they may be—his office safe, or his bank vault."

The policeman nodded impatiently; his eyes were on Lucy, pinning her to her chair with a remorseless calculation. Lucy shrank back, her fingers fumbling with a button on her dress.

"That was beastly of Joe," cried Mrs. Gimball passionately. "This… this creature his beneficiary, his wife… I simply refuse to believe it. It's not the money. But the callousness, the bad taste—"

"Hysterics won't help, dear lady," observed Ellery. He had removed his pince-nez and was scrubbing the lenses with an absent vigor. "Tell me, Mr. Finch; you haven't breathed a word of this beneficiary change to anyone?"

"Naturally not," growled Finch, still offended. "Joe asked me to keep quiet about it, and I did so."

"Of course, Gimball himself wouldn't have told anyone," mused Ellery. "He stood apparently at some emotional crossroad; he had taken action and was making up his mind how to break the news. You know, it all tenors snugly. Bill Angell received a wire from Wilson—I suppose we should continue to differentiate between his personalities—yesterday morning, requesting him to come here last night on a matter of extreme urgency. He was in trouble, he wired. It's obvious he meant to tell Bill the whole story, make a clean breast of his predicament, and ask his advice as to future procedure. I don't doubt his own mind was made up, for he had changed his beneficiary to Lucy. But he was probably uneasy about how she would take the revelation that he was another man altogether. What do you think, Bill?"

"I'm past thinking," said Bill dully. "But I imagine you're right enough."

"And that bulky envelope he left with you Friday? Has it occurred to you that it may contain the eight policies?"

"It has."

"Well, it won't take genius to determine that—"

"Mrs. Wilson," said De Jong rudely. "Look at me."

Lucy obeyed as if mesmerized; the bewilderment, the pain, the shock had not yet drained away from her sweet, strong features.

Bill growled: "I don't like that tone of yours, De Jong."

"Then lump it. Mrs. Wilson, did you know that Gimball was insured?"

"I?" she faltered. "I knew? No, really I didn't… Joe didn't carry any insurance. I'm sure he didn't. I once asked him why, and he said he didn't believe in such things."

"Not the reason at all, of course," drawled Ellery. "Insurance as Joe Wilson meant a medical examination, the signing of documents. And a man living constantly in the fear that his double life might be exposed would avoid signing his name whenever possible. That explains why he didn't carry a checking account—a remote risk, but he must have been in the last stages of nervous exhaustion over the constant strain of maintaining the deception. I daresay he wrote as little as he could get by with."

"You not only knew he carried insurance, Mrs. Wilson," snapped De Jong, glaring at Ellery, "but maybe you persuaded him to change his beneficiary from Mrs. Gimball to yourself, hey?"

"De Jong—" warned Bill, stepping forward.

"Keep quiet, you!" The three people from New York were frozen. All at once something menacing had invaded the shabby room. De Jong's face was very red, and the arteries in his temples bulged.

"I don't know what you mean," whispered Lucy. "I've told you I didn't know he was anybody… I mean, anybody but Joe Wilson. How could I know about this lady?"

De Jong sneered, his nostrils derisive. Then he stepped to the side-door, opened it, crooked his finger. The small brown man who had brought Lucy to the shack came in, blinking a little in the light. "Sellers, tell me again for the benefit of these good people what you did when you drove up to Mrs. Wilson's house in Philly last night."

"I found the house, all right, got out of my car, and rang the bell," replied the detective in a tired voice. "No answer. House dark. Just a private house, see? I waited on the porch a while, then I thought I'd take a look around. The back door was locked, like the front; cellar, too. I nosed around the garage. Doors shut. Iron staple across the door rusted and broken, no lock there at all. I opened the doors and switched on the light. Two-car garage, empty. Closed the doors again and went back to the porch and waited until Mrs. Wilson came—"

"That's all, Sellers," said De Jong; and the brown man went out. "Well, Mrs. Wilson, you didn't drive into town to see that movie; you said yourself you took the trolley. Then where's your car?"

"My car?" echoed Lucy feebly. "Why, that can't be. He—he must have looked in the wrong garage. I was out driving by myself a bit yesterday afternoon and got back in the rain and put the car into the garage and closed the door myself. It was there. It is there."

"Not if Sellers says it isn't. Don't know what happened to it, do you, Mrs. Wilson?"

"I just told you—"

"What make and year is it?"

"Not another word, Lu," said Bill quietly. He strode forward until he stood chest to chest with the big policeman, and for a moment they glared into each other's eyes. "De Jong, I don't like the damned nasty implications in those questions of yours, d'ye understand? I forbid my sister to say another word."

De Jong considered him in silence; then he smiled crookedly. "Now, hold your horses, Mr. Angell. You know this is just routine stuff. I'm not accusing anybody. Just trying to get at the facts."

"Very laudable." Bill turned abruptly to Lucy. "Come on, Lu; we're getting out of here. Ellery, I'm sorry; but this bird's just impossible. I'll see you tomorrow here in Trenton—if you're still with us."

"I'll be here," said Ellery.

Bill helped Lucy into her coat and then led her like a child to the door.

"Just a moment, please," said Andrea Gimball.

Bill stood still, the tips of his ears reddening. Lucy looked at the young girl in ermine as if she were seeing her for the first time, with a dazed curiosity. Andrea went to her and took her large soft hand. "I want you to know," she said steadily, avoiding Bill's eyes, "that I'm frightfully sorry about… everything. We're not monsters, really we're not. Please forgive us, my dear, if we've—we've said anything to hurt you. You're a very brave and unfortunate woman."

"Oh, thank you," murmured Lucy. Her eyes filled with tears and she turned and ran out.

"Andrea!" said Mrs. Gimball in a shocked, furious voice. "How dare you—how can you—"

"Miss Gimball," said Bill in a low voice. She looked at him then, and for a time he did not speak. "I won't forget this." He turned on his heel and followed Lucy. The door banged, and a moment later they heard Bill's Pontiac puffing off in the direction of Camden. There was a defiant snort to the exhaust, and De Jong was white with rage. He lit a cigar with a trembling hand.

"Ave atque vale," said Ellery. "You dislike him, De Jong, but he's a very estimable young man. Like all male animals, dangerous when his females are threatened… In the name of friendship, Miss Gimball, may I thank you? And now, may I inspect your hands?"

She raised her eyes slowly to his face. "My hands?" she whispered.

De Jong muttered something under his breath and stamped away.

"Under less painful circumstances," said Ellery as he raised her hands, "this would be a pleasure of considerable proportions. If I possess an Achillean heel, Miss Gimball, it's paradoxically my weakness for the well-kept hands of a woman. Yours, it's needless to remark, are of the essence of manual perfection… Did I understand you to say that you are engaged to be married?"

Under his fingers he felt her palms go moist; there was the merest suggestion of a tremble in the soft flesh he was holding. "Yes. Yes."

"Of course," murmured Ellery, "it's none of my business. But is it the latest mode for the wealthy young bride-to-be to eschew the symbol of plighted troth? Syrus said that God looks at pure, not full, hands; but I didn't know our upper classes had taken up the classics." She said nothing; her face was so pale he thought she was going to faint. Mercifully, Ellery turned to her mother. "By the way, Mrs. Gimball, I'm a hound for verifications. I noticed that your—er—husband's hands, since we're on the subject, showed no nicotine stains, nor were his teeth discolored. And there are no tobacco shreds in the crevices of his pockets, and no ashtrays here. It's true, then, that he didn't smoke?"

De Jong came back. "What's this about smoking?" he growled.

The society woman snapped: "No, Joseph didn't smoke. Of all the idiotic questions!" She rose and offered a limp arm to the tall man. "May we go now? All this…"

"Sure," grunted De Jong. "I'd like you people to come back in the morning, though. Certain formalities. And I've just heard that the prosecutor—that's Pollinger—wants to talk to you."

"We'll be back," said Andrea in a low voice. And she shivered again, drawing her wrap more closely about her. There were pale smudges under her eyes. She glanced surreptitiously at Ellery, and quickly away.

"There's no chance," insisted Finch, "of suppressing the story of this… I mean, this prior marriage? It's so terribly awkward, you know, for these people."

De Jong shrugged; his mind seemed on other things. The three stood forlornly at the front door; Mrs. Gimball's sharp chin was forward, although her thin shoulders sagged like weighted panniers.

Then, in a rather oppressive silence, they left. Neither man spoke until the thunder of their motor died away. "Well," said De Jong at last, "that's that. One hell of a mess."

"Messes," remarked Ellery, reaching for his hat, "are what you make 'em, De Jong. This is a fascinating one, at any rate. It would delight the heart of Father Brown himself."

"Who?" said De Jong absently. "You're going back to New York, eh?" He made no effort to conceal his ponderous wistfulness.

"No. There are elements in this puzzle that cry for elucidation. I shouldn't sleep if I dropped out now."

"Oh." De Jong turned to the table. "Well, goodnight, then."

"Goodnight," said Ellery pleasantly. The policeman was stowing away in a paper bag the plate on the table, with its contents. The broad back was surly and antagonistic. Ellery went out to his car whistling and drove back to the Stacy-Trent.

Mr. Ellery Queen left the hotel Sunday morning with a guilty feeling. The soft arms of his bed had betrayed him; it was after eleven.

Downtown Trenton was deserted in the young sun. He walked to the corner and turned east, crossing the street, into a narrow thoroughfare quaintly named Chancery Lane. In the middle of the block he found a long low three-story building that looked remarkably like Army barracks. Before it, on the sidewalk, there stood a tall old-fashioned lamppost topped with lantern-glass; and on the post a square white sign announced in block letters, POLICE HQRS—NO PARKING.

He turned into the nearest doorway and found himself in a narrow dingy reception room with streaky walls, a long desk, and a low ceiling; a room beyond was crowded with green steel lockers. There was a prevailing brown decrepitude and an odor of rancid masculinity in the air that depressed him. The desk sergeant directed him to Room 26, where he found De Jong in earnest conversation with a short skinny man with pale features pinched by cleverness and dyspepsia; and Bill

Angell in a chair, red-eyed and disheveled, looking as if he had neither slept nor taken his clothes off all night.

"Oh, hello," said De Jong without enthusiasm. "Queen, meet Paul Pollinger, prosecutor of Mercer County. Where've you been?"

"Drinking weary childhood's mandragora." Ellery shook hands with the skinny man. "Anything new this morning?"

"You've missed the Gimball crowd. They've come and gone."

"So soon? Hi, there, Bill."

"Hello," said Bill. He was staring at the prosecutor.

Pollinger lit a cigar. "As a matter of fact, this man Finch wants to see you at his office tomorrow morning." He surveyed Ellery over the cocked match.

"Really?" Ellery shrugged. "Have you had the autopsy report yet, De Jong? I'm perishing of curiosity."

"Doc told me to tell you he didn't find any burns."

"Burns?" frowned Pollinger. "Why burns, Mr. Queen?"

Ellery smiled. "Why not? Just one of my usual aberrations. That's all your medico reported, De Jong?"

"Oh, nuts! What's the diff? He did say something about the knife having been stuck into Gimball by a right-handed blow, but that's the regular baloney."

"And how about the envelope Wilson… Gimball—damn the fellow!—left with Bill Angell here?"

The prosecutor flipped a sheaf of documents on De Jong's desk over with his forefinger. "You guessed it. They're the eight policies. Revised to make Lucy Wilson the beneficiary. I imagine Gimball meant to leave them in Angell's keeping for the further protection of Mrs. Wilson. There's no question in my mind about his intention to tell Angell all about his other personality."

"Maybe," grinned De Jong, "the beneficiary change was part of a deal. He knew his wife's brother would be hopping mad, and he figured if he threw a million bucks at 'em it would sort of smooth things over."

Bill said nothing, but he transferred his attention from Pollinger to the chief of police. The hand on his knee was trembling.

"I think not," observed Ellery. "No man deliberately submits himself to a life of mental torture for eight years without overwhelming emotional cause. What you say, De Jong, might be true if Gimball considered Lucy Angell a mere plaything. But he married her ten years ago, and for at least the last eight years he resisted the natural temptation to solve his problem by quietly divorcing her, or simply disappearing, when by staying he was making life a complex hell for himself."

"He loved her," said Bill harshly.

"Oh, unquestionably." Ellery fished for his brier and began to stuff the bowl with tobacco. "He loved her so much that he endured a veritable Proustian life to keep her. The man wasn't a callous libertine; his face and history show that. The worst you can say about him is that he was weak. And then compare Lucy Wilson with Jessica Gimball. You haven't seen Lucy, Pollinger; but De Jong has, and even that ophidian pulse of his must have quickened. She's a remarkably attractive young woman; while Jessica Gimball… Well, it's considered unkind to refer to a lady's wrinkles."

"All that may be true, Queen," said Pollinger. "But if it is, why the devil did he commit bigamy with this society woman?"

"Ambition, perhaps. The Bordens are multi-millionaires. And while Gimball came of blooded stock, I seem to recall that of late years they've been comparatively impoverished. And then old Jasper Borden has no sons. A weak but ambitious man might not be able to resist the temptation—possibly the pressure laid on by a mother of the type he had. Old lady Gimball was a virago; she used to be called by the boudoir gossips the Old Battle-Axe of the Republic. I shouldn't be surprised if, unaware of the mess he was in, she pushed him into the bigamous marriage."

The two Trenton men glanced at each other. "Probably true,"

remarked the prosecutor. "I talked with Mrs. Gimball this morning and from all indications it was one of those marriages of convenience—at least on Gimball's side."

Bill Angell stirred. "I don't see what all this has to do with me. May I go now?"

"Wait a minute, mister," said De Jong. "How about Wilson? I mean, as Wilson did he make a will?"

"I'm sure he didn't. If he had, he would have come to me."

"Everything's in your sister's name?"

"Yes. Both cars, the house—he owned that free and clear."

"And the million." De Jong sat down in his swivel-chair. "And the million. Nice wad for a good-looking young widow."

"One of these days, De Jong," smiled Bill, "I'm going to ram that damned hyena grin of yours down your filthy throat."

"Why, you—"

"Now, now," said Pollinger hastily. "There's no need for this sort of thing. You've brought your sister's marriage certificate, Mr. Angell?"

Glaring at the policeman, Bill threw a document on the desk. "Hmm," said Pollinger. "We've already checked with the Philadelphia records. No question about it. He married Lucy Angell two years before his marriage with this Borden woman. It's a mess."

Bill snatched back the certificate. "Damned right it's a mess—with my sister on the receiving end of the swill!"

"Nobody is—"

"Furthermore, we want custody of that body. He was Lucy's husband and it's our legal right to bury him. There's going to be no argument about that. I'm getting a court order tomorrow. There's not a judge in this State who wouldn't award the burial right to Lucy on this evidence of marriage priority!"

"Oh, now, look here, Angell," said Pollinger uneasily. "After all, isn't that rubbing it in? These New York people are rather powerful; and he was Joseph Kent Gimball, you know. It wouldn't be right—"

"Right?" said Bill grimly. "Who's thinking of my sister's rights? Do you think you can wipe out ten years of a woman's life with one smear? Do you think I'm afraid of that crowd just because they've got position and money? I'll see 'em in hell first!" And he stamped out, his mouth working. The three men remained silent until the clatter of his footsteps on the stairs ceased.

"I told you," remarked Ellery, "that Bill Angell was a man of parts. And don't underestimate his ability as a lawyer, either."

"Now what do you mean by that?" snapped the prosecutor.

Ellery picked up his hat. "To garble Cicero a little—prudence is the knowledge of things to be shunned as well as those to be sought. Beware the Ides of March, and all that sort of thing. 'Voir."

It was nine-thirty on Monday morning when Ellery, in natty olive gabardine and Panama, presented himself at the executive offices of the National Life Insurance Company in its handsome house on lower Madison Avenue in New York. He had spent a cloistered Sunday at home, mulling over the case between the alimentary ministrations of Djuna and the rather cynical comments of his father the Inspector; and despite the vernal gaiety of his costume he was far from cheerful.

A brisk young woman with a toothpaste smile, in the anteroom to the office lettered Office of the Executive Vice-President, raised her brows at his card. "Mr. Finch wasn't expecting you so early, Mr. Queen. He isn't down yet. Wasn't your appointment for ten?"

"If it was, I wasn't informed. I'll wait. Any notion what your precious Mr. Finch wants to see me about?"

"Ordinarily," she smiled, "I should say no. But since you're a detective, I suppose there's no point in dissembling. Mr. Finch telephoned me at home yesterday afternoon and told me all about it. It's about this frightful business in Trenton, and I believe Mrs. Gimball is to be here, too. Won't you wait in Mr. Finch's private office?"

Ellery followed her into a palatial blue-and-ivory room that looked like a motion-picture set. "I seem to be moving in golden circles these days," he observed. "That's metaphoric, not literal, Miss Zachary—isn't that the name?"

"However did you know? Have a seat, Mr. Queen." She hurried to the oversized desk and brought back a box. "Cigaret?"

"No, thanks." Ellery sank into a blue leather chair. "I believe I'll smoke my pipe."

"Would you like to try some of Mr. Finch's tobacco?"

"That's one invitation no confirmed pipe-smoker turns down." The young woman brought him a large jar from the desk, and he filled his pipe. "Mmm. Not bad. Very good, in fact. What is it?"

"Oh, dear, I don't know; I'm stupid about these things. It's a special blend, foreign or something, sold by Pierre of Fifth Avenue. Would you care to have me send you some?"

"Oh, now, really—"

"Mr. Finch won't mind. I've done it before. Oh, good-morning, Mr. Finch." The young woman smiled again and went out.

"Bright and early, I see," said Finch as they shook hands. "Well, well, this business becomes more sickening by the hour. Have you seen the morning papers?"

Ellery grimaced. "The usual orgy."

"Frightful." The tall man put away his hat and stick, sat down, fiddled with his mail, lit a cigaret. Suddenly he looked up. "See here, Queen, there's no point in beating around the bush. I talked to Hathaway and some of the directors early yesterday. We've agreed that, from the company's standpoint, action must be taken."

"Action?" Ellery raised his brows politely.

"You must admit that on the surface the thing looks suspicious. We're making no accusations, but... Excuse me. That must be Jessica." Miss Zachary opened the door to admit Mrs. Gimball, Andrea, and two men.

In thirty-six hours Andrea's mother had become an old woman, Ellery saw at once. She leaned heavily on her daughter's arm, and the eyes she raised in greeting were lifeless. In the clear light cleaving Finch's windows Ellery read the strangulation of a narrow, proud, and inhibited spirit. She could barely walk, and in silence Finch led her to a chair.

When he straightened, his face was troubled. "Mr. Queen, meet Senator Frueh, the Borden attorney." Ellery shook the flaccid hand of a florid, paunchy little man whose shrewd eyes appraised him coldly from a face chiefly remarkable for its beard. Frueh was well-known to him by reputation: an ex-Senator of the Federal Congress, his private practice was arrogantly gilt-edged, and his bearded face was constantly being displayed in the news columns. It was an Olympian brush of the bifurcated variety, reddish in color, and reaching to his chest. He seemed proud of it; his fat hand played with it incessantly. "And this is Burke Jones, Miss Gimball's fiancé. I didn't expect to see you today, Burke."

"I thought I might be of service," said Jones in what Ellery thought was a peculiar diffidence. He was a large young man with calfish empty eyes, a skin burned walnut by the sun, and a slouch. His right arm was trussed in a sling. "Hullo. So you're Queen, eh? I've been reading your books for years." He said it as if Ellery were one of the better-known monstrosities of a freak show.

"I hope the disillusionment won't make you stop the practice," chuckled Ellery. "As a matter of fact, I'm not unfamiliar with your own exploits. Nasty spill you took at Meadowbrook two weeks ago. Papers were full of it."

Jones grimaced. "Lousy pony. Bad blood somewhere. Blood tells in polo ponies as well as human beings. First time I've ever broken anything at the game. Lucky it wasn't a leg."

"Shall we sit down?" said Finch fretfully. "Miss Zachary, we are not to be disturbed. I was telling Mr. Queen," he continued when they were seated, "what we had decided."

"I don't quite know why I'm honored with all this attention," remarked Ellery. "It's a little overwhelming. My blood isn't bad, Mr. Jones, but it's of the common variety, and I can't help wondering if I'm a little out of my class this morning."

Andrea Gimball stirred. Out of the corner of his eye Ellery noticed that, under the skilful make-up, she was an extraordinarily worried young woman. She had not once glanced at young Jones since their entrance into the office; and as for Jones, there was a pettish line between his thick brows that was curiously unlover-like. They sat stiffly side by side like children angry at each other.

"Before you proceed, Finch," announced Senator Frueh in a gruff voice, "I want Queen to understand I'm not in favor of this."

"Of what?" smiled Ellery.

"Of this deliberate confusion of motives," snapped the bearded lawyer. "Finch has an axe to grind for his blasted company; and we've another entirely different. I agreed, Finch, as I told you last night, only because Jessica and you insisted. If Jessica took my advice—and Andrea's— which she won't, she'd keep strictly out of this stinking tangle."

"No," said Mrs. Gimball in a low voice. "That woman robbed me of everything—my good name, Joe's love. I'll fight. I've always permitted everyone to step over me—father, Joe, even Andrea. This time I'm going to defend myself."

Ellery thought that the woman was stretching the probabilities a little. He could not visualize her as she painted herself. "But there's very little you can do, Mrs. Gimball," he said. "There's no doubt whatever concerning Lucy's—I mean Mrs. Wilson's legal status. She was his lawful wife. The fact that she was his wife under an assumed name doesn't alter the case at all."

"I've been telling mother that," murmured Andrea. "It can't lead to anything but more notoriety. Mother, won't you please—?"

Jessica Gimball's lips compressed. Some strange quality in the undertones of her voice made them silent. "That woman," she said, "killed Joe."

"Oh, I see," said Ellery gravely. "I see. And on what basis do you make this accusation, Mrs. Gimball?"

"I know it. I feel it."

"I'm afraid," he replied in dry tones, "that our courts won't take cognizance of such evidence."

"Please, Jessica," said Grosvenor Finch with a frown. "Look here, Queen. Mrs. Gimball is naturally not herself. Of course hers is no reason at all. But I speak now for the company. The point is that the National Life as such has no personal motive against this woman which might strike anyone as persecutive. It's interested only in determining the facts."

"And since I am also," drawled Ellery, "presumably an objective agent aiming at the same goal, you want my puny assistance?"

"Please. Let me finish. Let me state Hathaway's position; he would have been here to talk to you himself, except that he's ill. Mrs. Wilson became the beneficiary of one of our policy-holders a matter of mere days before his death by violence. True, he created her his beneficiary himself, but there is no proof that she did not beguile or coerce him into making the change."

"Nor proof that she did."

"Very true, very true. Nevertheless, the contingency from our standpoint exists. Now, this contract calls for payment of one million dollars to the new beneficiary. There are peculiar contributory circumstances. The new beneficiary was the secret wife of the insured—at least secret from point of view of his real identity. If she suddenly discovered his perfidy, even granting a genuine love for him prior to that discovery, she would be inhuman if her love did not turn to hate. Add the fact that she was his beneficiary to the tune of a million—that's omitting completely the possibility that her hatred led her to wheedle him into altering his beneficiary—we have a dual motive for murder. Surely you see our position?"

Senator Frueh stirred restlessly in his chair as he fingered his beard. Ellery said apologetically, "I could make out almost as strong a theory—forgive me—to implicate Mrs. Gimball. Discovering that her husband was married to another woman, that indeed she had never been his legal wife, that moreover he had heaped the last indignity upon her of making this other woman his beneficiary... Voilà."

"But the point is that Mrs. Wilson is the beneficiary and the million does go to her. As I say, in the face of these circumstances, the National would be remiss in its duty to its policyholders if it did not hold up payment of the policy pending an investigation."

"Why come to me? Surely you have your own corps of trained investigators?"

"Oh, of course." Finch paused delicately. "But there the personal element enters. I feel that an outside agent, specially employed for the purpose, could be depended upon to exercise more—er—discretion. And then you were on the scene from the beginning..."

Ellery drummed lightly on the arm of his chair. Their eyes watched him. "You know," he said at last, "this is an odd position for me. This woman whom you propose to pillory is the sister of an old chum. I really should be in the other camp. The only element of your request that appeals to me is that you're interested not in a preconceived result but in simply fixing the truth. You could depend upon my discretion, Finch, but not my silence."

"What d'ye mean by that?" demanded Senator Frueh.

"Well, it logically follows, doesn't it? In my pitiful way I try to live up to my Messianic complex. If I should discover the truth, I can't guarantee that it will be a respecter of persons, you see."

Finch rummaged in the papers before him, extracted one, uncapped his fountain-pen, and began to write. "All the National wants," he said quietly, "is reasonable proof that Lucy Wilson did or did not murder or cause to be murdered her husband." He blotted what he had written, rose, circled his desk. "Will this do as a retainer, Mr. Queen?"

Ellery blinked. The piece of paper was a cheque, and above Finch's signature in its distinctive green ink there was stamped the sum of five thousand dollars. "Very handsome," he murmured. "But suppose we defer the question of remuneration until I've had a chance to look around a bit. I haven't quite decided, you see."

Finch's face fell. "As you wish, of course."

"A question or two, please. Mrs. Gimball, have you any idea what the present condition of your—of Gimball's estate is?"

"Estate?" she repeated blankly, almost as if she were annoyed.

"Joe was a poor business man," said Andrea bitterly. "He had nothing in his own name. Poor in that as in everything else."

"If it's his will you're after," grunted the lawyer, "I can tell you that he leaves everything to Jessica Borden Gimball. But since he's left virtually nothing but debts and his insurance, under the circumstances that's a rather cynical bequest."

Ellery nodded. "By the way, Senator, I suppose you knew nothing of Gimball's decision to change his beneficiary?"

"Nothing whatever. The idiot!"

"You, Mr. Jones?"

"I?" The young man raised his brows. "How would I know? We weren't on what you'd call intimate terms."

"Ah, your prospective father-in-law didn't care for you, Mr. Jones, or was it merely lack of common interest?"

"Please," said Andrea wearily. "What good does this sort of thing do, Mr. Queen? Joe hadn't anything to say about it, anyway."

"I see." Ellery rose. "You understand, Finch, that if I accept your assignment there are to be no strings whatever on my activity?"

"I took that for granted."

Ellery picked up his stick. "I'll let you know my decision in a day or so, when more facts leak out of Trenton. Good-morning."

It was growing dark Monday evening when Ellery rang the Borden-Gimball bell on the eleventh floor of a rather staggering Park Avenue pile. A fish-faced man in tails admitted him to the living-room of a duplex apartment in the grand manner. As he lounged about waiting to be announced, inspecting the canvases and the authentic period furniture, he wondered idly out of whose pocket the cost of all this magnificence had come. The apartment itself must lease for between twenty and thirty thousand a year, he judged; and the appointments must have run into six figures, if the room he was in was a criterion. It smacked more of old Jasper Borden than the slight, poetic gentleman he had left on a slab in the Trenton morgue the day before.

The fish-faced man conducted him noiselessly to a suite mysterious with dim lights and velvet hangings, in the midst of which sat a gigantic old man on a wheelchair, enthroned like a dying king. A nurse with forbidding eyes stood guard behind him. There was a brocade dressing-gown over his wing-collar and ascot tie, and a heavy ring with a curious seal on the finger of his gnarled right hand. For an octogenarian he was remarkably well-preserved, Ellery thought, until he noticed the peculiar rigidity of the old man's left side. The muscles on the left side of his face did not move, and even his left eye stared unwinkingly ahead as the right swam about. It was as if he were composed of two bodies, one alive and one dead.

"How do you do, Mr. Queen," he said in a rusty bass voice out of the side of his mouth. "Please excuse me for not rising. And let me thank you for your kind and courteous message Saturday night. To what do I owe the pleasure of this visit?"

There was a mustiness in the dark air that was almost necropolitan. Ellery saw that this man was already in his tomb. The cobalt orbits in which his eyes lay were huge and dead. But, studying that grim chin and rhamphoid nose, imbedded in a face the color of unwatered earth, it came to Ellery that old Jasper Borden was still a force to reckon with. The one fierce moving eye made him as uncomfortable as if it had been a potential convulsion of nature. "Good of you to see me, Mr. Borden," he said quickly. "I shan't waste time in amenities that can only be painful to you. You know the nature of my interest in the death of your son-in-law?"

"I have heard of you, sir."

"But Mrs. Gimball—?"

"My daughter has told me everything."

Ellery paused. "Mr. Borden," he said at last, "truth is a curious thing. It will not be denied, but one can hasten its inevitability. Since you've heard of me, it's unnecessary for me to assure you that my concern with such tragedies as this is completely detached. Will you answer my questions?"

The sunken moving eye steadied. "You realize, Mr. Queen, what this means to me—to my name, my family?"

"Quite."

The old man was silent. Then he said, "What do you want to know?"

"I want to know when you first learned that your son-in-law was leading a double life."

"Saturday night."

"You had never heard of Joseph Wilson—the man or the name?" The ponderous head shook once, slowly. "Now, I believe you were responsible for your son-in-law's taking out the million-dollar policy?"

"I was."

Ellery cleaned the lenses of his pince-nez. "Mr. Borden, did you have any special reason for doing so?"

He fancied that a faint smile lifted the grim blue lips at the right side. "Of a criminal nature, no. My motive was purely one of principle. My daughter did not need her husband's financial protection. But," the rusty voice hardened, "in these modern days, when every man is godless and every woman a shameless gadabout, it is good that someone enforce the old-fashioned virtues. I'm a man of the past, Mr. Queen, an anachronism. I still believe in God and the home."

"And very properly, too," Ellery hastened to reply. "By the way, of course you did not know that your son-in-law—"

"He was not," rumbled the octogenarian, "anything of the sort."

"That Gimball, then—"

79

Borden said quietly, "He was a dog. A carnal beast. A shame and a degradation to everything people of quality stand for."

"I understand your feeling thoroughly, Mr. Borden. I meant to ask if you had known of the change he made in his beneficiary?"

"Had I known," growled the old man, "feeble and chained to this foul chair as I am, I should have throttled him!"

"Mr.—would it be too personal to ask, sir, precisely under what circumstances Gimball courted and married your daughter?" Ellery coughed. "You must understand I use the conventional terms for lack of a more precise phraseology."

For an instant the fierce eye flashed, then the lid drooped. "These are strange days, Mr. Queen. I never liked Joseph Gimball. It always seemed to me that he was a weakling, a shell of a man, too handsome and irresponsible for his own good. But my daughter fell madly in love with him, and I could not deny my only child her chance for happiness. My daughter, you know," the bass voice paused, "was unfortunate in her first marriage. Married young, she suffered the tragedy of seeing her first husband, a very worthy young man of unimpeachable family and position, die of lobar pneumonia. When, years later, Gimball came along, Jessica was already forty." The great right shoulder twitched. "You know how women are."

"And Gimball's financial condition at this time?"

"A pauper," Borden grunted. "His mother was a cunning she-devil, and I'm sure her ambition drove him to the decision to risk bigamy. Joseph Gimball didn't have the gumption to resist a louse, let alone a creature like his mother. Jessica had a substantial fortune in her own right—a combination of her first husband's estate and a legacy from my dear wife—and of course I could not permit her to marry without… He had nothing. I took him into my own business. I thought it might work. I gave him every chance." The voice died off in a dangerous mutter. "The dog, the ungrateful dog. He could have been my son…" The nurse signaled imperiously.

"He managed your affairs, Mr. Borden?"

"That part of them to which he could do the least damage. I have considerable holdings. I presented him with several directorships in corporations I control. In the crash of '29 and '30 he lost everything I'd given him. On Black Friday he must have been off in that den of his in Philadelphia, carousing with that woman!"

"And you, Mr. Borden?" asked Ellery with bland respect.

"I was still active then, Mr. Queen," replied the old man grimly. "They didn't catch Jasper Borden napping. Now—" the shoulder twitched again—"now I'm nothing, a living corpse. They don't even let me smoke my cigars any more. They feed me with a spoon like a cursed—"

The nurse was furious; her thumb was stabbing toward the door.

"One thing more," said Ellery hastily. "Have you always had conscientious objections to divorce, sir?"

For an instant Ellery feared the old millionaire might suffer another stroke. His good eye roved in terrifying circles and his face became suffused with dark blood. "Divorce!" he shouted. "Sinful contrivance of the Devil! No child of mine—" Then he fell silent, muttering. After a while he said in almost a mild voice, "My creed forbids divorce, Mr. Queen. Why do you ask?"

But Ellery murmured: "Thank you, Mr. Borden, you've been very kind. Yes, yes, Nurse, I'm going," and backed to the door.

Someone said behind him, "Mr. Queen," in a dull voice, and he turned to find Jessica Gimball in ghastly black behind him. The tall figure of Finch loomed nearby.

The dark air was stifling. Ellery said, "Sorry," and stepped aside. She drifted past him, already unconscious of his presence. Finch sighed as he followed her.

As he walked off he could not help overhearing old Jasper Borden growl pettishly, "Jessica. Get that dying look off your face! Do you hear?" and the middle-aged woman's submissive, "Yes, Father."

He went down the stairs furiously thoughtful. Much of the background was clear now that had been obscure. And not the least illuminating fact was that Jasper Borden, dying hulk that he was, still ruled his household with an unweakened scepter.

The fish-faced man downstairs looked annoyed, insofar as it was possible for him to express any emotion whatever, when Ellery politely asked to be announced to Miss Andrea Gimball instead of leaving the sacred domain. When Andrea appeared from an inner chamber he stood to one side, stiffly, as if it were his duty to protect her from invasion. At her heels shambled Burke Jones in a dinner jacket, his arm rather sumptuously trussed in a black silk sash.

"Ah, there, Queen," said Jones. "Sleuthing, eh? By George, I envy you chaps. Lead a dashed exciting life. Any luck?"

"None visible," smiled Ellery. "Good evening, Miss Gimball. That man's here again."

"Good evening," said Andrea. She had gone strangely pale at sight of him. Her black low-cut evening gown with its daring lines might have caused another young man to stare with admiration, but Ellery was what he was, and he chose to study her eyes instead. They were wide with fear. "You—you wanted to speak to me?"

"On my way up," remarked Ellery casually, "I noticed a cream-colored car parked at the curb. Sixteen-cylinder Cadillac…"

"Oh," said Jones, "that must be my car."

Ellery caught the instant wave of sheer horror that swept across Andrea's face. She cried involuntarily, "Burke!" and then bit her lip and groped for the back of a chair.

"What the devil's up, Andy?" demanded Jones, his brows drawing together.

"Yours, Jones?" murmured Ellery. "Strange. Bill Angell saw a cream-colored sixteen-cylinder Cadillac roadster leave the driveway in front of the hideaway in which Joseph Gimball was murdered on the very night of the crime. Very strange indeed. Nearly ran Bill down."

Jones's walnut skin went gray. "My—car?" he said at last, moistening his lips. His empty eyes went to Andrea and jerked back. "I say, Queen, that's not possible. I attended that charity jamboree at the Waldorf Saturday night with the Gimball party, and my car was parked on the Avenue all evening. Must be another car."

"Oh, no doubt. And, of course, Miss Gimball can vouch for that."

The girl's lips barely moved. "Yes."

"Oh," said Ellery, "you do vouch for it, Miss Gimball?"

Her hands fluttered a little. "Yes," she whispered. Jones was trying not to look at her. He seemed drawn in upon himself, his big shoulders a little hunched, as if he faced a struggle but did not quite know what course of action to take.

"In that case," said Ellery gravely, "you leave me no choice, Miss Gimball, but to ask to see your engagement ring."

Jones stiffened. His eyes darted from Ellery to Andrea's left hand, and remained fixed there with horror. "Engagement ring?" he muttered. "What earthly reason could—"

"I imagine," said Ellery, "Miss Gimball can answer that."

From somewhere above came the sound of voices. Jones took a short step toward Andrea. "Well?" he said harshly. "Why don't you show it to him?"

Her eyes closed. "Burke…"

"I said," his voice became thick, "why don't you show it to him? Andrea, where is it? Why is he asking? You never told me—"

A door banged on the balcony above; Mrs. Gimball and Grosvenor Finch appeared. "Andrea!" cried Mrs. Gimball. "What's the matter?"

Andrea's hands went to her face; the fourth finger of the left was still bare. And she began to sob.

Mrs. Gimball swooped down the stairs. "Stop that silly crying!" she said sharply. "Mr. Queen, I insist on an explanation."

"I merely asked," said Ellery patiently, "your daughter to show me her engagement ring, Mrs. Gimball."

"Andrea," rasped Jones, "if you've got me into a mess…"

"Andrea," said Mrs. Gimball. "What—?" Her face was livid and old. Finch ran down the stairs; he was obviously distressed.

"Oh," sobbed Andrea, "is everyone against me? Can't you see I—I—?"

Mrs. Gimball said coldly, "If my daughter won't answer your silly questions, Mr. Queen, she won't. I don't understand your motive, but I see now that you're protecting that precious sister of that nauseating young man from Philadelphia. You're not working with us. You know she murdered him!"

Ellery sighed and went to the door. "Oh, yes," he said, disappointing the piscatorial flunky beside him. "Finch."

"This is childish," said Finch hastily. "Why not talk this over—"

"Words are women, deeds are men. I believe I shall revert to my natural masculinity."

"I don't—"

"Well, under the circumstances," said Ellery in a regretful tone, "it's manifestly impossible for me to go to work on this case under the aegis of the National Life Insurance Company. No co-operation, you understand. Such a perfectly simple question! So I must refuse the assignment."

"If the fee—" began the tall man helplessly.

"A fig for the fee."

"Ellery," said a low voice. Ellery turned. Bill Angell was standing in the doorway. The fish-faced man looked almost angry. Then he almost shrugged. Finally, with his nose in the air, he stepped aside and Bill came in.

"Well, Bill," said Ellery slowly, his eyes narrowing. "So you've come at last. I thought you would."

Bill looked unhappy, but his handsome chin was hard. "I'm sorry, El. I'll explain some other time. Meanwhile," he said, raising his voice and staring calmly about, "I should like to speak to Miss Gimball—alone."

Andrea was on her feet, her hand on her throat. "Oh, you shouldn't have come."

"Andrea—" began Mrs. Gimball shrilly.

Jones said in a curt voice: "I've stood for about as much mystery as I intend to. Andrea, you've played me off long enough. I want an immediate explanation or, damn it all, it's all off between us! Who is this fellow? Where's your ring? What the devil did you do with my car Saturday night? If you're mixed up in this murder…" For a moment Andrea's eyes glittered. Then they fell, and a little color came into her cheeks.

Bill said blankly, "Your car?"

"Now you see," murmured Ellery, "why candor is the better part of romance, Bill. I could have told you last night that Andrea Gimball doesn't own or drive a cream-colored Cadillac roadster. Most elementary; a mere judicious inquiry in the right place. May I suggest the door be closed and that we all sit down and discuss this like sensible people?"

Finch muttered something to the flunky, who looked grieved, shut the door, and vanished. Mrs. Gimball sat down angrily, with pursed lips, as if she wanted to say something nasty but did not quite know what. Jones glowered at Andrea, and Andrea kept looking at the floor. She was no longer pale. As for Bill, he suddenly became conscious of his feet. He shuffled them about and looked miserable. "Just what," asked Ellery quietly, "were you intending to discuss with Miss Gimball, Bill?"

Bill shook his head. "That's up to Miss Gimball. I have nothing to say." Andrea gave him a shy, queerly pained little glance.

"It seems to me," observed Ellery after a moment of strained silence, "that I shall have to do the talking, after all. I should have preferred listening. You've both acted very oddly—you, Miss Gimball, and you, Bill. Childishly, when it comes to that." Bill flushed. "Shall I tell you what happened? On Saturday night, while I was examining the rug in the shack, your eye happened to catch sight of something imbedded in the nap which glittered. You put your foot over it. When you thought no one was looking, you pretended to tie your shoelace and picked it up. I was watching, and I saw it. It was a large cut diamond of at least six carats."

Bill stirred, and Andrea uttered a little gasp. Jones's skin was gray again, his cheekbones tight with wrath. "I thought—" began Bill in a mutter.

"You thought you were unobserved. But, you see, Bill," said Ellery gently, "it's part of my training to see everything, and part of my creed not to permit friendship to stand in the way of the truth. You didn't know whose diamond it was, but you were afraid to say anything about it to De Jong because you thought it might in some mysterious way involve Lucy. Then Miss Gimball came, and you saw a ring on her finger with the stone gone. It couldn't have been coincidence. You realized she must have been in that shack. But, you see, Bill, I noticed it, too."

Bill laughed a little glumly. "I'm a prize fool, of course. My abject apologies, Ellery." His shoulders lifted in a secret sign to Andrea, as if to indicate his helplessness. Through her tension and pain she managed a ghost of a smile. Jones saw it, and his thin lips tightened.

"You drew her aside into a shadow," continued Ellery as if nothing had happened, "and, since there was a convenient shadow adjacent, I exercised the prerogative of outraged friendship and eavesdropped. Shall I go on?"

Andrea made a little sound. Then she suddenly looked up; her eyes were clear. "No need for that any more, Mr. Queen," she said steadily. "I see how futile it was. I'm not very good at—well, at that sort of thing, I suppose. Thank you, Bill Angell; you've been swell." He flushed again and looked uncomfortable.

"You borrowed my car during the afternoon Saturday," muttered Burke Jones. "Damn it, Andrea, you've got to clear me of that."

Her eyes were scornful. "Don't worry, Burke, I shall. Mr. Queen, on Saturday afternoon I received a telegram from—from Joe."

"Andrea," said Mrs. Gimball feebly.

"Don't you think, Andrea," began Finch in a low voice, "that it's unwise to—"

Her lids veiled her eyes. "I've nothing to conceal, Ducky. I didn't kill him, if that's what you're all thinking." She paused. "The telegram asked me to meet him in that shack on an urgent matter. It gave me instructions for getting there. It set the time for nine."

"I'll bet it was a duplicate of mine," muttered Bill.

"I borrowed Burke's car—we were out during the afternoon and he couldn't use it. I didn't tell Burke where I was going."

"Why don't you tell them you drove?" growled Jones. "I couldn't drive with this broken wing."

"Please, Burke," she said quietly. "I think Mr. Queen understands that. I got out there early. There was no one there, so I went for a spin, going off toward Camden. When I got back—"

"What time," asked Ellery, "did you reach there the first time?"

"Oh, I don't know. Eight, perhaps. When—"

"And what time did you reach there the second time?"

She hesitated. "Oh, I don't remember. It was almost dark. I went inside—there was a light on—and..."

Ellery stirred. "Forgive me for interrupting, Miss Gimball. When you arrived at the shack the second time, you saw nothing suspicious?"

"No, no, nothing." She said it so quickly that he repressed another question and lit a cigaret. "Nothing at all. I went in and there was Joe. He was on the floor. I thought he was dead. I—I didn't touch him. I couldn't. The blood... I suppose I screamed. Then I ran out. I saw another car near the house on the road and grew frightened. I jumped into the Cadillac and drove off. Of course, now I know it was Mr. Angell I almost ran down." She paused. "That's all."

In the silence that followed Burke Jones cleared his throat. There was a new and embarrassed quality to his voice. "Well. Sorry, old girl. If you'd only told me... When you asked me Sunday not to say anything about having taken my car—"

"It was very sweet of you, Burke," she said coldly. "I'll always remember your generosity."

Grosvenor Finch went to her and patted her shoulder. "You've been a foolish child, Andrea, as Mr. Queen has said. Why didn't you confide in me, in your mother? You did nothing wrong. For that matter, Mr. Angell received a telegram and was there, too, without witnesses, and yet you see he had no hesitation…"

Andrea closed her eyes. "I'm very tired. I wonder if—"

"And the stone, Miss Gimball?" asked Ellery casually.

She opened her eyes. "I seem to remember banging my hand against the door as I went out. I suppose the stone was dislodged then. In my—well, I didn't notice that it was missing until Mr. Angell called it to my attention later that night."

"I see." Ellery rose. "Thanks very much, Miss Gimball. If you took my advice you would tell your story to Pollinger—"

"Oh, no!" she cried in alarm. "Not that. Oh, please, you won't tell him? To have to face those men…"

"It's not really necessary, Ellery," said Bill in a low voice. "Why complicate matters? It can't do any good, and it will only get Miss Gimball a lot of unwelcome notoriety."

"Angell's right, Mr. Queen," said Finch eagerly.

Ellery smiled a little. "Well, I seem to be overruled by sheer weight of numbers. Goodnight."

He shook hands with Finch and Jones. Bill stood rather awkwardly by the door. His eyes met Andrea's and came away. Then he followed Ellery out of the apartment with a despondent set to his shoulders.

Neither man spoke much on the journey to Trenton. Once, when they had left the General Pulaski Skyway and the lights of the Newark Airport behind, Bill muttered, "I'm sorry about not having told you, El. Somehow—"

"Forget it."

The Pontiac rumbled along. "After all," said Bill out of the darkness, "it's so obvious she told the truth."

"Oh, is it?"

Bill was silent for a moment. Then he said quickly: "What do you mean? Anyone can see that girl is the real stuff. You don't think she—Why, that's ridiculous! I'd no more consider her a murderess than I would my own sister."

Ellery lit a cigaret. "It seems to me," he remarked, "that you've undergone a startling change of heart in the past few days, my son."

"I don't get you," mumbled Bill.

"Really? Now, now, Bill, you're brighter than that. Really a smart young man. Only Saturday evening you were ranting against the rich, and rich young women in particular. Now, Andrea Gimball is so clearly a member of that parasitical class you detest, that I wonder at the consideration you've shown her."

"She's—" Bill paused lamely. "She's—well, different."

Ellery sighed. "If it does that to you…"

"If what does what to me?" glared Bill in the darkness.

"Peace, friend." And Ellery smoked away. Bill stepped on the accelerator. They accomplished the rest of the journey in silence.

De Jong's office in Chancery Lane was deserted. Bill drove around to South Broad, parked the Pontiac near Market Street, and they hurried into the dark lobby of the Mercer County Court House. In the office of the County Prosecutor on the second floor they found the small, dyspeptic Pollinger and the police chief with their heads together. The heads separated with the celerity of guilt. "Well, look who's here," said De Jong in a queer tone.

"The very man." Pollinger was nervous. "Have a seat, Angell. Just drove down from New York, Mr. Queen?"

"Yes. I thought I'd get whatever developments there were at first hand. Bill happened to be with me. Any news?"

Pollinger glanced at De Jong. "Well," said the prosecutor casually, "before we discuss that, I'm rather curious to hear your views, Mr. Queen. That is, of course, if you have any."

"Quot homines, tot sententiæ," chuckled Ellery. "So many men, so many opinions. I suppose I have one—a poor thing, but mine own."

"What did Finch want to see you about?"

"Oh, that." Ellery shrugged lightly. "He wanted to hire me to investigate this business for the National Life."

"The beneficiary angle, eh?" Pollinger drummed on his desk. "I thought they'd do that. Glad to help you, of course. We can work together."

"I didn't," murmured Ellery, "accept."

"Really?" Pollinger drew his brows up. "Well, well, let's hear your views, anyway. I'm not one of those short sighted lawyers who disdain the advice of amateurs. Fire away."

"Sit down, Bill," said Ellery. "Apparently we've run into something." Bill obeyed. His eyes had become watchful again.

"Well?" drawled De Jong in a half-amused way.

Ellery took out his pipe. "I'm at a disadvantage. Obviously you men have information of which I'm ignorant. At the moment, I can offer no theory which focuses upon an individual. The facts don't lend themselves to solution, at least the facts at my disposal. But, from the instant I identified Wilson as Gimball, it struck me that there was one line of investigation which might prove fruitful. I suppose you gentlemen have seen your local papers recently?"

Pollinger pulled a long face. "They've had a field day of it."

"There was one story by a fellow-townswoman of yours," continued Ellery, "which I confess impressed me. I refer to the work of that charming young hoyden with the red hair who writes special features for the Trenton Times."

"Ella Amity's all right," said De Jong indifferently.

"Oh, wake up, De Jong. That's faint praise. The woman's grasped something which has escaped all of you. Do you recall her sobriquet for the shack in which Gimball met his death?" The two officials looked politely blank. Bill was sucking a knuckle with absorption. "She named it," observed Ellery, "Halfway House."

"Halfway House." Pollinger looked impatient. "Oh, yes."

"It doesn't strike sparks," said Ellery dryly. "But it should. She put her canny finger on the very heart of the problem."

De Jong sneered. "It sounds plain screwy to me."

"Your loss. The phrase is a positive inspiration. Don't you see its significance?" He exhaled a cloud of smoke. "Tell me. Whose murder are you investigating?"

"Whose—" The prosecutor sat up sharply.

"It's a riddle," grinned De Jong. "I'll bite. Mickey Mouse?"

"Not bad, De Jong," said Ellery. "I ask once more: Who has been murdered?" He waved his long fingers. "And if you can't give him a name, it's going to be more difficult to find his killer."

"What are you driving at?" snapped Pollinger. "Joseph Kent Gimball, of course. Or Joseph Wilson, or Henry Smith, or any other damned name you want to call him by. We've got the man, the body; that's the important thing; and we know who he is. What difference does his name make?"

"Possibly all the difference in the world. Old Shakespeare unfortunately didn't live in the days of criminological science. You see, you don't know. Gimball or Wilson—precisely. This man was Wilson in Philadelphia and Gimball in New York. He was polished off in Trenton…. Halfway House, says our Ella. Very apt indeed. Now in Halfway House, to push the conceit a little further," continued Ellery soberly, "you found Gimball clothes and Wilson clothes, a Gimball car and a Wilson car. In Halfway House this man was both Gimball and Wilson, you see. And so I ask again: In what personality was the man murdered? As Gimball or as Wilson? Whom did the murderess think she was dispatching—Joseph Kent Gimball of New York or Joe Wilson of Philadelphia?"

"I never thought of it in that way," muttered Bill. Pollinger rose and began to patrol the floor behind his desk.

De Jong jeered. "Nuts and double-nuts. Hifalutin' stuff."

Pollinger halted. He shot a peculiar look at Ellery from under his sparse brows. "And in what personality do you think he was killed?"

"That," sighed Ellery, "is indeed the question. I can't answer it. Can you?"

"No." Pollinger sat down. "No, I can't. But it seems to me to be still a purely academic question. I can't see how… Look here."

"Here it comes," said Bill. His hands hung loosely between his knees, perfectly controlled. Ellery smoked calmly.

The prosecutor's slender fingers played with a paper-cutter on his desk. "De Jong's made a major discovery. He's found the car used by the person who murdered Gimball Saturday night—the small car with the Firestone tires."

Ellery glanced at Bill. It was odd how Pollinger's simple statement affected the young man. It tightened his skin like a caustic, making it look dry and old. He sat in a lump as if he were afraid the slightest movement would precipitate an avalanche. "Well?" He cleared his throat. "Well?"

Pollinger shrugged. "Abandoned. Had an accident."

"Where?" demanded Ellery.

"And don't think," drawled De Jong, "there's any doubt about it, gents. It's the bus, all right."

"An Olympian utterance. How can you be certain?"

Pollinger opened the top drawer of his desk. "By reason of three quite conclusive facts." He tossed over a bundle of photographs. "The impressions of the tires. We've made casts of the middle set of marks from the mud in front of the shack, and compared them with the tires of the car we found—'32 Ford, by the way, coupé black paint job. Well, casts and tires coincide. That's number one."

Bill was blinking as if the green-shaded light hurt his eyes. "And number two?"

"Number two," replied the prosecutor, putting his hand into the drawer again, "is this." He brought out the rusty figurine of the naked woman which De Jong's man had found in the main driveway on the night of the murder—the radiator-cap which had snapped off at the ankles of the figure. And then he placed beside it another object made of the same rust-flecked metal—the plug of the cap, with two jagged ends of metal sticking up from its top. "Examine them. You'll find that the broken edges of the metal ankles fit exactly into the broken ends of the metal feet on the cap."

"The cap comes from this Ford coupé?" asked Ellery intently.

"If it doesn't," said De Jong, "I was dreaming when I unscrewed it."

"Of course," continued Pollinger in an odd tone, "this is almost as sound evidence as a fingerprint. Now, number three." For the fourth time his hand went to the drawer; when it emerged, it was swathed in some dark filmy material.

"The veil!" exclaimed Ellery; he reached for it. "Where did you find this, by thunder?"

"On the driver's seat of the coupé." Pollinger leaned back. "You can see how important this veil is as evidence. The tire marks and the broken radiator-cap establish the Ford as having visited the scene of the crime on Saturday evening. The veil serves to fix guilt. Found in the Ford, it sets up a reasonable presumption that the Ford was driven by the criminal. For the victim himself told Angell with his dying breath that his murderess wore a veil. And veils aren't common these days."

Bill was glaring at the veil. "As a lawyer," he said hoarsely, "of course you realize that's the frailest kind of circumstantial evidence? You haven't connected. Where's your eye-witness? That would be a case. Or have you checked the times involved? How do you know the car wasn't abandoned long before the crime-period? How—"

Pollinger said slowly: "My dear young man, I know the law very well indeed." He rose and began pacing again.

There was a knock on the door, and the thin little man whirled about. "Come in!"

Sellers, the small brown man attached to De Jong's staff, opened the door; there was another detective behind him. The brown man seemed a little surprised at the sight of the two visitors. "Well?" barked De Jong. "Everything go off all right?"

"Fine."

De Jong flashed a glance at Pollinger. The prosecutor nodded and turned away. Bill was gripping the arms of his chair, looking wildly from face to face. Sellers mumbled something and the other man vanished. A moment later he reappeared with his hand on the arm of Lucy Wilson. All the blood seemed permanently to have deserted her skin. There were large violet arcs under her splendid eyes. Her hands were fists and her high breasts rose and fell in surges. There was something so bedraggled and woebegone in her appearance that for a long moment no one seemed able to find his tongue. Then she said, in a weak voice: "Bill. Oh, Bill darling," and she stumbled toward him.

Bill sprang from his chair like a catapult released. "You skunk!" he shouted at De Jong. "What the hell d'ye mean by dragging my sister down here this time of night?"

De Jong gestured to the brown man, who stepped forward and touched Bill's arm. "Come on now, Angell. We don't want any trouble with you."

"Lucy." Bill brushed the man aside. He gripped Lucy's shoulders and shook her. "Lucy! Why did you let them bring you into New Jersey? They can't do that. They can't cross a State line without extradition papers!"

She whispered: "I feel so… I don't know. Oh, Bill, they—they said Mr. Pollinger wanted to talk to me. They said—"

"You tricky shyster!" yelled Bill. "You've no right—"

Pollinger stalked forward with a sort of bantam dignity. He thrust something into Lucy's hands. "Mrs. Wilson," he asked formally, "do you recognize this automobile?"

"Don't answer!" cried Bill.

But she said with a tired frown: "Yes. Yes, that's my car. That's the Ford Joe gave me for my birthday a few years ago. Joe gave me…"

"Do you still deny knowing how this car of yours happened to get out of your garage Saturday?"

"Yes. No. I mean I don't know."

"It was found jammed against a tree off the road in Fairmount Park, Philadelphia," droned the prosecutor. "Not five minutes away from your home, Mrs. Wilson. Didn't you have an accident there Saturday night—returning from Trenton?"

Something stark in the scene—the harsh green light, the standing silent men, the stiff rows of law books on the shelves, the cluttered desk—penetrated to her brain. Her nostrils quivered and perspiration sprang out on the bridge of her small nose. "No," she whispered. "Good God, Mr. Pollinger, no!" Her black eyes were shiny with terror.

Pollinger picked up the dark veil. "And isn't this black veil yours?"

She stared at it without seeing it. "What? What?"

"You won't get anything out of her, Pollinger," said De Jong gruffly. "She's a smart gal. Let's get this over with." A clock ticked noisily away on the wall. The brown man's clutch tightened on Lucy Wilson's sleeve. Bill stood in a half-crouch, his fingers curved and his eyes liquid with fear.

"Gentlemen," said Ellery sharply. "I warn you not to offer this poor woman up as a sacrifice to public opinion. Bill, be still!"

"I know my duty, Mr. Queen," said the prosecutor stiffly. He reached for a document on his desk.

Bill shouted: "Don't! Damn you, you can't—"

"Lucy Wilson," said Pollinger in a tired voice, "I hold here a warrant for your arrest. It charges you in the name of the people of New Jersey with the murder with malice aforethought of one Joseph Wilson, also known as Joseph Kent Gimball, in Mercer County, State of New Jersey, on the night of Saturday, June the first, 1935."

The woman's black eyes rolled over as she slid, fainting, into her brother's arms.

III

THE TRIAL

*"Eye me, blest Providence, and
square my trial
To my proportion'd strength."*

THE MERCER COUNTY Court House in which Lucy
Wilson is about to go on trial for her life, charged with the
murder of her husband Joseph Wilson, otherwise Joseph
Kent Gimball, prominent New York financier and social luminary,'
wrote the AP man with the flair for statistics, 'stands on South Broad
Street in Trenton near the corner of Market, a weather-beaten stone
structure adjoining the County Jail on Cooper Street where Lucy Wilson
lies nursing her strength for the epic struggle to come.

'The chamber in which her brother, Attorney William Angell of
Philadelphia, will begin her legal defense on Monday morning against
the accusations of the State of New Jersey lies at the north end of
the building on the second floor in Room 207, housing the Court
of Common Pleas where murder trials in Mercer County are usually

96

held. It is a deep wide room entered from the rear, with a high ceiling punctured by two sets of square-paneled, frost-glass skylights.

'The bench from which Justice Ira V. Menander, veteran jurist, will preside is high and wide, almost concealing the tall Judge's chair. On the wall behind the bench are three doors, one at the extreme right leading to the jury room, one at the extreme left leading to the Bridge of Sighs, and one directly behind the Judge's chair leading to His Honor's chambers.

'To the right of the bench is the witness box and beyond lies the jury box, composed of three rows of four chairs each. Before the bench,' continued the AP man, warming to his work,' there is a narrow space for the court clerks and a large open area in which stand two round tables for the use of the defense and prosecution.

'The spectators' section, which consumes the remaining space in the courtroom, is divided in two by an aisle. Each side contains ten long wooden benches in five rows. Since each bench holds from six or seven persons, the capacity of the room is between 120 and 140 spectators.'

Miss Ella Amity, feature writer for the Trenton Times, scorned such dry details. Writing tearfully and copiously in the issue of Sunday, June the twenty-third, she plunged into the heart of matters.

'Tomorrow morning at 10 o'clock Daylight Saving Time,' she wrote, 'a beautiful woman, glowing with youth and life, with a face and figure unspoiled by the dissipations of our hectic times, will be led from the County Jail on Cooper Street across the box-like Bridge of Sighs into a small, bare, grimy vestibule which opens into the court-room where Mercer County tries its most hardened criminals.

'She will be shackled to a deputy like a slave-girl of ancient times, to be placed on the block of Justice and sold to the higher bidder—the State of New Jersey in the person of Paul Pollinger, prosecutor of Mercer County, or her devoted and brilliant brother, William Angell of Philadelphia, who is directing her defense.

'It will be for a jury of her peers to decide whether it was Lucy Wilson, young Philadelphia housewife, who thrust the keen point of a paper-cutter into her husband's heart, or another woman. It is the opinion of many that Lucy Wilson must be judged by a jury who are truly her peers, or justice will not be done.

'For it is not Lucy Wilson who is on trial for her life, it is Society. Society, which makes it possible for a man of wealth and position to marry a poor girl of the lower classes in another city under a false name, take ten of the most precious years of her life, and then—when it is too late—decide to tell the truth and confess his hideous sin to her. Society, which makes it possible for such a man to commit bigamy, to have a poor wife in Philadelphia and a rich one in New York, to spend his time calmly between the two wives and the two cities like a commuter. Innocent or guilty, Lucy Wilson is the real victim, not the man who lies buried in a Philadelphia cemetery under the name of Joseph Wilson, not the heiress of millions who took his real name of Gimball in vain at St Andrew's Cathedral in New York in 1927. Will Society protect Lucy from itself? Will Society make amends for the ten years it took from her life? Will Society see that the crafty forces of wealth and social power do not crush her beneath their cruel heels? These are the questions which Trenton, Philadelphia, New York, the whole nation are asking themselves today.'

*

Bill Angell grasped the edge of the jury box with such vehemence that his knuckles whitened. "Ladies and gentlemen of the jury, the law gives to the defense the same privilege of announcing in advance and in general terms what it will prove as it gives to the prosecution. You have just heard the prosecutor of your county. I shall not take so long. My learned friend the prosecutor, His Honor the Judge, can tell you that in most instances in trials for murder the defense waives its right to address the jury in advance, because in most instances the defense has something to conceal or must build its case out of the ragged remnants of the prosecution's case. But this defense has nothing to conceal. This defense addresses you out of a full heart, confident that justice can be done in Mercer County and that justice will be done in Mercer County.

"I have merely this to say. I ask you to forget that I am the brother of this defendant, Lucy Angell Wilson. I ask you to forget that Lucy is a beautiful woman in the prime of her life. I ask you to forget that Joseph Wilson did her the cruelest wrong in the power of any man. I ask you to forget that he was really Joseph Kent Gimball, a man of millions, and that she is Lucy Wilson, a poor loyal woman who comes from just such a walk of life as your worthy selves. I ask you to forget that during the ten peaceful years of their married life, Lucy Wilson did not derive a single penny's worth of benefit from Joseph Kent Gimball's millions.

"I would not ask you to forget these things if for the space of a single instant I entertained the most minute doubt of Lucy Wilson's innocence. If I thought she were guilty I would emphasize these things, play upon your sympathies. But I do not think so. I know Lucy Wilson is not guilty of this crime. And before I am finished, you will know that Lucy Wilson is not guilty of this crime.

"I ask you to remember only that murder is the most serious charge which a civilized State can level against any individual. And, because this is so, I ask you to keep in mind during every moment of this trial that the State must prove Lucy Wilson a red-handed murderess beyond the last faint shadow of a reasonable doubt. His Honor will no doubt charge you that in a circumstantial case, such as this, the State must prove, step by step, without the slightest gap, the movements of the defendant until the very moment of the commission of the crime. There must be no gaps left to guess-work. That is the law of circumstantial evidence, and you must be guided by it. And remember, too, that the burden of proof is wholly upon the State. His Honor will instruct you in this.

"Ladies and gentlemen of the jury, Lucy Wilson asks you to keep this principle constantly in mind. Lucy Wilson wants justice. Her fate lies in your hands. It lies in good hands."

*

"I," said Ella Amity, "want a drink of whatever is in that bottle."

Ellery did things with cracked ice, soda, and Irish whisky, and passed the red-haired young woman the result. Bill Angell, his coat off and his shirt-sleeves rolled up, shook his head and went to the window of Ellery's room. The window was open wide; the Trenton night outside was hot and noisy and as turbulent as a carnival.

"Wall," said Ellery, regarding Bill's silent back, "what do you think?"

"I'll tell you what I think," said Ella, crossing her legs and setting down the glass. "I think there's a large black gentleman in the wood-pile here."

Bill turned sharply. "What makes you say that, Ella?"

The uppermost leg swung in an impatient arc. "Look here, Bill Angell. I know this town and you don't. Do you think Pollinger's a complete fool? Give me a butt, somebody."

Ellery obeyed. "I'm inclined to agree with the press, Bill. Pollinger wasn't born yesterday."

Bill frowned. "I'll admit the man struck me as capable enough. But, damn it all, the facts are there! He simply can't have anything important which he hasn't disclosed."

Ella snuggled deeper into the Stacy-Trent armchair. "Listen to me, you idiot. Paul Pollinger has one of the keenest minds in this State. He was weaned on a lawbook. He knows old Judge Menander the way I know the facts of life. And he's an expert on juries in this county. Do you think a prosecutor like that would pull such a boner? I'm telling you, Bill—watch your step."

Bill flushed angrily. "All right, all right. Will you kindly tell me what I can expect this magician to pull out of his hat? I know this case like the palm of my own hand. Pollinger's been misled by his own eagerness to get a conviction in a sensational case. It's been done before, and it always will be."

"You feel, then," asked Ellery, "that there's no chance for a conviction?"

"Not a chance in the world. I tell you this case won't even go to the jury. The law's the law in Jersey as anywhere else. When Pollinger rests the State I'll make the usual motion for dismissal, and I'll bet you every cent I've got that Menander throws the case out then and there."

The newspaperwoman sighed. "You poor, poor egomaniac. Maybe that's why I'm wasting all this time and energy on you. Confidence! I adore you, Bill, but there's a limit even to my patience. You're playing around with your sister's life. How the devil can you be so cocksure of yourself?"

Bill stared out the window again. "I'll tell you," he said at last. "Neither of you is a lawyer and so you can't see my point. All you can see is the usual layman's misconception of circumstantial evidence."

"It sounds pretty strong to me."

"It's weak as hell. What has Pollinger got? A dying declaration, which unfortunately I myself was responsible for bringing to light. This declaration, admittedly made by the victim in the full knowledge that he was dying—an important point legally—accused a veiled woman of stabbing him. He has the treads of the tires of a Ford car in the dirt before the scene of the crime. I'll even grant for the sake of argument that he can make out a positive expert's identification of Lucy's Ford as the one which made those tire marks. So what? Her car was used by the criminal. In her car was found a veil—not even hers; I know it isn't hers, because she's never worn or had a veil. So he can't possibly prove it's hers. He has, then, her car used by the criminal, who was a veiled woman. Possibly he has someone who can testify to seeing this veiled woman in the Ford near the scene of the crime. But whoever the witness is, he can't conceivably identify Lucy as the woman in the Ford. Even if he lies, or testifies to a positive identification under a mistaken impression, it will be child's play to break down his credibility. The mere fact that a veil was worn makes positive identification in the legal sense an incredibility."

"She has no alibi," pointed out Ellery, "and a theoretical double motive of uncomfortable potency."

"All embroidery." Bill's tone was savage. "We don't need an alibi, legally speaking. Even at that, though, I'm in hopes that I can get the cashier of the Fox theatre to identify her. At any rate, that's the extent of his case. And will you tell me, please, where in this set of facts there is anywhere the slightest implication of Lucy in person? You don't know the law. Circumstantial evidence strong enough to convict must place the accused at the scene of the crime, above all other evidence. You tell me how Pollinger's going to prove that Lucy Wilson, herself, in the flesh, was in that shack on the night of June first!"

"Her car—" began Ella.

"Rats. Her car doesn't put her there. Anybody could have stolen her car. As a matter of fact, that's what happened."

"But the inference—"

"The law doesn't countenance such inferences. Even if Pollinger produced an article of her clothing in that shack—a handkerchief, a glove, anything—that wouldn't be proof she was there. I mean proof within the rules of circumstantial evidence."

"Well, don't throw a fit over it, Bill," sighed the red-haired woman. "It sounds good the way you put it, but…" She frowned and, picking up her glass, took a long drink.

Bill's face softened. He went to her and seized her free hand. "I want to thank you, Ella—I haven't had a chance before. Don't think I'm ungrateful. You've been a pillar of strength, and your newspaper articles have unquestionably swayed public opinion. I'm damned glad you're on our side."

"Hey, that's my job," she said lightly, but her smile was tender. "I don't believe Lucy knifed that ape. All's fair in love and murder trials, isn't it? And the class-angle on this case was too tempting... I hate the guts of that Park Avenue crowd, anyway." She pulled her hand free.

"So," murmured Ellery, "does Bill."

"Now listen—" began Bill. "Just because I recognize a certain human balance doesn't mean..." He stopped, flushing.

Ella Amity glanced at him with raised brows. "Aha," she said. "Snoop Scents Romance. What's this, Bill—another case of the Montagues and the Capulets?"

"Don't be silly," he snapped. "You two have the most annoying faculty for making mountains out of molehills! The girl's engaged to be married. Hell, she's 'way out of my class. I'm just..."

Ella's left eyelid drooped at Ellery. Bill champed his jaws in a helpless fury and turned away. Ella rose and refilled her glass. None of them spoke for a long time.

*

In the jammed courtroom Paul Pollinger launched the State's case with a fanged rapidity, as cold and sure as if the trial were an inconsequential formality to the fore-ordained conviction. Even though the tall windows and skylights were open and the electric fans going, the room was suffocating with the heat of packed bodies. Pollinger's collar was a rag, and Bill's face steamed. Only Lucy Wilson's at the defense table, flanked by two hard-eyed State troopers, seemed impervious to the heat. Her skin was dry and pallid, as if already the vital processes of perspiration had ceased. She sat stiffly, her hands in her lap, staring at the seamed face of Judge Menander and avoiding the embarrassed glances of the mixed jury.

'By the end of the first day,' typed the cross-eyed reporter from the Philadelphia Ledger, 'Prosecutor Pollinger demonstrated once more in a murder trial his genius for lightning construction of vital elements. Mr. Pollinger built his case rapidly. During the day he put on the witness-stand Coroner Hiram O'Dell, Defense Counsel William Angell, Chief of Police De Jong, Grosvenor Finch of New York, John Sellers, Arthur Pinetti, Sergeant Hannigan, and Lieutenant Donald Fairchild of the New York Police Department. Through the testimony of these witnesses he succeeded in establishing an insurance motive against the defendant, primary facts concerning the discovery of the body, and a number of important exhibits, including the broken halves of the radiator-cap alleged to come from the defendant's Ford coupé. In the opinion of trained observers Mr. Pollinger scored a damaging blow when he was able, over the constant hecklings and objections of Mr. Angell, to inject into the record the testimony of his experts concerning the all-important Firestone tire prints in the mud before the shack where Joseph Kent Wilson was stabbed to death. The entire afternoon was consumed by the direct testimony and cross-examination of Sergeant Thomas Hannigan of the Trenton police, who first examined the tire impressions, of Chief De Jong, who found the Ford coupé alleged to belong to Mrs. Wilson, and of Lieutenant Fairchild. Lieutenant Fairchild is a recognized authority on the science of automobile-tire identification.'

'On the stand,' clicked out the telegrapher in the press-room, continuing his transmission of the Ledger man's story, 'Lieutenant Fairchild resisted all Mr. Angell's savage attempts to cast doubt upon his findings, substantiating to the last detail Sergeant Hannigan's testimony. The New York expert compared photographs and plaster casts of the tire prints from the roadway with the actual tires of Mrs. Wilson's Ford, exhibited in the courtroom by the State.

"'In the case of worn automobile tires," testified Lieutenant Fairchild in summing up his findings, "it is possible to make as positive identification as in the case of human fingerprints. No two tires which have seen service for any length of time will be found to leave the same impressions in a plastic surface. These Firestones are several years old and their treads are scarred and gashed. I have carefully run the defendant's car over the driveway before the scene of the crime, under conditions exactly similar to those on the night of the murder. I found that these tires left scar-prints, gash-prints, worn areas and so on identical with those in these plaster casts."

"'And your conclusion from this, Lieutenant?" asked Mr. Pollinger.

"'In my opinion there is no doubt whatever that the impressions from which these photographs and casts have been taken were made by the four tires in evidence."

'An attempt by Defense Counsel Angell to insinuate that the "four tires in evidence" were not the tires from Mrs. Wilson's car but had been deliberately substituted by the police was effectually resisted by Mr. Pollinger in re-direct examination.'

*

"No fireworks yet," said Bill Angell to Ellery on the evening of the third day. They were in Bill's room at the Stacy-Trent. Bill was in his undershirt, bathing his cheeks in cold water. "Whew! Have a drink, Ellery. Soda's on the dresser. Ginger ale, if you like."

Ellery sat down with a groan; his linen suit was crumpled and his face was caked with dust. "No, thanks. I just had a couple of exquisitely lousy lime concoctions downstairs. What's happened?"

Bill picked up a towel. "The usual. To tell the truth, I'm getting a little worried myself. Pollinger can't conceivably hope to get a conviction on the case he's presenting. He hasn't connected Lucy at all. Where've you been all day?"

"Gadding about."

Bill flung the towel away and pulled on a fresh shirt. "Oh," he said. He seemed vaguely disappointed. "Decent of you to come back at all. I know this mess must be cutting into your own plans."

"You don't understand," sighed Ellery. "I went to New York on a little inquiry for you."

"El! What?"

Ellery reached over and picked up a thick sheaf of mimeographed papers. They constituted the official transcript of the day's testimony. "Chiefly nothing. I had an idea, but it didn't pan out. Mind if I go through this transcript? I want to know what's happened in my absence."

Bill nodded gloomily, finished dressing, and left; Ellery was already intent on the transcript. He took the elevator up to the seventh floor and knocked on the door numbered 745. It was opened by Andrea Gimball.

They were both embarrassed, and for a moment Bill's complexion matched the pallor of the girl's skin. She was dressed in a simple frock with a high neck, caught at the throat by a pearl clasp; the effect was severe, and for an unguarded instant it flashed through Bill's mind that Andrea was suffering. There were alarming circles about her blue eyes and she looked peaked and ill. Her slender form drooped against the jamb. "Bill Angell," she said, with a catch in her throat. "This is a—a surprise. Won't you come in?"

"Come in, Bill, come in," yelled Ella Amity's voice from within. "Make this a real party!"

Bill frowned, but he stepped into the room. It was a sitting-room filled with fresh flowers, and Ella Amity sprawled in the most capacious chair with a glass at her elbow and a cigaret between her fingers. Tall Burke Jones glowered at him from a window-ledge, his trussed arm jutting forward like a danger-signal.

"Oh, I'm sorry," said Bill, stopping short. "I'll come around some other time, Miss Gimball."

"What's this," said Jones, "a social call? I thought you fellows stayed on the other side of the fence."

"My business," said Bill stiffly, "is with Miss Gimball."

"You're with friends," said Andrea with a wan smile. "Please sit down, Mr. Angell. I haven't had the opportunity of… well, it's been a little awkward, hasn't it?"

"Hasn't it?" said Bill foolishly, sitting down and wondering why he had done so. "What are you doing here, Ella?"

"Little Ella's on the trail. Seeing how the other half lives. Get a story, maybe. Miss Gimball has been sweet, but Mr. Jones thinks I'm a spy, so it's just perfect." The newspaperwoman chuckled.

Jones rose from the ledge with an impatient movement of his muscular body. "Why the devil don't you people let us alone?" he growled. "Bad enough we've got to stay down here in this filthy hole."

Andrea glanced at her hands. "I wonder… Burke, do you mind?"

"Mind? Mind? Why should I mind?" He strode to an inner door, jerked it open, and slammed it behind him.

"Naughty, naughty," murmured Ella. "Boy-friend has a temper. That lad will need a heap of training, darling. In fact, I think he's a heel." She rose lazily, drained her glass, gave them both a bewitching smile, and drifted out.

Bill and Andrea sat in silence for a moment. The silence became oppressive. They did not look at each other. Then Bill cleared his throat and said, "Don't mind Ella, Miss Gimball. She means well. You know how these newspaper people are…."

"I don't mind, really." Andrea kept studying her hands. "You wanted—?"

Bill rose and jammed his hands into his pockets. "I know this is rotten for both of us," he said, scowling. "Jones is right. We are on opposite sides of the fence. I shouldn't be here at all."

"Why not?" murmured Andrea. Her hands strayed to her hair.

"Well… It's not proper. I shouldn't permit—"

"Yes?" She looked at him then, squarely.

Bill kicked a chair. "All right, I'll say it. Personal considerations. Can't be locked up for telling the truth. I suppose I like you. Damned fool to… I didn't mean that. I mean that my sister is fighting for her life. I've got to use any weapon that comes to hand. As a matter of fact, that's just what I'll probably be forced to do."

She went a little pale, and moistened her lips before she spoke. "Please tell me. There's something on your mind. It isn't—"

Bill sat down again and boldly took one of her hands. "Listen to me, Andrea. I came here tonight against all my instincts and training because I—well, I didn't want you to be sore at me. After." He drew a long breath. "Andrea, I may have to put you on the stand."

She snatched her hand away as if it burned. "Bill! You wouldn't!"

He passed his hands over his eyes. "The situation may demand it. Please try to understand my position. It's Lucy's attorney speaking now, not plain Bill Angell. Pollinger's not far from through. On the basis of what he's already shown, he hasn't a case. But before he rests, he may pull something which will completely change the complexion of things. In that event, I'll be forced to go through with the defense."

"But what has that to do with me?" she whispered. He did not see, as he doggedly studied the rug, the terror in her eyes.

"The defense here, as in so many murder cases, is negative. It must consist in confusing the issue. It must try to put into the minds of the jury as many doubts as possible. Now, there's no question in my mind that Pollinger knows perfectly well you visited the scene of the crime simply from having traced the Cadillac. I don't know whether he's talked to you about it or not." He paused, but she did not answer. "Naturally, he wouldn't put you on the stand. It could only hurt the State's case." He tried to take her hand again, but could not. "But don't you see that if it hurts the State's case, it helps the defense?"

She rose, and Bill, looking at her, knew that she meant to be haughty, imperious, outraged. But she was not. She bit her lip and felt for the chair. "Bill… Please don't. Please. I—I'm not used to begging. But I must beg now. I don't want to go on the stand. I can't go on the stand. I mustn't!" Her voice rose to a wail.

For the first time a cold shower drenched Bill's brain, leaving it crisp and clean and shining. He got to his feet and they stood face to face. "Andrea," he said in a low voice, "why mustn't you?"

"Oh, I can't explain! I—" She bit her lip again.

"You mean you're afraid of the notoriety?"

"Oh, no, no, Bill! Not that. Do you think I care—"

"Andrea." His voice hardened. "You're in possession of some fact of importance!"

"No, no, I'm not. I'm not."

"You must be. I see it all now. You've been playing me for a sucker. Playing on my sympathies." In his anger he glared at her, and seized her shoulders; she shrank back and buried her face in her hands. "All that good-wishes bunk! This will teach me a lesson. Stay in your own back-alley. You thought you'd put one over on me, get me off my guard, get me to keep quiet—while my own sister is on trial for her life! Well, you're mistaken. I won't be fooled again. My dear Miss Gimball, you're going on that stand, and God help you if there's something you know that you're withholding which would free my sister!"

She was sobbing now, and he took his hands from her shoulders as if contact with her was unbearable. "You don't understand," she said in a muffled voice. "Oh, Bill, how can you say such things? I—I wasn't acting. I can't… free your sister. What I know—"

"Then you do know something!" he cried.

The brimming horror in her eyes caught him up. He had never seen such a look on a human face. He drew back, his anger beginning to drain away. "I don't know anything," she said hurriedly, in a breathless and tumbling whisper. "I don't know what I'm saying. I'm—I'm upset. I don't know anything at all, do you hear? Oh, Bill, please…"

"Andrea," he said in a low voice. "What is it? Why don't you confide in me, let me help you? You're in trouble. Are you mixed up in this thing? Did you… kill him?"

She sprang away. "No. I tell you I don't know anything. Nothing at all. And if you're going to put me on the stand, I'll—I'll run away! I'll leave the State! I'll—"

He drew a long breath, relaxing. "Very well," he said quietly. "I know how to deal with such a situation. For your own good, Miss Gimball… I warn you. Do something rash, and I'll hound you to your dying day. I'm on the spot, and so are you; but Lucy is closest to a horrible fate. Stay put, and I'll be as easy with you as I can. Do you hear me?" She did not reply; she was sobbing into the cushion of a divan. He regarded her for a long time, the muscles of his cheeks twitching; then he turned on his heel and went away.

When Ellery had gone through the transcript once, he deliberately took off his coat, lit a cigaret, and buried himself in the pages once more. In a mass of testimony one section stood out. The witness had been called in late afternoon. Ellery went over the testimony slowly, word by word, and his frown deepened as he read.

DIRECT EXAMINATION BY MR. POLLINGER

Q. Your full name?

A. John Howard Collins.

Q. You operate a gasoline filling-station, Mr. Collins?

A. Yes.

Q. And where is your filling-station located?

A. I have my place on lower Lamberton Road, about six miles from Trenton. That's between Trenton and Camden. I mean it's closer to Trenton.

Q. I point to a certain spot on this map, Mr. Collins. Is this about where your gasoline station lies? A. Just about. Yes, sir.

Q. You know this section well?

A. Sure. Had my place on that spot for nine-ten years. Lived near Trenton all my life.

Q. Then you know where the Marine Terminal is? Can you place it on this map?

A. Yes, sir. (Witness takes pointer and points to Marine Terminal on map.) Right here.

Q. That's correct. Back on the stand, please. Now, Mr. Collins, how far from the Marine Terminal is your place of business?

A. Three miles.

Q. Do you recall the evening of June first this year, a little less than a month ago?

A. Yes, sir.

Q. Clearly?

A. Yes, sir.

Q. How is that you recall that particular evening so clearly?

A. Well, a lot of things made me remember it. First place, it rained all afternoon and there was practically no business. Second place, I had an argument with my helper around half past seven and fired him. Third place, I'd run low on gas late Friday night and called up the gas people first thing Saturday morning to send a truck out, special, right away. I didn't want to get caught low on Sunday. Truck didn't come, though, all day Saturday.

Q. I see. Then all these things made you remember that day very clearly, Mr. Collins. Now, I show you State's Exhibit 17, a photograph of an automobile. Have you ever seen the car in this photograph?

A. Yes, sir. It drove up to my place that night at five after eight.

Q. How do you know this photograph represents the identical car that drove up to your filling-station at 8.05 pm June first?

A. Well, it's a Ford coupé '32 model, and the one that drove up was, too. I wouldn't be able to swear it's the very same car, though, if I hadn't also took down the license-number. And this picture here shows the same license-plate.

Q. You noted down the license-plate number, Mr. Collins? Why did you do that?

A. Because there was something phony-looking about the woman that drove it. I mean the Ford. I mean the woman was funny. She acted like she was scared of something. And then she was wearing a veil that hid her whole face. You don't see veils these days, I mean veils like that. It all looked so screwy to me I thought maybe I'd better not take any chances, so I took down her plate-number.

Q. Tell the jury what happened when this veiled woman drove up.

A. Well, sir, I come running out of my office and I says to her: "Gas?" She nods her head. I says: "How many?" And so forth. So I pumped five gallons of gas into her.

THE COURT. The Court will tolerate no demonstrations of this disgraceful sort. There is no occasion for this unseemly laughter. Bailiff, eject any of the people who disturb the orderly conduct of this proceeding. Go on, Mr. Prosecutor.

Q. And what happened after you poured five gallons of gasoline into the Ford's tank, Mr. Collins?

A. She gave me a one-dollar bill and drove off without waiting for her change. Oh, yes, that's another thing that made me remember her.

Q. In what direction did she drive off?

A. Towards that shack near the Marine Terminal where the murder was.

MR. ANGELL. I object, Your Honor, to the answer as suggesting an unwarrantable conclusion. According to the witness's own testimony, his gasoline station lies three miles from the Marine Terminal. Besides, the form of the answer is clearly prejudicial.

MR. POLLINGER. If the car drove off in the direction of Trenton, Your Honor, it also drove off in the direction of the scene of the crime. We're dealing with directions, not destinations.

THE COURT. That is true, Mr. Pollinger, but there is an implication nevertheless. Strike the answer out.

Q. Did the Ford drive off in the direction of Camden?

A. No, sir, it came from Camden way. It drove off toward Trenton.

Q. Mr. Collins, I show you State Exhibit 43. Do you know what it is?

A. Yes, sir, that's the woman's veil found in the abandoned car in Philly which—

MR. ANGELL. Object—

MR. POLLINGER. Don't expand, Mr. Collins. I want answers only to the extent of your personal knowledge and observation. Very well, it's a woman's veil. Do you recognize this veil?

A. Yes, sir.

Q. Where did you see it last?

A. On the face of the woman who drove up to my gas station that night.

Q. Will the defendant please rise? Now Mr. Collins, take a good look at the defendant. Have you ever seen her before?

A. Yes, sir.

Q. Where, when, under what circumstances?

A. She was the one who drove up in the Ford that night for gas.

Bailiff. Order in the court. Order in the court.

Mr. Pollinger. Your witness, Counsel.

CROSS-EXAMINATION BY MR. ANGELL

Q. Mr. Collins, since you have maintained your gasoline filling-station at that single location on Lamberton Road for nine years, is it fair for me to assume that you have a busy station?

MR. POLLINGER. I object, Your Honor.

Q. Never mind. Do you do a good business, Mr. Collins?

A. It's all right.

Q. Good enough for you to remain in business there for nine years?

A. Yes.

Q. Thousands of cars stop at your station annually for gasoline and other automobile services?

A. Well, I suppose so.

Q. You suppose so. How many cars would you say? Just an estimate. How many cars would you say have stopped for gas at your place in the past month?

A. That's hard to say. I don't keep no records of that.

Q. Surely you must have some idea? A hundred? A thousand? Five thousand?

A. I can't say, I tell you. I don't know. A great many.

Q. You can't tell us more exactly? A hundred cars a month would be how many per day?

A. About three. It's more than that.

Q. More than three per day. Thirty per day?

A. Well, I don't know exactly, but I suppose you could say so, yes.

Q. Thirty cars per day. That's roughly a thousand cars per month?

A. Sure.

Q. You have serviced for gasoline, then, about a thousand cars since the evening of June first?

A. If you put it that way, yes.

Q. And still, after one month, after speaking to one thousand drivers, after pouring gasoline into the tanks of one thousand cars, you remember one particular car so clearly as to be able to describe it and its driver here and now?

A. I told how I came to remember. It was raining that day.

Q. It has rained exactly five days since June first, Mr. Collins. Do you remember the events of those five days just as clearly?

A. No, but I also fired my helper—

Q. Firing your helper made you remember a passing motorist one thousand cars ago?

A. And my call to the gas people—

Q. Is that the only time your storage tanks have run short of fuel, Mr. Collins, on May thirty-first and June first of this year?

A. No.

Q. I see. Mr. Collins, you testified that you noted down the license-plate number of the Ford coupe you have just identified. May I see that note, please?

A. I haven't got it on me.

Q. Where is it?

A. In my other suit.

Q. Where is your other suit?

A. Home.

BAILIFF. Order in the court. Order in the court.

MR. POLLINGER. The witness will produce the note as soon as he can.

MR. ANGELL. May I ask the prosecutor to be so kind as to leave the conduct of this cross-examination to defense counsel?

A. I'll bring the note tomorrow.

Q. The very same note, Mr. Collins?

A. Sure.

Q. Not a copy?

MR. POLLINGER. Your Honor, I strongly object to counsel's insinuation. The State is in a position to authenticate the note this witness will produce. It is only by an unfortunate oversight that the note has not been produced this afternoon.

MR. ANGELL. And I strongly object, Your Honor, to the prosecutor testifying.

THE COURT. I think you might leave off this line of examination temporarily, Counsel. It can be resumed when the exhibit is produced.

Q. Mr. Collins, from the time this veiled woman drove up to your gas station until she drove away, how many minutes elapsed?

A. About five.

Q. About five minutes. Now you testified that you poured five gallons of gasoline into the tank of her car. How long did that take you to do?

A. How long? Most of the time, I guess. Say about four minutes. I had a little trouble getting the cap off and putting it on. Threads were rusty and stuck.

Q. For four of the five minutes, then, you were busy at the tank of the car. Where was the tank on the car?

A. At the back, of course.

Q. At the back. And did this veiled woman get out of the car at any time during this five-minute period?

A. She just sat behind the wheel all the time.

Q. Then you didn't see her at all for four of the five minutes?

A. Well, no.

Q. Then you would say you actually saw this woman for only one minute altogether?

115

A. Well, if it figures that way.

Q. If it figures that way. What do you think? Doesn't it figure that way? Four from five leaves one?

A. Yes.

Q. All right, then. Now, how much of this veiled woman's figure was visible to you during the one minute you saw her?

A. A whole lot.

Q. Can't you be more specific?

A. Well—

Q. Did you see her waist?

A. Well, not that. She was sitting behind the wheel, I said. She didn't open the door. I saw her from the chest up.

Q. As far as you could see, what was she wearing?

A. A big floppy hat and a coat of some kind.

Q. A coat of what kind?

A. A loose sort of coat. Cloth coat.

Q. What color was it?

A. I can't say for sure. Dark.

Q. Dark? Blue? Black? Brown?

A. I can't say exactly.

Q. Mr. Collins, it was still daylight when this woman drove up, wasn't it?

A. Yes, sir. According to Standard Time it would be only a little past seven.

Q. And still you can't say what color her coat was, seen in daylight?

A. Not exactly. The coat was dark, I tell you.

Q. Do you mean that you can't remember what color her coat was?

A. I remember it was dark.

Q. You saw her coat though, didn't you?

A. I just said so.

Q. Then on the evening of June first you knew what color her coat was, but you don't know today what color it was?

A. I didn't know it, the way you say it. I didn't especially notice the color. Only that it was a dark coat.

Q. But you noticed her appearance?

A. Well, sure.

Q. You noticed her appearance closely enough to sit in that witness chair and identify this defendant as the woman you saw in that Ford coupe a month ago?

A. Yes.

Q. But you don't remember the color of her coat?

A. No.

Q. What color was her hat?

A. I don't know. Floppy—

Q. Did she wear gloves?

A. I don't remember.

Q. And you saw her only from the chest up?

A. Yes.

Q. And you saw her altogether for only one minute?

A. About.

Q. And she wore a heavy veil completely concealing her face?

A. Yes.

Q. And despite this you still identify the defendant as the woman you saw in that Ford car?

A. Well, they're the same build.

Q. Oh, they're the same build. You mean by that, of course, the same build from the chest up?

A. Well, I guess so.

Q. You guess so. Are you testifying by guess or from knowledge?

MR. POLLINGER. Your Honor, I respectfully object to Counsel's heckling of my witness. This futile kind of cross-examination—

THE COURT. Counsel has the right, Mr. Prosecutor, to test the credibility of the witness's memory in identification on cross-examination. Proceed, Counsel.

Q. Mr. Collins, you have said that this Ford coupe drove up to your gas station at five minutes after eight on the evening of June first. Was that

117

a positive statement, or were you guessing about that, too?

A. No, sir. I was not. It was five after eight by my office clock. To the second.

Q. You looked at your clock when the car drove up? Is that a habit of yours, Mr. Collins?

A. I was looking at it just as it drove up. I told already how I was on the wire talking to the gas people when it drove up. I was kicking about why they hadn't sent the truck all day after my morning 'phone call, and I said: "Look, it's five after eight already." You see, I was looking at the clock.

Q. And just then this Ford car drove up outside?

A. That's it.

Q. And then you left your office and went outside and asked how many gallons of gas the woman wanted?

A. Yes, sir, and she held up five fingers. So I filled up the tank.

Q. She held up her hand, and you don't remember whether she was wearing gloves or not? You remember one thing, but not the other?

A. She held up her hand. I don't remember about the gloves.

Q. I see. You filled up the tank, you say? Filled it up? With five gallons of gas?

A. Right.

Q. Now, Mr. Collins, don't you know what the capacity of a Ford gasoline tank is?

A. Sure I know. Around eleven gallons.

Q. Then you made a mistake when you said you filled the tank up with five?

A. No, sir, I did fill her up. Or pretty near.

Q. Oh, you mean the tank wasn't empty? Or very low?

A. That's right. It had around five gallons in it already, because when I put in my five the gas came almost up to the cap.

Q. I see, I see. In other words, when this woman drove up and signified by spreading five fingers that she wanted five gallons of gas, her tank wasn't empty, or nearly empty? It still was about half full? She could have gone on for quite a way on what was in the tank?

A. Yes, sir.

Q. Didn't it strike you as strange that a motorist should stop for gas with a half full tank?

A. I don't know about that. Some folks are leery about being caught without gas on a trip. But still I remember I did think it was sort of queer.

Q. You thought it was sort of queer. Didn't it strike you why it was queer?

MR. POLLINGER. Object. What the witness thought.

The Court Strike it out.

Q. Mr. Collins, you said a moment ago that the woman held up five fingers to indicate how much gasoline she wanted. Didn't she speak at all?

A. Not a word.

Q. You mean she didn't open her mouth to utter a syllable during the entire five minutes you were attending to her and her car?

A. She didn't say a single word.

Q. Then you didn't hear her voice at all, at any time?

A. No.

Q. If this defendant rose in this courtroom and said something you would not be able to identify her as the driver of that car by reason of her voice alone?

A. Sure not. How could I? I didn't hear the driver speak.

Q. You have identified this defendant as the driver of that car solely because of a resemblance in physique, in build, from the chest up? Not by reason of her voice or face, which was covered?

A. Yes. But a big woman, husky like she is—

Q. Now, this veil you identified. You testified, I believe, that it is positively the same veil you saw the woman in the car wearing?

A. Positively.

Q. It couldn't be a different veil that just looks the same?

A. Sure it could. But I ain't seen a veil like that on a woman in twenty years. And then I took particular notice of the—the—I don't know how you would say it—that word—

MR. POLLINGER. The mesh?

MR. ANGELL. Will the prosecutor kindly refrain from putting the answer into the witness's mouth?

A. That's it. The mesh, the weave, like. I took particular notice of it. Like waves set so close together you couldn't see anything behind it. I'd know that veil anywhere.

Q. You'd know the veil, you remember the design of the mesh, but you don't remember the color of her coat or hat, or whether she was wearing gloves?

A. I told you a hundred times already.

Q. You testified before that the Ford drove up from the direction of Camden?

A. Yes.

Q. But you were in your office when the car stopped outside for gas?

A. Yes, but—

Q. You didn't actually see it coming down Lamberton Road from Camden?

A. It was stopped when I came out, but it was facing the Trenton way. So it must have come from the Camden way.

Q. But you didn't actually see it coming?

A. No, but—

Q. It could have come from the direction of Trenton and driven into your station to park in such a manner that it would seem to have come from the direction of Camden?

A. I suppose so, but—

Q. You're sure this car drove up on the night of June first, not May thirty-first or June second?

A. Oh, sure.

Q. You don't remember the color of the driver's coat, but you do remember the exact date?

A. I told you before—

MR. ANGELL. That is—

MR. POLLINGER. May I suggest that counsel permit the witness to finish what he has to say? He's been trying to explain to counsel for five minutes now without any success.

MR. ANGELL. Do you think five more minutes would result in better success, Mr. Pollinger? If so, I'll gladly extend my questions. Besides, the prosecutor didn't permit counsel to finish himself. I was about to say: That's all.

RE-DIRECT EXAMINATION BY MR. POLLINGER

Q. Mr. Collins, aside from the question of identification of the driver, you're positive that she drove the identical car as shown in Exhibit 17?

A. Positive, sir.

Q. You're also positive it drove up at 8.05 on the night of June the first for the good and sufficient reasons you gave?

A. Positive.

Q. There was no one else in the car with the woman?

A. No, sir.

Q. She was all alone?

A. Yes, sir.

Q. And she wore this very veil I hold in my hand?

A. Yes, sir.

Q. And, no matter from what direction she came, at least she did drive off toward Trenton?

A. Yes, sir.

Q. You stood there and watched her drive off toward Trenton?

A. Till she was out of sight.

MR. POLLINGER. That's all, Mr. Collins.

RE-CROSS-EXAMINATION BY MR. ANGELL

Q. You say the woman was all alone in the car, Collins?

A. That's what I said, sure. It's the truth.

Q. This was a coupé was it not, with a rumble-seat in the rear?

A. Sure.

Q. Was the rumble-seat open?

A. No. It was shut tight.

Q. It was shut tight. Then it was possible for someone to have been hiding in the closed rumble-seat compartment without your suspecting it? You can't swear the woman was all alone in the car?

A. Well—

MR. POLLINGER. I object to both the form and substance of the question, Your Honor. Counsel is trying—

MR. ANGELL. Now, now, let's not argue about it, Mr. Pollinger. I'm satisfied. That's all, Collins.

Witness excused.

*

"It's coming," muttered Bill to Ellery the next morning in court.

The man himself was an enigma. Pollinger was a slight dyspeptic fellow with shrewd eyes and the ageless air of the professional gambler. He was the coolest person in the jammed courtroom, thin and small and immaculate, as alert and harmless-looking as a sparrow.

Jessica Borden Gimball sat on the leather-upholstered witness bench behind the prosecutor's table, her gloved hands folded. She was dressed in widow's black, unadorned by any ornaments. With her sallow pinched face, unrelieved by cosmetics, her hollow eye-sockets and dry skin, she almost gave the illusion of a woman aged by a hard and uncertain lower-class existence. Andrea sat beside her, pale as death.

Bill's lips were grim as he regarded mother and daughter across the room. Under cover of the table-top he patted his sister's hand. But Lucy's expression of hypnotic intensity did not change; and she did not take her eyes from the face of the older woman on the bench.

"Philip Orleans to the stand."

The murmur that rose stilled like a subsiding wave. Every face was taut; even Judge Menander looked graver than usual. A tall thin man with the bony head and brilliant eyes of an ascetic took the stand quietly after being sworn in. Bill leaned forward, cupping his chin on one hand; he was as pale as Andrea. Behind him, on the witness bench, Ellery stirred a little and sank lower into the cushions. His eyes were on Pollinger, the keystone. Pollinger was superb. There was no hint of anything unusual in his manner. If anything, he was cooler and calmer than ever.

"Mr. Orléans, you are a citizen of the Republic of France?"

"I am." The tall thin man spoke nasally, with the suggestion of a Gallic accent. But his voice was cultured and assured.

"What is your official capacity in your own country?"

"I am of the Parisian Sûreté. I hold what corresponds to your portfolio of Chief of the Bureau of Criminal Identification in this country."

Ellery saw Bill stiffen with horrified recognition. He found himself sitting straighter on the bench. He had not for a moment connected the name with the man. But now it came back to him. Orléans was one of the most famous names in the annals of modern criminological history—a man of international reputation, of unimpeachable honesty, with decorations for services rendered, from a dozen governments.

"You qualify, then, as an expert in criminal identification?"

The Frenchman smiled a little. "I shall be honored to relate to your court my credentials, Monsieur."

"If you will be so kind."

Ellery saw Bill licking his lips nervously; it was evident that the summoning of this distinguished witness had caught him completely off guard.

"I have made the science of criminal identification," said Orléans easily, "my life work. For twenty-five years I have done nothing else. I studied under Alphonse Bertillon. I have the honor to be a personal friend and colleague of your Inspector Faurot. The cases in which I have lent my professional assistance—"

Bill was on his feet, pale but steady. "The defense grants the qualifications of the expert. We shall not challenge."

The corner of Pollinger's mouth lifted to the height of a millimeter. It was the only sign of triumph he made. He walked over to the exhibit table and picked up the paper-cutter found on the scene of the crime. A tag was attached to the haft, and its blade still showed dark streaky traces of Gimball's blood. It was wonderful how cautious Pollinger was in handling the thing. He held it by its very tip, apparently undisturbed by the fact that his fingertips grasped a surface stained by human blood. And he waved it gently before him, like a conductor's baton. Every eye in the room was fixed on the knife, as if the courtroom were indeed a concert hall and the audience a dutiful orchestra. "By the way, Mr. Orléans," murmured Pollinger, "will you please explain for the benefit of defense counsel and the jury how you came to be a witness in this case?"

Bill's eyes, like all others, were rooted on the knife; his skin had turned from gray to yellow. Lucy was staring at the blade with parted lips.

"Since May twentieth," replied the Frenchman, "I have been touring your police departments. On June second I chanced to be in Philadelphia. I was visited by Chief De Jong of your city and asked for my opinion, as an expert, concerning certain evidence in this case. I was given several objects to examine. I am here to testify."

"You were completely unaware, were you not, Mr. Orléans, of the prior findings of the Trenton police?"

"Completely."

"You are receiving no fee for your services, sir?"

"A fee was offered." The famous expert shrugged. "I declined. I do not accept emoluments while my duty lies elsewhere."

"You are unacquainted with any of the persons—defendant, counsel, prosecution—in this case?"

"That is so."

"You are testifying purely in the interests of truth and justice?"

"Precisely."

Pollinger paused. Suddenly he brandished the paper-cutter before the expert. "Mr. Orléans, I show you State's Exhibit 5. Is this one of the objects which you examined?"

"It is."

"May I ask the exact nature of your examination?"

Orléans smiled faintly, his teeth gleamed. "I tested for fingerprints."

"And you found?"

The man had a flair for drama. He did not reply at once. His brilliant eyes coolly surveyed the courtroom. Under the chandelier the skin of his bony forehead shone. The room was very still. "I found," he said at last in a clear, emotionless voice, "the fingerprints of two persons. Let me designate them momentarily as A and B. There were more of A's prints than of B's. The exact number is as follows." He consulted a memorandum. "Of A on the blade of the knife: One print of the pollex, two of the index, two of the medius, two of the annularis, one of the auricularis. Of A on the haft: One pollex, one index, one medius. Of B on the blade: One pollex, one index, one medius. Of B on the haft: One index, one medius, one annularis, one auricularis."

"Let us confine ourselves to B, Mr. Orléans," said Pollinger. "In what position did you find B's prints on the haft of the knife? Were the prints scattered, or were they in any order?"

"Will you hold the knife up, please?" Pollinger did so, in such a way that the weapon was vertical to the floor, the haft uppermost. "B's prints on the haft ranged from top to bottom in the order I have given: index highest, medius directly below index, annularis below medius, auricularis below annular is. They were all grouped very closely."

"Suppose we translate the technical terms into their more familiar forms, Mr. Orléans. Is it correct to say that on the haft of this weapon, reading from top to bottom as I now hold it, you found the imprints of four fingers—forefinger, middle finger, ring finger, and little finger?"

"That is correct."

"You have said these four were closely grouped. What is your inter-pretation, as an expert on fingerprints, of this grouping?"

"I should say there is no question but that B grasped the haft of this weapon in the usual manner in which a person would grasp it for a blow. The thumb-print would not show, since the thumb in this position normally overlaps the other fingers."

"Were these all clear fingerprints? There is no possibility of their having been misread, so to speak?"

The Frenchman frowned. "The specific prints I have designated were clear enough. However, there were many indications of smudges which were unreadable."

"Not on the haft?" asked the prosecutor hastily.

"Chiefly on the haft."

"However, there is no possible doubt concerning the clear prints you have named belonging to B?"

"None whatever."

"There are no other prints overlapping those prints of B's on the haft?"

"No. There is a slight smudge here and there. But the prints are not covered with other prints."

Pollinger's eyes were narrow. He went to the exhibit table and picked up two little folders. "I show you now State's Exhibit 10, the finger-prints taken from the dead hands of Joseph Kent Gimball, otherwise known as Joseph Wilson. Did you employ this set of fingerprints for comparison purposes in analyzing the prints on the weapon?"

"I did."

"Will you please clarify your findings for the jury as regards these arbi-trary classifications of the two sets of prints on the knife as A and B?"

"The prints I have designated as A are the prints of your Exhibit 10."

"In other words, A's prints were Joseph Kent Gimball's prints?"

"That is so."

"Would you care to explain in greater detail?"

"There is this to say. On both haft and blade of the knife appear prints of the fingers of both Gimball's hands."

Pollinger paused. Then he said: "I now show you, Mr. Orléans, State's Exhibit 11. Will you follow the same procedure as regards this exhibit?"

Orléans said evenly: "The prints I have designated as B are identical with those recorded in State's Exhibit 11."

"Any clarification?"

"Yes. B's prints on the blade come from the left hand. B's prints on the haft come from the right hand."

"May I ask you to read for the benefit of the jury the caption on State's Exhibit 11?"

Orléans took the little folder from Pollinger's hand. He read quietly: "State's Exhibit 11. Fingerprint recording. Lucy Wilson."

Pollinger walked away, saying between his teeth, "You may examine, Counsel."

Ellery sat unmoving as Bill Angell placed his palms on the surface of the round table, pushed in a tired way, and rose. He looked like a dead man. Before he left the table he turned and smiled down at his sister, who seemed turned to stone. The smile was so grotesque, so courageous, so mechanical, that Ellery averted his eyes. Then Bill walked to the witness box and said, "Mr. Orléans, there is no reservation in the minds of the defense regarding your authority as a fingerprint expert. We appreciate your unselfish services in the interests of truth. For that reason—"

"I object," said Pollinger coldly, "to Counsel's making a speech."

Judge Menander cleared his throat. "I suggest that you proceed with your cross-examination, Counsel."

"I mean to do so at once, Your Honor. Mr. Orléans, you have testified that Lucy Wilson's fingerprints appear on the knife with which Joseph Kent Wilson was murdered. You have also testified that on the knife there were many indications of smudged prints which were unreadable, have you not?"

"That is not quite what I said, sir," replied Orléans courteously. "I said there were many indications of smudges."

"Not smudges such as might have been made by fingers?"

"The smudges were unreadable. They could not have been made by naked fingers."

"But they could have been made by fingers encased in some manufactured substance?"

"Conceivably."

"Such as fingers encased in gloves?"

"It is possible."

Pollinger looked angry; a little color seeped back into Bill's cheeks. "You also testified, Mr. Orléans, that most of these smudges were on the haft?"

"Yes."

"It is by the haft that a person wishing to wield a knife in the normal manner will grasp it?"

"Yes."

"And there were smudges of this peculiar nature over the fingerprints of Lucy Wilson on the haft?"

"Yes." The expert stirred. "But I must refuse to go on record, sir, as specifying the nature of those smudges. I cannot tell what made them. I do not believe science can tell. The best we can do is hazard a guess."

"Ware these smudges on the haft in the shape of fingertips?"

"They were not. They were blurring marks in irregular shapes."

"Such as might have occurred if a gloved hand grasped the haft?"

"I say again: It is possible."

"And these smudges are over Lucy Wilson's prints?"

"Yes."

"Indicating that someone handled that haft after she did?"

The Frenchman showed his teeth again. "I cannot say that, sir. The smudges may have been caused by no human agency. If the knife had been wrapped loosely in tissue, for example, and placed in a box, and the box had received a shaking, the smudges may have so occurred."

Bill paced up and down. "You have also testified, Mr. Orléans, that Lucy Wilson's prints on the haft were so grouped as to suggest she grasped the knife for a blow. Don't you believe that pushes forward an unwarrantable conclusion?"

Orleans frowned. "I beg your pardon?"

"Might not a person pick up a knife merely to examine it and still leave such prints grouped as you found them?"

"Oh, naturally. I was merely exemplifying the nature of the grouping."

"Then you cannot as an expert certainly say that Lucy Wilson used that knife for lethal purposes?"

"But of course I cannot. My concern is with the fact, sir. The fact you cannot change. The interpretation—" He shrugged.

As Bill walked away Pollinger leaped to his feet. "Mr. Orléans, you found Lucy Wilson's prints on this knife?"

"Yes."

"You have sat in this courtroom and heard it testified that the knife was purchased only the day before the crime by the victim himself, that it was found not in his Philadelphia home but in the shack in which he was murdered, in its original wrappings, with a gift card made out in the hand not of Lucy Wilson but of the victim, with—?"

"Object!" stormed Bill. "Object! This is not proper—"

"That's all," said Pollinger with a quiet smile. "Thank you, Mr. Orléans. Your Honor," he paused and drew a deep breath, "the State rests."

Bill whirled and demanded a dismissal of the charges. But the testimony of the French fingerprint expert had completely changed the complexion of the case. Judge Menander refused. Bill was flushed; he was very angry and breathing hard. "Your Honor, the defense requests an adjournment. The testimony of the last witness comes as a complete surprise. We have not had an opportunity to examine into the subject-matter of the testimony, and ask for one."

"Granted." The Judge rose. "Adjourned until tomorrow morning at ten o'clock."

When Lucy had been taken away and the jury had filed out, the pressbox exploded. With feverish haste the newspaper people scrambled out of the courtroom.

Bill looked limply at Ellery; then his eyes flashed across the room. Andrea Gimball was staring at him with a cloudy, tight-lipped anguish. He looked away. "Bombshell. Lucy didn't say—"

Ellery took his arm gently. "Come on, Bill. There's work to do."

*

The red-haired woman found Ellery smoking thoughtfully on a bench behind the Old State House overlooking the placid river. Bill Angell patrolled the walk before the bench with a ceaseless and inhuman energy. The night sky was smoky with heat.

"So there you are," she said cheerfully, dropping beside Ellery. "Bill Angell, you'll wear your soles away. In this swelter, too! And I don't mind telling you that every news hawk in the world is looking for you. Eve of the defense, and what not… I suppose," she said suddenly, "I ought to shut up."

There was a gaunt and indrawn look imprinted on the yellowed skin of Bill's face. His eyes were two sullen lights at the bottom of red-rimmed wells. All afternoon and evening he had been calling in experts, sending out investigators, rounding up witnesses, conferring with colleagues, making innumerable telephone calls. He should have been reeling with fatigue.

"You're not doing yourself or Lucy any good, going on this way, Bill," said Ella in a subdued voice. "First thing you know you'll wake up in a hospital, and then where will the poor thing be?"

Bill's legs continued to pump. The red-haired woman sighed and crossed her long legs. From the river came a girl's empty shout and the deep laughter of a man. The State House behind them was quiet, squatting on the dark lawns like an old bullfrog. Bill flung his hands up suddenly and waved them at the smoky sky. "If only she had told me!"

"What does she say?" murmured Ellery.

Bill made a snorting, desperate sound. "Simplest explanation imaginable—so simple no one will believe it. Joe brought that damned desk-set home with him Friday night. Naturally, she wanted to see it. So she unwrapped it and looked it over. And that's how her prints got on the metal parts. Beautiful, eh?" He laughed shortly. "And the only witness who can corroborate her statement is dead!"

"Oh, come now, Bill," said Ella Amity in a light tone, "that does sound reasonable. Who wouldn't believe that a gift from two people would be handled by both? The desk-set was from Joe and Lucy and, lo! Joe's and Lucy's prints are found on it. Why should a jury disbelieve that?"

"You heard that Wanamaker clerk on the stand. The set was bought by Joe—alone. It was wiped clean by the wrapper before being handed over. Joe wrote the gift card in the store himself. No hint of Lucy yet, is there? Then what? Joe went home. Can I prove that? No! True, he'd told me he was leaving Philadelphia the next morning, which implies that he meant to spend the night with Lucy; but implication isn't proof and, considering the source, it's biased testimony. No one saw him come home Friday night, no one saw him leave home Saturday morning. No one but Lucy, and you can't expect a prejudiced jury to believe the unsupported word of a defendant."

"They're not prejudiced, Bill," said the red-haired woman quickly.

"Good of you to lie. Have you been watching the pan of Juror Number 4? When I approved her I thought I had fertile ground there—fat, fifty, definitely middle-class, domestic.... Now she turns raging female! Lucy's too damned beautiful; she makes every woman who sees her squirm with envy. The others—Number 7's got a tendency to cramps. How the hell was I to know that? He's sore at the world. Ah, nuts." Bill waved his arms.

They were silent, finding nothing to say. After a while Bill muttered, "It's going to be a fight, all right."

"You're putting Lucy on the stand?" asked Ellery quietly.

"Heavens, man, she's my only hope! I can't dig up a witness to support her movie alibi nor one for the fingerprint business, so she's got to testify herself. Maybe she'll make a sympathetic witness." He dropped onto a bench opposite them and ruffled his hair. "If she doesn't, God help us both."

"But, Bill," objected Ella, "aren't you being too pessimistic? I've pumped some of the legal talent floating around town, and they all think Pollinger's got a poor jury case. It is circumstantial evidence, after all. There's certainly enough reasonable doubt…"

Bill said patiently: "Pollinger's a crack prosecutor. And he has last whack at the jury, don't forget that—State sums up after the defense. Any experienced trial lawyer will tell you he'll concede half his case just to leave the last impression on the minds of the jury. And then public opinion—" He scowled.

"What about public opinion?" demanded the woman indignantly.

"Oh, you've been a trump, Ella. But you haven't the legal slant. You've no idea what harm was done by that insurance business."

Ellery shifted on the bench. "The what?"

"Even before the case went to trial it leaked out that the National was withholding payment of the insurance to Lucy on grounds of suspicion that the beneficiary might have murdered the insured. Page one stuff. Old Hathaway made a speech about it to the reporters; he didn't put it quite that way, but the inference was plain. Naturally, I tried to patch up some of the damage by filing suit in New York to compel payment of the policy. But that's routine: the pivotal point is the outcome of the trial. Meanwhile, every potential juryman in the county read that story. The gang over at the Court House denied it, but they did."

Ellery flipped a cigaret away. "What's the defense, Bill?"

"Lucy herself to explain the fingerprint mess, her alibi, so on. You to bring out discrepancies unaccounted for by the prosecution. You'll do that, of course, Ellery?" Bill asked suddenly.

"Don't be a greater ass than you can help, Bill."

"There's one angle you can be of service on, El. The match-stubs."

"Match-stubs?" Ellery blinked a little. "What about them? How?"

Bill jumped off the bench and began pacing again. "There's no question that those stubs prove the murderess smoked while lying in wait for Gimball. It will be easy for me to prove that Lucy doesn't smoke and never has. If I put you on the stand—"

"But, Bill," said Ellery slowly, "there is a question about that. A very large question. So large, in fact, that there's every logical indication that you're completely wrong."

Bill halted. "What's that? Not smoking?" he seemed bewildered; his eyes had sunken even deeper into his head.

Ellery sighed. "I went over that room with a fine comb, Bill. I found a large number of burnt match-stubs on the plate. All right; it's natural to think of smoking at once. But what are the facts?"

"Lesson Number One in how to be a detective," chuckled the red-haired woman, but she was watching Bill with anxiety.

"Smoking," frowned Ellery, "means tobacco. Tobacco means ashes and butts. What did I find? Not the minutest trace of ashes or butts, not the most fragmentary shred of tobacco, consumed or otherwise. No burns anywhere, no signs on the plate or table that a cigaret had been ground out, not the faintest indication in the fireplace or on the rug of a burn or ashes or butts—and I went over that rug inch by inch, examining every thread. And finally, no butts or ashes outside the windows on the ground or anywhere in the vicinity, showing that none had been flicked out of the windows from inside the shack." He shook his head. "No, Bill. Those matches were employed for any purpose but smoking."

"So that's out," said Bill, and fell silent.

"Wait a minute." Ellery waved another cigaret. "There's something out, true, but by the same token there's something in. Something that may help you in your general plan of attack. Before I go into that, however," he squinted through the smoke, "may I ask what you intend to do about Miss Andrea Gimball?"

A woman, tall and cool in lawn, was strolling along the walk on the arm of a man. The group at the benches grew very still. The woman's face was dim, but it was evident that she was listening to her escort, whose burly body jerked restlessly from side to side as if he were in a passion about something. Then the pair came within range of an overhead lamp, and they recognized Andrea Gimball and her fiancé. Burke Jones halted abruptly, glowering. So did Andrea; and she looked at Bill as if he had been a ghost. Then the yellow of Bill's skin began to redden; he closed his hands and stared down at the resulting fists. Andrea turned like a wraith and ran off down the walk in the direction from which she and her escort had come. Jones stood irresolute for a moment, glaring from Bill to the running girl; and then he too broke into a run, his trussed arm swinging swiftly against his coat.

Ella Amity jumped to her feet. "Bill Angell, I could shake you!" she cried. "What in the name of common sense has got into you? You fool! You've picked a sweet time to act like a kid with his first crush!"

Bill's fingers opened. "You don't understand, Ella. None of you understands. The girl means nothing to me."

"Tell that to the Marines!"

"I'm interested in her because I've discovered that she's concealing something."

"Oh," said Ella in a different voice. "What?"

"I don't know. But it's so important to her that she's frantic at the mere thought of going on the stand. So,"—he opened and shut his hands rapidly—"that's exactly where she's going. Fool, am I?" His eyes strained after the stumbling figure far down the walk. "I'll show her who's a fool. She's important to me—to poor Lucy. So important I'm saving her to be my final witness!"

"Bill, darling. That's the old Blackstone speaking. Good for you, counselor. Is this for publication?"

"Not officially," said Bill grimly. "But it might be rumored. There's nothing Pollinger can do about it. I've subpoenaed her."

"Rumored it is. Your Worship. Seein' you, darling!" And Ella snapped her fingers and scurried off after the vanished pair.

"Bill," said Ellery. Bill sat down, averting his eyes. "I think I know what that decision means to you."

"Means? Why should it mean anything to me? I'm glad of it for Lucy's sake! You people give me a pain. Means!"

"Of course you are, Bill," said Ellery soothingly. "And so am I. For more reasons," he added in a thoughtful voice, "than one."

*

When the jury retired after Judge Menander's charge opinion among the initiate varied. Many thought that the verdict would come swiftly for acquittal. Others predicted a long session ending in a disagreement. Only a handful envisioned conviction.

Lucy, it is true, had made a poor witness. From the first, she was nervous, jumpy, scared. While Bill led her through her testimony she was quiet enough, answering readily, even smiling faintly at times. Through his sympathetic questions she told of her life with the man she had known as Joseph Wilson, his kindness to her, their love, a detailed account of their meeting, courtship, marriage, daily life.

Gradually Bill worked her around to the period just before the crime. She related how they had discussed buying something for Bill's birthday; how Wilson had promised to get something on Friday, the day before his death, in Wanamaker's; how he had brought the desk-set home with him that night and she had unwrapped it and examined it; and how he had taken the gift with him on leaving Saturday morning, promising to stop off and give it to Bill that very day. She was on the stand during direct examination for a day and a half, and by the time Bill had finished with her she had explained everything and denied all of the State's allegations. Then Pollinger sprang to the attack.

Pollinger assailed her story with consummate viciousness. The man was a human question-mark, with savage gestures and infinite variations in tonal insinuation. He sneered at her protestations of honesty. He derided her statement that she had never known or even suspected her husband's real identity, pointing out that no jury would believe that a woman could live with a man for ten years—especially when he 'suspiciously' spent most of his time away from home—without coming to learn everything there was to learn about him. His cross-examination was merciless; Bill was continuously on his feet shouting objections.

At one point Pollinger snarled, "Mrs. Wilson, you had an opportunity to make a statement—a hundred statements—long before today, did you not?"

"Yes."

"Why haven't you told this story about how your fingerprints got on the paper-cutter before? Answer me!"

"I—I—no one asked me."

"But you knew your fingerprints were on that knife, didn't you?"

"I didn't realize—"

"You do realize, though, don't you, what a bad impression you are making by suddenly pulling this flimsy explanation out of your bag of tricks—after you know how dark things look for you and have had an opportunity to talk things over with your counsel?"

The whole question was stricken out at Bill's enraged objections, but the blow had told. The jury were frowning. Lucy was wringing her hands.

"You have also testified," snapped Pollinger, "that your husband promised to stop in at your brother's office that Saturday morning and hand over this gift, haven't you?"

"Yes. Yes."

"But he didn't, did he? The gift was found in its original wrappings in that isolated shack miles from Philadelphia, wasn't it?"

"I—He must have forgotten. He must have—"

"Don't you realize, Mrs. Wilson, that it's quite obvious to everyone here that you lied about that gift? That you never did see it at your own home? That you first saw it at the shack—"

By the time Pollinger was through with her, despite all Bill could do to have accusatory questions stricken out, Lucy was completely unstrung, weeping, at times flaring into anger, and constantly—through the traps of pure language Pollinger set—contradicting her own testimony. The man was very clever about it; his ferocity was all on the surface, a calculated emotion nicely adjusted to the instability of the witness. Beneath he was as cool and relentless as a machine. It was necessary to recess until Lucy could recover from hysteria.

Bill grinned doggedly at the jury and plunged ahead with the defense. He summoned witness after witness—neighbors, friends, trades-people—to corroborate Lucy's claim of untroubled felicity with the dead man until the very eve of his death. All testified that there never had been a suspicion in their minds concerning Wilson's double life, that Lucy had never evinced the slightest sign of knowledge. He called several witnesses to testify to Lucy's unfailing habit of attending a motion picture show in town on Saturday nights when her husband was presumably away on a 'sales trip'. He established through friends and clerks in apparel shops she patronized that she had never bought or worn a veil. Through all this Pollinger moved with calm and sure interference, quick to catch a weakness in testimony or a predisposition to bias.

Then Bill went to work on the car. He had long since pointed out, during the testimony of one of Pollinger's witnesses—the department fingerprint expert who examined the Ford—that there was no significance in the fact that only Lucy's fingerprints had been found in the car. It was hers, she alone had driven it for years, and it was natural that her prints should be all over it. He had also tried, with uncertain success, to have certain smudges on the wheel and gear-shift interpreted as evidences of gloved hands, but this the witness had refused to concede.

Now Bill put a succession of experts on the stand to bring out that very point—all attacked in business-like fashion by the prosecutor, either on the score of the expert's unreliability, poor previous trial record, or outright bias. The authenticity of the tire tracks Bill left severely alone. Instead, he put on the stand an expert in metals, employed in the Federal Bureau of Standards.

This witness testified that in his opinion the Ford's radiator-cap could not have 'fallen off' by the process Pollinger had claimed: a rusty area so weakened by the car's vibration that it finally snapped through on the scene of the crime without human agency. The expert said that he had analyzed the broken halves of the radiator-cap and that nothing less than a sharp blow could have caused the little metal woman to snap off at the ankles. He went into details of strains and metal-aging. This opinion Pollinger subjected to a searching cross-examination; finally promising to produce during rebuttal an expert who would testify to an opinion precisely opposite.

And then Bill, on the fourth day of the defense, put Ellery on the stand. "Mr. Queen," said Bill after Ellery had sketched a little of his semiprofessional background, "you were on the scene of the crime before even the arrival of the police, were you not?"

"Yes."

"You examined the scene of the crime thoroughly, out of a purely professional interest in the case?"

"Yes."

Bill held up a small, nondescript object. "Do you remember having seen this during your examination?"

"Yes." It was a cheap plate.

"Where was it situated when you examined the room?"

"On the only table there, the table behind which the dead man lay."

"It was in a prominent position, then; it couldn't be missed?"

"No."

"Was there anything on this plate, Mr. Queen, when you saw it?"

"Yes. A number of paper match-stubs, all showing evidences of having been burnt."

"You mean that the matches had been struck and extinguished?"

"Yes."

"You have heard the complete case presented by the State? You've sat in this courtroom since the beginning of the trial?"

"I have."

"Has this plate," asked Bill grimly, "or the match-stubs which you saw on it at the scene of the crime, been so much as mentioned once by the prosecution?"

"No."

Pollinger leaped to his feet and for five minutes he and Bill argued before Judge Menander. Finally Bill was permitted to proceed. "Mr. Queen, you are well known as an investigator of crime. Have you anything to offer this jury in explanation of the burnt match-stubs so carefully ignored by the prosecution?"

"Oh, yes."

There was another argument, more protracted this time. Pollinger fumed. But Ellery was permitted to go on. He went through the reasoning he had outlined to Bill a few nights before concerning the logical impossibility of the matches having been used for smoking purposes.

"You have just shown, Mr. Queen," said Bill swiftly, "that the matches could not have been employed for smoking purposes. Is there anything you found on your examination of the shack which explains to your own satisfaction why the matches were used?"

"Indeed, yes. There was an object examined not only by me but by Chief De Jong and his detectives that very night. Its condition makes the conclusion, under the circumstances, inevitable."

Bill brandished something. "Is this the object you refer to?"

"Yes." It was the charred cork found on the paper-knife.

There was another argument, more violent this time. After a bitter exchange it was settled by the Judge, who permitted the cork to be placed in evidence as a defense exhibit. "Mr. Queen, this cork had been charred by fire when you found it?"

"Unquestionably."

"It was found on the tip of the knife which killed Gimball?"

"Yes."

"Have you, as a criminologist, any theory to account for this?"

"There is only one possible interpretation," said Ellery. "Obviously when the knife was plunged into Gimball's heart the cork was not on its tip. Therefore the cork must have been placed on the tip by the killer after the murder and then charred by repeated applications of the little paper-matches found on the plate. Why did the criminal do this? Well, what is the effect of a charred cork stuck on the point of a knife? It becomes a crude but effective writing implement. The knife provides leverage, the carbonized cork on its tip provides an edge capable of leaving legible marks. In other words, the killer after her crime wrote something for some purpose of her own."

"Why in your opinion didn't the killer employ a simpler device?"

"Because there wasn't any. There were no ink-filled pens, pencils, or other writing tools anywhere in the shack or on the person of the victim—except for the desk-set, which had a pen and inkwell. But this pen and well were also dry, being new and never having been filled with ink. If the criminal wished to write, then, and had no writing implement on her own person, she would have to manufacture one, which was what she did. The cork, of course, came from the desk-set; she had already had to remove it, in all probability, to commit the crime. So she knew about it in advance of the necessity for writing. As for thinking of the device, the use of burnt cork in the theater, for example, is so universally known that it would not take brilliance to see the possibilities."

"Have you heard the prosecution so much as mention this burnt cork in presenting its case against the defendant?"

"No."

"Was a note found, or any sort of written message?"

"No."

"Your conclusion from this?"

"Patently, it was taken away. If the killer wrote a note, it must have been to someone. It is logical to suppose, therefore, that this person took the note away, that there is a new factor in this case which has not heretofore been suspected. Even if the killer took her own note away, which is absurd, the mere fact introduces an element in no way accounted for by the prosecution."

For an hour Ellery and Pollinger sparred across the rail of the witness box. It was Pollinger's point that Ellery was a poor witness for two reasons: that he was a personal friend of the defendant, and that his reputation was based on 'theory, not practice'. When Ellery was finally excused they were both dripping with perspiration. Nevertheless, it was conceded by the press that the defense had scored an important point. From that time on Bill's whole manner changed. A bright confidence crept into his eyes which began to infect the jury. Number 2, a sharp-looking business man of Trenton, was observed whispering hotly to his neighbor, who had the blank features of one wholly aloof from the vicissitudes of the world. The blankness disappeared under a cloud of painful thought. Others in the jury box looked more interested than they had appeared for days.

On the last morning, after several sessions with relatively unimportant defense witnesses, Bill came into court with a squareness to his jaw that was remarked by everyone within eyeshot. He was pale, but not so pale as he had been; and there was a truculence in the glance with which he swept the courtroom that made Pollinger look thoughtful.

He wasted no time. "Jessica Borden Gimball to the stand!"

Andrea, behind the prosecutor's table, gave a little gasp. Mrs. Gimball looked nauseated, then bewildered, and finally furious. There was a hasty conference at the table in which Senator Frueh, who had sat with Pollinger from the beginning of the trial, took the leading role. Then the society woman, striving to soften her features, took the stand.

Bill raked her with fierce questions, met Pollinger's interruptions swiftly, put her through a scathing examination that left her white with rage. When he was through with her, despite all her acid protestations, the impression had accreted that Mrs. Gimball possessed far greater motive for killing Gimball than anyone else in the universe. Pollinger softened the blow by painting her, on cross-examination, as a gentle, misunderstood, and bewildered woman who had not even the consolation of marriage to repay her for the wrong Gimball had done. And he brought out her movements on the night of the murder, her attendance at the Waldorf charity ball—which Bill had questioned—and the improbability of the insinuation that she could have slipped away and driven some eighty miles and back without having been missed.

Bill instantly summoned Grosvenor Finch to the stand. He made the insurance executive admit that Mrs. Gimball had been Gimball's beneficiary until a few weeks before his death. Although Finch denied it, the possibility was broached that Mrs. Gimball had learned of this beneficiary change through him. To cap the point, Bill recalled to Finch his statement to De Jong on the night of the murder—to the effect that 'any of us could have slipped away and killed Joe.'

Pollinger retaliated with a stenographic transcript of the exact statement: 'If you mean that any of us could have stolen off, driven out here, and stabbed Joe Gimball to death, I suppose you would be hypothetically correct.' Then he asked: "What did you mean by that, Mr. Finch?"

"I meant that theoretically anything under the sun was possible. But I also pointed out the absurdity of it—"

"Are you in a position to state whether Mrs. Gimball was away from the Waldorf ballroom that evening for any length of time?"

"Mrs. Gimball did not leave the hotel all that evening."

"Did you ever tell Mrs. Gimball that the man she thought her husband had suddenly made someone else his insurance beneficiary?"

"Never. I have testified to that effect innumerable times. There is not a single person in this world who can come forward and assert with truth that I so much as hinted that Gimball had changed his beneficiary."

"That's all, Mr. Finch."

Bill got to his feet and said clearly: "Andrea Gimball." The girl walked toward the witness box as if she were treading the last long mile. Her eyes were downcast and her hands, clasped tightly before her, were trembling. There was no color whatever in her cheeks. She swore to the formal oath and sat down to become so completely still that she might have been in a trance. The courtroom on the instant sensed hidden drama. Pollinger was gnawing his nails. Behind him the Gimball group showed unmistakable signs of nervousness.

Bill leaned over the box and stared at her until her eyes, as if drawn by a magnet, came up to meet his. Whatever bitter message flashed across the ionized inches of space between them no one ever knew; but both went even paler after a moment and their glances passed, Bill's to come to rest on the wall behind, hers to go to her hands.

Then Bill said in a strangely flat voice, "Miss Gimball, where were you on the evening of June first?"

Her answer was just audible. "With my mother's party at the Waldorf in New York."

"All evening, Miss Gimball?" His tone almost caressed her, but it was the soft and savage caress of a stalking animal. She did not reply, but caught her breath and her lip in one convulsive gasp. "Answer the question, please!" She choked back a sob. "Shall I refresh your memory, Miss Gimball? Or shall I summon witnesses who will refresh it for you?"

"Please…" she whispered. "Bill…"

"You are under oath to tell the truth," he said stonily. "I am entitled to an answer! Don't you remember where you spent that part of the evening during which you were not at the Waldorf?"

In the commotion at the prosecutor's table Pollinger snapped, "Your Honor, counsel is obviously impeaching his own witness!"

Bill smiled at him. "Your Honor, this is a trial for murder. I have summoned a witness who is hostile. I have the right directly to examine a hostile witness whose testimony I could not place on the record by cross-examination during the State's presentation for the simple reason that the State did not present this witness. It is pertinent testimony, important testimony, and I shall connect it at once if I am given the opportunity by the prosecutor." He added between his teeth: "Who seems strangely reluctant to have me do so."

Judge Menander said, "It is perfectly proper for defense counsel to call and examine a hostile witness. Proceed, Mr. Angell."

Bill growled, "Read the question, please."

The stenographer obeyed. Andrea replied in a tired, hopeless way, "Yes."

"Tell the jury where you spent the early part of that evening!"

"At the—the house by the river…"

"You mean the shack in which Gimball was murdered?"

She whispered, "Yes."

The room exploded. The Gimball party was on its feet, shouting. Only Pollinger was unmoved. During the commotion Bill did not change expression, and Andrea closed her eyes. It took several minutes to quiet the courtroom. Andrea told her story then in a lifeless voice: how, upon receipt of her stepfather's telegram, she had borrowed her fiance's Cadillac roadster and driven to Trenton; how, upon realizing that she was an hour early, she had driven off for a spin and returned at deep dusk to find the shack empty except for Gimball, lying still on the floor.

"You thought he was dead, when as a matter of fact he was still alive?" asked Bill harshly.

"Yes."

"You didn't touch his body, Miss Gimball?"

"Oh, no, no!"

As she went on to explain her shock, her scream, and her flight from the house, Ellery quietly scribbled a few notes on a sheet of paper and had it passed to Bill. Andrea stopped in her recital, her eyes widening with a milky fear that turned them from blue to gray.

Bill's lips tightened queerly. The paper in his fingers jerked a little. "How long were you in the shack—on your second visit?"

"I don't know. I don't know. Minutes." She was thoroughly frightened now, her shoulders a little drawn up as if to protect herself.

"Minutes. When you came the first time, at eight o'clock, was there a car in either driveway?"

It was almost as if she were thinking things out in her distress, choosing the unuttered words with a painful care. "There was no car in the main driveway. There was an old sedan—that Packard—in the side drive, parked against the little porch at the side."

"The Wilson car; that's right. Now, when you came back—if it was only a matter of minutes, by the way, that you spent in the shack, you must have got there the second time around nine? I saw you leave, remember, at eight after."

"I... suppose so."

"When you returned at nine, then, the Packard was still there, of course; but was any other car standing in either driveway?"

Very quickly she said, "No. No. Not at all."

"And you say," Bill went on relentlessly, "you saw no one inside the house either the first time or the second time?"

"No one. Not a soul." She was breathless now. At the same time she raised her eyes, and they were so full of pain, so reproachful, so choked with a mute plea, that Bill colored a little.

"Didn't you see automobile tracks in the main driveway the second time?"

"I—I don't remember."

"You have testified that, having come early, you drove off on Lamberton Road toward Camden for about an hour. Do you recall having passed a Ford coupé driven by a veiled woman on either the outward or the return trip?"

"I don't remember."

"You don't remember. Do you remember what time you got back to New York that night?"

"About eleven-thirty. I—I went home, changed into evening things, drove down to the Wardorf where I joined my mother's party."

"Didn't anyone remark on your long absence?"

"I—No. No."

"Your fiancé was there without you, your mother was there, Mr. Finch, other friends, and no one remarked on your absence, Miss Gimball? You expect us to believe that?"

"I—I was upset. I don't recall… that anyone said anything."

Bill's lips curled; his face was toward the jury. "By the way, Miss Gimball, what did you do with that note the murderess left for you?"

Pollinger automatically sprang to his feet; then he seemed to think better of it, for he sat down without having said anything. "Note?" faltered Andrea. "What note?"

"The note written with the burnt cork. You heard Mr. Queen's testimony. What did you do with that note?"

"I don't know what you're talking about." Her voice rose a little. "I tell you there was no—I mean I know nothing about a note!"

"There were three people on the scene of that crime, Miss Gimball," said Bill tensely. "The victim, the murderess, and you. That's giving you the benefit of every doubt. The murderess wrote the note after the crime, so she didn't write it to her victim. She certainly didn't write it to herself! Where is that note?"

"I don't know anything about a note," she cried hysterically.

"I think," drawled Pollinger, rising, "that this has gone far enough, Your Honor. This witness is not on trial. She has given sufficient answer to what is certainly an objectionable question."

Bill replied at length, arguing passionately. But Judge Menander shook his head. "You have been answered, Mr. Angell. I think you had better proceed with your examination."

"Exception!"

"You may have it. Proceed, please."

Bill turned fiercely to the witness box. "Now, Miss Gimball, may I ask you to explain to this jury if you have ever told your story of that evening's adventures to any official investigator of this crime—Chief De Jong, Prosecutor Pollinger, or any of their men?"

Again Pollinger half-rose, but he sank back. Andrea glanced at him, moistening her lips.

"We want your own story, Miss Gimball," said Bill ironically. "You will oblige me by not looking for assistance from the prosecutor."

She fumbled with her gloves. "I—Yes, I did."

"Oh, you did. Did you tell them this story voluntarily? Did you come forward with it of your own free will?"

"No, I—"

"Oh, then, Chief De Jong or Mr. Pollinger came to you?"

"Mr. Pollinger."

"In other words, had Mr. Pollinger not approached you, you would not have gone to the authorities with your story? Just a moment, Mr. Pollinger. You waited until the authorities came to you! When was this, Miss Gimball?"

She shielded her eyes from the stares of the courtroom. "I don't remember exactly. Perhaps a week after it…"

"After the crime? Don't be afraid to say it, Miss Gimball. The crime. You aren't frightened by that word, are you?"

"I—No. No. Of course not."

"A week after the crime, the prosecutor came to you and questioned you. During that week you said nothing to the authorities about having visited the scene of the crime on the night of the murder. Is that correct?"

"It—it wasn't important. I couldn't contribute anything. I disliked getting involved—"

"You disliked getting involved in an ugly mess? Is that it? Now, Miss Gimball, while you were on the scene that night did you touch the knife?"

"No!" She was answering with more spirit now; her eyes flashed and were blue again. They glared at each other across the rail.

"Where was the knife?"

"On the table."

"You didn't so much as lay a finger on it?"

"No."

"Were you wearing gloves that night?"

"Yes. But I had my left glove off."

"Your right glove was on your hand?"

"Yes."

"Isn't it true that in fleeing from the shack you banged your hand against the door and dislodged the diamond of your engagement ring?"

"Yes."

"You lost it? You didn't know you had dropped it?"

"I—No."

"Isn't it true that I found it, and told you about it the very night of the crime, and that you pleaded with me desperately not to say anything about it to anyone?"

She was furious now. "Yes!" Her cheeks were fiery.

"Isn't it true," asked Bill in a hoarse, impassioned voice, "that you even kissed me in an effort to keep me from disclosing the fact to the police?"

She was so stunned she half-rose from the chair. "Why, you—you promised! You—you—" She bit her lip to keep back the tears.

Bill tossed his head, doggedly. "Did you see the defendant on the night of the crime?"

The fire in her cheeks was quenched. "No," she whispered.

"You didn't see her at any time—in the shack, near the shack, on the road between the shack and Camden?"

"No."

"But you admit that you visited the scene of the crime that night and said nothing to anyone about it until you were accused point-blank in private by the prosecutor?" Pollinger was on his feet now, shouting. There was a long argument.

"Miss Gimball," resumed Bill hoarsely, "didn't you know that your stepfather was leading a double life?"

"No."

"Didn't you know that he had shortly before June first removed your mother as beneficiary of his million-dollar policy?"

"No!"

"You hated your stepfather, didn't you?"

Another wrangle. Andrea was white now, white with rage and shame. At the prosecutor's table the Gimball group were flushed with indignation. "All right," said Bill curtly, "that's enough for me. Inquire."

Pollinger strode to the rail of the box. "Miss Gimball, when I came to you a week after the crime what did I say to you?"

"You said you had traced the roadster and found it belonged to my fiancé. You asked me if I hadn't visited the—the scene on the night of the crime and, if so, why I hadn't come forward and told you so."

"Did it ever strike you that I was trying to shield you, or suppress your story?"

"No. You were very severe with me."

"Did you tell me the story you have just told this jury?"

"Yes."

"What did I say to that?"

"You said you would check up on it."

"Did I ask you any questions?"

"A great many."

"Pertinent questions? About the evidence? About what you saw and did not see, that sort of thing?"

"Yes."

"And didn't I then tell you that your story in no way conflicted with what evidence the State had already amassed against the defendant, and that therefore I would spare you the annoyance and pain of putting you on the stand during the trial?"

"Yes."

Pollinger stepped back, smiling paternally. Bill stamped forward. "Miss Gimball, it's true, is it not, that the State did not call you as a witness in this trial?"

"Yes." She was weary now, sapped and limp.

"Although you had a story to tell that might conceivably put a reasonable doubt of the defendant's guilt into the minds of the jury?"

The defense rested.

*

As they waited for the verdict and the hours massed into a day, and then into two days, with still no word from the jury, it was remarked that opinion had shifted since the close of the State's case. The prolonged discussions in the jury room were a favorable sign for the defendant; at the very least, they seemed to indicate a deadlock. Bill was heartened; as the hours passed he even began to smile faintly.

The summations after the short session of rebuttal testimony had been swift. Bill, summing up first, had made out a strong indictment against Pollinger personally. He contended that not only had the defense reasonably explained away all the accusations of the State, but that Pollinger had been criminally remiss in his sworn duty. Pollinger, he thundered, had suppressed important evidence: the story of Andrea Gimball's visit to the scene of the crime. It was the function of the public prosecutor, he pointed out, not to persecute, not to hold back any facts, but to sift for the truth. And Pollinger had deliberately ignored two other very important facts which would have gone unmentioned if not for the alertness of the defense's witnesses: the burnt match-stubs and the charred cork. They had not been explained by the State and certainly had not been connected to the defendant. Moreover, the State had failed to prove that the veil was the defendant's, had failed to produce the source from which the veil had come.

Finally, Bill outlined the defense theory. Lucy Wilson, he said, had obviously been framed for the murder of her distinguished husband. The powers of wealth, of social position, he cried, had picked a poor defenseless victim: the woman who had received nothing from Gimball but his love. Someone was offering her up as a victim. In support of this theory he pointed to the 'crushing' testimony of the Federal expert on metals, who had testified that the radiator-cap would not have broken off by itself. Someone, then, had knocked it off. But if someone had knocked it off, it must have been done deliberately; and it could only have been so done with intent to implicate the owner of the car from which it came, Lucy Wilson.

Starting from this, Bill argued—in line with the fervent discussion he had had with Ellery the night before—it was child's play to reconstruct the devilish frame-up: the murderess stole Lucy's car; she stopped for gas for no other reason than to fix the car and the veiled driver firmly in the station owner's mind. "This is proved," he cried, "by the fact that she did not really need gas, that she could have gone on for sixty, eighty miles on the gas already in her car's tank!" She went to the shack, he continued, saw the paper-cutter with its gift card, killed Gimball with the knife, and finally drove back to Philadelphia and wrecked the car in a place where it would be—as it was—easily found by the police.

"If this defendant, my sister," he roared, "were the criminal, why did she wear a veil? She would know that the shack was isolated, that there was little chance of her being seen except by the victim, who would be dead. But the real criminal had every reason to use a veil if she were framing Lucy! Should her own face be seen, the frame-up was defeated. For that matter, if Lucy were this woman, why did she leave the veil to be found in the car? But the criminal had every reason to do so if she were framing the crime around Lucy.

"Furthermore, if Lucy were the criminal everything she did was almost unbelievably stupid. Would she leave an open trail to her own car, would she leave impressions of her tires in the mud, would she permit her car to be found, would she leave the veil, would she make no attempt to fix an alibi for herself, would she wield that knife without the precaution of wearing gloves? Stupid, stupid! So stupid that its very stupidity cries out," shouted Bill, "her innocence. But a woman framing Lucy would have every reason to leave such a plain trail!"

It was an impassioned summation, and it left a visible impression on the jury. Bill concluded more quietly on the note of reasonable doubt. If there was a single member of the jury, he said, who could honestly and conscientiously declare now that there was no reasonable doubt of the defendant's guilt… He flung up his hands and sat down.

But Pollinger had the last word. He derided the 'obvious' defense theory of a frame-up, "the whimper," he said, "of every weak defense." As for the defendant's stupidity, Pollinger remarked with a significant and open glance at Ellery, any practical criminologist knew that all criminals were stupid; it was only in books that criminals were masterminds. This defendant, he said, was not a habitual criminal; her motives had, as usual in the case of the vengeful woman, betrayed her into blind actions; she had left a trail without realizing that she had done so.

The State had amply proved, he said vigorously, her movements on the day of the crime up to its actual commission. She had been seen on the road leading to the shack only a few minutes before the murder. She had been seen driving her car toward that shack. Her car had then left its clear tire prints in the mud before the shack, under such circumstances that it was possible to prove, as the State had proved, that the car had visited that shack during the general period of the murder. This had placed the defendant, he went on, at the scene of the crime circumstantially. And, he pointed out, if there was any doubt concerning her identity as the driver of the Ford, it was completely and irrefutably dispelled by her fingerprints on the knife which killed her husband.

"Fingerprints," he said ironically, "aren't framed—except, perhaps, in those books I mentioned." The jury grinned. "This defendant had her hands on that knife in that shack. The State, then, has led her to the corpse." That was sufficient connection, he went on, in a circumstantial case, to remove all doubt. What was the answer of the defense to this all-important question of fingerprints on the knife? That her prints had got on the knife the night before in her own home! But where was the proof of this transparent story? There was not a single witness to support her explanation. There was not a single proof that the victim even spent that Friday night in his Philadelphia home… And when was this explanation given? After it was brought out that the fingerprints were on the knife! Didn't that show all the evidences of a hastily trumped-up story to explain away a damaging fact?

"I give you my word," said the prosecutor earnestly, "that my heartfelt sympathy goes out to this poor young man who has so ably defended his sister in this trial. He has toiled long and tirelessly to make the best of a bad, bad case. We are all deeply sorry for him. But that should not sway you, ladies and gentlemen, in your judgment of this case. A jury determines facts and ignores its sympathies. You must not permit yourselves to be influenced in your verdict by emotions which would defeat the ends of justice." Moreover, he added dryly, the defendant had been wholly unable to prove an alibi for the night of the crime.

When Pollinger was through outlining the motives he went briefly into the question of deliberation. "The motive here," he said, "was twofold, as I have shown: revenge on the man who had lied to her for ten years, and the natural desire to benefit, while punishing him for that awful living lie, from his death. To have known that he was Joseph Kent Gimball, to have known that he carried a million-dollar policy and had recently changed his beneficiary from Mrs. Gimball to herself, Mrs. Wilson must have had knowledge well in advance of June first. In fact, there is nothing to show that she did not compel Gimball to assign his insurance to her in 'payment' for the wrong he had done her; indeed, psychologically everything points to it. In the light of this, how can anyone doubt that this was a murder planned in advance?

"And if there is any doubt in your minds, consider that this defendant came disguised—clumsily, it is true, but there was an effort at concealment—to the shack in which she murdered her husband. The defense has tried to argue that the use of the newly-purchased paper-cutter as the killing weapon indicates in itself a spontaneous crime, a crime on the spur of the moment; and that, therefore, even if Lucy Wilson had killed her husband it could not be construed as anything but an unpremeditated murder. But how false that is when examined in the naked light! For if I adopt the defense's own theory— that Lucy Wilson was framed for this crime—you will see at once that the use of the knife was merely a convenient alternative for this defendant. If someone framed Lucy Wilson it could only have been with intent and plan far in advance of the actual commission. This flimsy 'someone' could not have known that Joseph Wilson would buy a desk-set the day before his death; therefore the so-called 'framer' must have planned to kill Wilson by some other means—a revolver, strangling, even a knife. But not this knife. Nevertheless, this knife was used. Wouldn't that seem to show that there was no framer? The argument is fallacious all along the line. It shows no such thing. Lucy Wilson came prepared to kill Joseph Kent Gimball with a gun, perhaps, or another knife. In the heat of the encounter she used a knife already on the scene. The point is meaningless."

His peroration was a masterpiece of shrewd persuasion. Then he sat down, quietly rubbing his neck with a handkerchief.

Judge Menander's charge to the jury was surprisingly short. It outlined the possible verdicts and explained the law of circumstantial evidence. It was observed with astonishment by trained spectators that the famous jurist refrained from injecting into his short charge—it took only twenty-five minutes—the slightest hint of his own convictions in the matter, an unusual phenomenon in a State which permitted its presiding justices in capital cases the widest latitude for the expression of their own views.

Then the case went to the jury.

*

During the seventy-first hour word was sent that the jury had at last arrived at a verdict. It came in late afternoon, during an impromptu conference with the press in Bill's room at the Stacy-Trent. The long delay had so convinced Bill of ultimate victory that he was his old self, a little gayer than was natural, perhaps, but cheerful and laughing and full of good Scotch whisky. There was ample reason for optimism. Six hours after the retirement of the jury word had leaked out that they stood 10-2 for acquittal. The delay could only mean that two jurors were stubborn; the announcement that a verdict had been reached could only mean that the two had finally been won over.

The summons to the County Court House sobered him like a cold shower. They left on the run.

Bill, waiting for Lucy to be brought back into the courtroom through the Bridge of Sighs from the adjoining jail, carefully looked around. Then he slumped back in his chair. "All over but the shouting," he sighed to Ellery. "Well, I see the Gimball bunch has skipped."

"Remarkable eyesight," said Ellery dryly, and just then Lucy was led in and they both became too busy for conversation. Lucy was in a semi-stupor, barely able to drag her legs to the defense table. Ellery stroked her hand while a doctor administered restoratives, and Bill talked to her so naturally and easily that her eyes became almost normal again and a faint color returned to her cheeks.

There were the inevitable delays. Pollinger could not be found. Then someone managed to get hold of him and he was hustled into the courtroom. The cameramen became involved in an argument with the Sheriff's staff. Somebody was ejected from the room. The bailiffs shouted for order.

The jury filed in at last. They were twelve tired, dripping people whose eyes seemed affected by an epidemic of shiftiness. Juror Number 7 looked ill and angry. Juror Number 4 looked haughty. But even these two kept their eyes away from the cleared space before the clerk's railing. From the instant he saw their faces Bill stiffened in his chair. His own face whitened.

In a silence so profound that the ticking of the big clock on the front wall was clearly audible, the foreman of the jury rose and in a trembling voice announced the verdict.

They had found Lucy Wilson guilty of murder in the second degree. Lucy fainted. Bill did not so much as move a finger; he seemed frozen to his chair. In fifteen minutes Lucy was revived and sentenced by Judge Menander to twenty years in the State penitentiary.

It appeared, as Ellery discovered later in the boiling crowds, that Jurors 4 and 7 had managed to achieve the astounding result, after

seventy hours and thirty-three minutes in a steaming room, of con-
verting an original 10-2 for acquittal to 12-0 for conviction. Rather
handsomely, Ellery thought, Jurors 4 and 7 had compromised from a
demand for death in order to win over their weaker brethren.

"It was those fingerprints on the knife did it," said Juror Number 4
later to the press. "We just didn't believe her." Juror Number 4 was a
large stout woman with a chin of iron.

*

There was a painful constriction of Mr. Ellery Queen's heart as he
packed his things, rang for a porter, and plodded down the corridor
to Bill Angell's room. He composed his features and knocked on the
door. There was no answer. He tried the knob; to his surprise the door
was unlocked. He opened it and looked in.

Bill was lying on the bed, half-dressed. His dusty shoes had left a
wide earthy stain on the sheet. His necktie was twisted around his collar,
and his shirt was wet all over, as if he had stepped under a shower without taking it off. He was staring up at the ceiling without expression.
His eyes were red, and it seemed to Ellery that he had been crying.

Ellery said, "Bill," in a gentle voice, but Bill did not stir. "Bill,"
said Ellery again, and he came in and shut the door to stand with his
back against it. "I suppose I don't have to tell you how…" He found
it surprisingly difficult to express himself. "What I mean to say is that
I'm leaving. I didn't want to duck out without telling you that I'm not
finished with this thing. In a way, it's lucky Lucy got what she did. If
it had been the Chair… Now there's no need for racing against time."

Bill smiled. It was very queer to see him smile, with his eyes red and
sunken and his face like a death-mask. "Have you ever been in a cell?"
he asked, quite conversationally.

"I know, Bill, I know." Ellery sighed. "But it's better than—well,
the other thing. I'm going to work, Bill. I wanted you to know it."

"Don't think," said Bill without turning his head, "I'm unappreciative, Ellery. It's just that…" His lips compressed.

"I've done nothing at all. It's been a most mystifying puzzle. It's even more mystifying now. But there's one ray of sunshine… Well, let's not discuss it now. Bill."

"Yes?"

Ellery scuffed the rug. "Er—how about money? This thing must have put you in debt to the whole world. An appeal, I mean. It costs a lot, doesn't it?"

"No, Ellery, I can't accept… I mean, thanks just the same. You're a brick."

"Well." Ellery stood there irresolutely for a moment. Then he went to the bed and patted Bill's damp shoulder and went out. As he shut the door behind him he turned to find Andrea Gimball leaning against the wall opposite Bill's room. For a moment he was shocked. Somehow, the spectacle of this girl standing outside Bill's room, her gown crumpled, a damp handkerchief in a ball in her fist, her eyes hollow and red—like Bill's—struck him as indecent. She should have been off with the others, smug in their satisfaction over the burnt offering.

"Well," he said slowly, "look who's here. Just in time, Miss Gimball, for the wake."

"Mr. Queen." Her tongue wet her lips.

"Don't you think you had better leave, Miss Gimball?"

"Is he…?"

"I don't think it's wise," said Ellery, "to attempt to see him at the moment, my dear. I imagine he'd rather be alone."

"Yes." She fumbled with the handkerchief. "I—I thought he would."

"Nevertheless, you're here. That's kind of you. Miss Gimball! Listen to me for a moment."

"Yes?"

Ellery strode across the corridor and seized her arm. Despite the heat, it was strangely cold. "Do you know what you've done to Bill, to that poor woman condemned to twenty years in prison?" She did not reply. "Don't you think it would be decent to try to remedy it—the harm you've done?"

"I—I've done?"

Ellery stepped back. "You won't sleep well," he said softly, "until you come to me with your story. Your real story. You know that, don't you?"

"I—" She stopped, her lips trembling.

Ellery stared at her. Then his eyes narrowed and, deliberately, he turned his back and stalked off down the corridor to his room. The porter was waiting for him, holding his bags, looking curiously at the girl slumped against the wall. He heard very clearly as he walked away what she said. But he knew that she'd said it without realizing that it took the form of audible words. It was a plea and a prayer, and it was so deep with anguish that it almost made him halt and go back: "What should I do? Oh, God, if I only knew what to do."

But he conquered the impulse. There was something in the girl's mind that could only come out by pressure from within. He signaled the porter and they went to the elevator. As he stepped in, he glanced again in Andrea's direction. He was intent and thoughtful.

Andrea stood where he had left her, twisting the limp handkerchief between her fingers, staring at Bill Angell's quiet door as if peace lay there, a peace that was just out of reach. Somehow, the picture of torment and despair she made was to linger in Ellery's mind for a long time. It only emphasized his conviction that around her slender figure shimmered the glowing imponderable that was to change the whole complexion of the sensational Wilson-Gimball case.

IV

THE TRAP

"Some… with arrows, some with traps."

WHAT," SAID INSPECTOR Queen with disgust, "again?" Ellery did not stop whistling as he labored over his bow-tie in the mirror above the bureau. "Seems to me," grumbled the Inspector, "that ever since those friends of yours got messed up in their private brand of hell in Trenton, you've turned into a regular Broadway punk. Where you going?"

"Out."

"Alone, I s'pose?"

"No, indeed. I have what is technically known as a date with one of the loveliest, wealthiest, most desirable and azure-blooded young females on the Island. Furthermore, she's engaged to be married. Not," he squinted critically at his reflection, "that I care a damn, you understand."

"You sound," growled the old gentleman, jabbing some snuff into his nostrils, "like anybody but the conceited pup I used to know. At least in the old days you were level-headed enough to lay off the women."

"Times," said Ellery, "have a deplorable habit of changing."

"The Gimball girl, hey?"

"None other. The name Gimball, by the way, is currently anathema in certain circles. It's Jessica and Andrea Borden, and don't let the Park Avenue crowd hear you call them anything else."

"Fat chance. What's the idea, El?"

Ellery slipped into his coat and fingered the satin lapels lovingly. "The idea," he remarked, "is largely exploratory."

"Ha, ha."

"No, really. Does a man good to get out into society once in a while. Gives you the temporary illusion of special privilege. I've been balancing it off with side-trips down to the East Side. Wonderful what a contrast there is."

"What," asked the Inspector grumpily, "are you exploring?"

Ellery began to whistle again. Djuna, their boy-of-all-work, clattered into the bedroom. "Again?" he shrilled with disapproval. Ellery nodded, and Inspector Queen threw his hands up. "I guess you got a girl," said Djuna blackly. "Here's somethin'."

"Something?"

"Package. Just came. Messenger. All dolled up like a general." The boy threw something large and grand on the bed and sniffed.

"See what it is, imp."

Djuna ripped away the wrappings, disclosing a chaste can, a flattish box, and a note on crested stationery. "You order tobacco from a guy by the name of Pierre?" he demanded.

"Pierre? Pierre? Oh, Lord—the incomparable Miss Zachary! That," grinned Ellery, seizing the note, "is what comes of hobnobbing with riches, dad."

The note said, "My dear Mr. Queen: Pray forgive the delay. My blend is made of foreign tobaccoes, and recent labor troubles in Europe held up the last shipment. I trust you will find the tobacco satisfactory and to your taste. Please accept the enclosed box of paper match-packets with my compliments. I have taken the liberty of having your name inscribed on each one, my usual custom. Should you find the tobacco too strong or too mild, we shall be glad in the future to make the required adjustment of blend. I remain, Yours Respectfully."

"Good old Pierre," said Ellery, tossing the note aside. "Put the stuff away in the family humidor, Djun'. Well, boys, I'm off."

"You're telling me," said the Inspector glumly. He looked positively anxious as Ellery adjusted his hat to a nicety, tucked a stick under his arm, and departed whistling.

*

"This," said Andrea in a severe tone later that evening, "is not the sort of thing I have come to expect from you, Ellery Queen. It's deadly after all those lovely dives you've been taking me to."

Ellery glanced around the quiet and elegant club in the night-sky above Radio City. "Well, I don't want to be precipitate, darling. These problems of social education require delicacy of handling. Too consistent a diet of bread and water…"

"Pish! Let's dance."

They danced in exquisite silence. Andrea gave herself up to the music with a fluid acquiescence of body that made dancing with her a physical pleasure. She floated in Ellery's arms, so light and responsive that he might have been dancing alone. But he was very conscious of the aroma of her hair, and he remembered with a guilty feeling the expression on Bill Angell's face the night she had stood so close to him outside the Trenton shack.

"I like dancing with you," she said lightly as the music stopped.

"Discretion," sighed Ellery, "warns me to thank you and let it go at that." He thought her glance was a little startled. Then she laughed and they strolled back to their table.

"Hello, you two," said Grosvenor Finch. He was grinning at them.

Beside him stood Senator Frueh, as stiff as his pudgy little figure could contrive, and openly disapproving. Both men were in evening clothes. Finch seemed embarrassed.

"Ah, we have company," said Ellery. He held out Andrea's chair and she sat down. "Waiter, chairs. Sit down, gentlemen, sit down. I trust you haven't had too bothersome a chase this evening?"

"Ducky," said Andrea coldly, "what does this mean?"

Finch looked sheepish; he sat down and ran his hand over his gray hair. Senator Frueh, toying with his soft and beautiful beard, hesitated; then he sat down, too, angrily. He glared at Ellery.

Ellery lit a cigaret. "Come, come, Finch; you look like an overgrown country boy caught in Farmer Jones's apples. Relax."

"Ducky!" Andrea stamped her foot. "I was speaking to you."

"Well," muttered the big man, rubbing his chin, "it's this way, Andrea. Your mother..."

"I thought so!"

"But, Andrea, what could I do? And then Simon here, blast him, sided with Jessica. It's rather a difficult position—"

"Not at all," said Ellery amiably. "We can take it, Andrea and I. What is it you suspect, gentlemen—a bomb in my right pocket and a copy of The Daily Worker in my left? Or is it simply that you consider me an immoral influence on a growing child?"

"Let me handle this, Mr. Queen," said Andrea through her small, white teeth. "Now, Ducky, let me get this straight. Mother sent you two skulking after me tonight?"

The Senator's fat fingers flew about in an outraged way among the hairs of his beard. "Andrea! You're insulting. Skulking!"

"Oh, stop it, Simon," said Finch, flushing. "You know that's virtually what it amounted to. Didn't care for the idea myself. But from what your mother tells me, Andrea—"

"And what," said Andrea dangerously, "has my mother told you?"

His hand described a vague arc. "Well... Slumming and things.

Queen's been taking you to what she considers—ah—improper places. She doesn't like it."

"Poor Mr. Rockefeller," said Ellery with a sad shake of his head as he glanced about the room. "I'm sure he'd be mortified by the epithet, Finch."

"Oh, not this place." Finch was growing redder. "Damn it all, I told Jessica… I mean, this is perfectly all right, of course, but those other places—"

"By the way, Andrea," drawled Ellery, "I almost took you down to the Rand School this evening. Think of the time you'd have had then, gentlemen. Those proletarian intellectuals are a hard lot."

"You think you're funny," growled Senator Frueh. "Look here, Queen, why the devil don't you let Andrea alone?"

"Why the devil," said Ellery pleasantly, "don't you mind your own business?"

Finch was ruddy to the roots of his gray hair now. "Blessed if we don't deserve that, Queen," he said with a wry grin. "Oh, come on, Simon; it was a rum idea in the first place."

The lawyer's beard trembled over the white cloth like a waterfall suddenly arrested in its course. "Queen's no fool. If Andrea is—"

"That," said Andrea, "is just about the last straw!"

"Be quiet, Andrea. We can talk plainly to this man. Queen, what are you after?"

Ellery blew smoke; but his eyes were bright with mockery. "What is any man after? A little home in the country, a garden, kiddies—"

"Stop clowning. You don't fool me for a moment, Queen. You're still nosing around that Wilson case, aren't you?"

"Is that an interrogatory question or a rhetorical one?"

"You know what it is!"

"Well," murmured Ellery, "it's really none of your affair; but since you're kind enough to ask—yes. And what has that to do with you?"

"Simon," said Finch uneasily.

"Don't be a jellyfish, Grosvenor. Just this. As friends of Andrea's—"

"No friends of mine," said Andrea in a frigid tone. But her palms were stroking the cloth and she was pale.

"—we know that it isn't mere desire for her company that's made you hound her this way ever since that woman was convicted up in Trenton. Now what the devil is it you want?"

"Peace," sighed Ellery, "and a complete abruption of intercourse as far as you and I are concerned. Is that fair enough?"

"Why are you hanging around Andrea? What is it you suspect her of?"

"I think," said Andrea grimly, "that this has gone quite far enough. You forget yourself, Senator Frueh. As for you, Ducky, I'm surprised that you would permit yourself to be… But I suppose it's Mother again. She always could twist you around her little finger."

"Andrea," said the tall man miserably.

"No! And you forget, Senator, that I'm a grown woman with presumably a mind of my own. No one takes me out by force, I assure you. If I've chosen to spend my time with Mr. Queen that's my business, not yours. I know what I'm doing; or if I don't," she added with a faint and bitter smile, "I'll find out soon enough. Now will you please—both of you—go away and let us alone?"

"Of course, Andrea, if that's the way you feel about it," said the fat man, bouncing out of his chair. "I'm merely discharging my duty to your family. After this—"

Ellery rose and waited politely. No one said anything. So he murmured, "I thought your role was legalistic, Senator. Have you turned detective, too? If so, let me welcome you into the ranks."

"Buffoon!" snarled Senator Frueh, tugging at his beard. "You watch your step." He flounced off.

"I'm sorry, Andy," said Finch, taking her hand.

"It's not really your fault, Ducky" She smiled at him, but withdrew her hand. He sighed, nodded to Ellery, and followed his stout companion.

"I suppose," said Ellery, not sitting down, "you'd rather go home, Andrea? The evening must be spoiled for you."

"Don't be silly It's just begun. Shall we dance?"

*

Ellery let out the Duesenberg. It roared with steadily mounting violence, as if it were an ancient lion and he had tweaked its tail. It fled down the concrete road as if all the devils in hell were after it. "Wheel" squealed Andrea, holding on to her hat. "How are your reflexes, mister? I'm still young, and life is sweet."

"I am," Ellery assured her as he pawed around precariously for a cigaret, "a veritable tower of strength."

"Here, stop that!" she screamed, sticking her own into his mouth. "This chariot may steer by itself, but I'd rather not chance… Not," she said suddenly, "that I'd care."

"Really? Care about what?"

She slumped down beside him, squinting along the spurting ribbon of road without really seeing it. "Oh, about anything. Well, let's not get maudlin. Where are we going?"

Ellery waved the cigaret. "Does it matter? The broad highway, a lovely companion of the opposite sex, no traffic to speak of, the sun beaming heroically… I'm happy."

"Good for you."

"Why?" he said, glancing at her. "Aren't you?"

"Oh, of course. Deliriously." She closed her eyes. Ellery drove peacefully After a while she opened her eyes and said in a gay voice, "Guess what. I found a gray hair this morning."

"Curses! So soon? You see, Senator Frueh was right. Did you remove it?"

"Idiot. Of course I did."

"As if," he said dryly, "grief could be assuaged by baldness."

"Now what is that supposed to mean? It's cryptic."

"Oh, it's more than that. Tusculanarum Disputationum, in fact. If you'd spent more time learning something than being 'finished' at school, you'd know that that's a pearl tossed off by Senator Cicero. It's foolish, he remarked, to pluck out one's hair for sorrow—as if, and so forth."

"Oh." She closed her eyes again. "You think I'm unhappy, don't you?"

"My dear child, who am I to judge? But if you want my opinion, I think you're going very rapidly to pot."

She sat up straight with indignation. "I like that! I suppose you don't realize that I've seen more of you in the past few weeks than of anyone else."

Ellery flicked the Duesenberg around a heat-swollen crevice in the concrete. "If I've contributed to your unhappiness, I should be drawn and quartered. I think I know several worthy persons who would assist in the operation. But while I'm not the most cheerful companion in the world, I don't believe it's my influence that's done it to you."

"Oh, don't you!" Andrea retorted. "You should have heard what Mother had to say on the subject last night—after I got home and she'd had the eminent Senator's report."

"Ah, your mother," sighed Ellery. "No, I don't flatter myself that that worthy dowager approves of Inspector Queen's little boy. Just what is it she suspects me of—designs on your virtue, your bankroll, or what?"

"Don't be coarse. It's these little excursions."

"Not my connection with the tragedy of Ella Amity's Halfway House?"

"Please," said Andrea. "Let's forget that, shall we? No, after you took me to see Waiting for Lefty and to that settlement house on Henry Street and the city lodging-house she simply exploded. She thinks you're poisoning my mind."

"A not unreasonable suspicion. Has the virus worked?"

"I won't say it hasn't. I never realized what misery…" Andrea shivered a little and took her hat off. Her hair, glinting in the sun, began to whip about her head. "She thinks you're simply the most terrible person in the world. Not that I care what she thinks—about you."

"Andrea! This is so sudden. When did it happen?"

"Mother," frowned Andrea, "is a good deal like those dreadful flying people in that Faulkner book you gave me—you know, Pylon? What was it the reporter said about them? If you squished 'em, they'd squirt cylinder oil instead of blood?"

"I fail to see the analogy. What liquid would your mother squirt?"

"Old wine—wine with a pedigree, you understand—old wine which has unaccountably and tragically turned to vinegar. Poor Mother! She's had a bruising life; she doesn't really know what's happened to her."

Ellery chuckled. "Described with remarkable point. Nevertheless, Andrea, that's an extremely unfilial speech."

"Mother is—well, Mother. You wouldn't understand."

"I think I would. Believe it or not, I had a mother once."

Andrea did not speak for a long time. "Grandfather," she said at last in a dreamy voice. "Let's see, now. Yes, of course. All you'd squeeze out of his poor broken body would be leucocytes. Not a trace of red left in him."

"How about Ducky? You know him better than I do."

"He should be easy," said Andrea, sucking the tip of her forefinger. "Ducky, Ducky… Port! No, that's wine again. Yes! Spirits of camphor. Doesn't that sound awful?"

"Sickening. Why camphor?"

"Oh, Ducky's so right. I suppose you don't see what I mean. My mind—such as it is—always associates camphor with stuffy YMCA bedrooms and colds in the head. Don't ask me why. It must have been poor conditioning as a child."

"Andrea, I believe you're tight. Only alcohol would link that bloated plutocrat with the YMCA."

"Don't be foul. You know I don't drink. That's why mother's so shocked; I'm the old-fashioned girl on a sudden bender. Now: Tolstoy."

"Who?"

"The Senator. I once saw a drawing of Tolstoy that reminded me of him. That obscene beard! He takes better care of it than a woman does of her new permanent. Of course you know what he has in his veins?"

"Tomato juice?"

"No! Pure formaldehyde. If he ever felt an honest emotion, it's been pickled stiff for forty years. And that," she sighed, "is the end of the story. What shall we talk about now?"

"Wait a minute," said Ellery. "How about friend Jones?"

She was very quiet for a moment. "I'd rather not… I haven't seen Burke for two weeks."

"Good heavens. If I've been the cause of breaking up the social alliance of the century—"

"Please. I'm not fooling. Burke and I are—" She stopped and rested her head against the top of the seat, staring down the road.

"Definitely?"

"Is anything definite in this world? Once—I was so sure. He seemed everything a girl could wish for in a man. Big—I've always had a weakness for big men—not too handsome, built like Max Baer, perfect manners…"

"He didn't impress me," said Ellery dryly, "as a prince of breeding."

"He—he was a little upset. Good family, loads of money…"

"And utterly devoid of gray matter."

"You would say something nasty. Well, I suppose it's true. I see now that all that was a silly girl's notion. Those things don't count, do they?"

"I don't believe they do."

"Once—" she smiled a queer, pained little smile—"I wasn't much better myself, you see."

Ellery drove for some time in silence. Andrea's lids drooped again. The miles slid into the gullet of the Duesenberg and spewed out behind in a smooth and soporific stream. Ellery stirred. "You've forgotten yourself."

"What?"

"If someone—Bill Angell, for example—should step on you, to continue the nauseating metaphor…"

"Oh." After a moment she laughed. "I may as well judge myself nobly; no one else does. The milk of human kindness."

"Slightly curdled?" asked Ellery in a gentle voice.

She sat up swiftly. "Now, just what does that mean, Ellery Queen?"

"Don't you know?"

"And why Bill Angell?"

Ellery shrugged. "I beg your pardon. I thought we were playing according to the established rules of honesty, but I see I was mistaken." He kept looking at the road. She kept looking at his calm, immobile profile. And finally her lips quivered and she looked away. "Corking day, isn't it?" observed Ellery at last.

"Yes." Her voice was low.

"Sky blue. Countryside green. Road oyster-white. Cows brown and red—when you see 'em." He paused. "When you see 'em."

"I don't—"

"I said. When you see 'em. Not everybody does, you know."

She was so quiet that he thought she had not heard; he glanced quickly at her. Her cheeks were whiter than the road. The strands of blond hair curling madly about her face seemed to be straining away from the wind. And her fingers plucked steadily at the hat in her lap.

"Where," she asked in a thick undertone, "are you taking me?"

"Where would you like to go?"

Her eyes flashed. She half rose in the seat; the wind clutched at her, and she grasped the top of the windshield for support. "Stop the car! Stop the car, I say!"

Obediently the Duesenberg rolled toward the soft shoulder of the road and, after a while, came to a stop.

"Here we are," said Ellery gently. "Now what?"

"Turn around!" she cried. "Where are you going? Where are you taking me?"

"To visit someone," he said in a quiet way, "who hasn't your visual advantages. I doubt if this unfortunate can glimpse a bit of sky larger than you could cover with this small palm of yours. I thought it might be kind if someone played the vicarious eye today… for her."

"For her?" she whispered. He took her hand; it lay limp and cold between his palms.

They sat that way for many minutes. Occasionally, a car rushed by; once a large young man in the horizon-blue uniform of the New Jersey State Police slowed up as his motorcycle whizzed past, looked back, scratched his head, and sped on again. The sun was hot in the motionless car; a film of perspiration sprang up on Andrea's forehead and little nose. Then her eyes fell, and she pulled back her hand. She did not speak.

Ellery threw the Duesenberg into gear again and the big car moved off, continuing in the direction in which they had been going. There was a faint and anxious line between his brows.

*

The Amazon in uniform stared at them, heaved aside, and motioned to someone in the dark corridor with a hand as large and abrupt as a traffic officer's.

They heard Lucy's feet before they saw her. The sound was a dreadful shuffle, slow, scraping, funereal. They had to strain their eyes as the shuffle became louder. In their nostrils was an indescribable, disagreeable odor: it seemed composed of fragments of smells coarsely blended: carbolic acid, sour bread, starch, old shoes, and the stench of wash.

Then Lucy came in. Her lifeless eyes flickered a little as she blinked at them standing behind the steel-mesh partition, clutching at the mesh like monkeys in a zoo but not chattering, so fixed and quiet that they might have been spectators at a play.

The shuffle quickened; she came to them in her clumsy prison shoes, hands outstretched a little. "I'm so glad. This is so good of you." Her eyes, deep-set and framed in violet pain, touched Andrea's set face almost shyly. "Both of you," she said softly. It was hard to look at her. It was as if she had been run through a wringer and all the sap and vigor of her generous body squeezed out. Her dark skin was olive no longer, but slate, an earthy color that suggested death rather than life.

Andrea groped for her voice before she found it. "Hello," she said, trying to smile. "Hello, Lucy Wilson."

"How are you, Lucy? You're looking well," said Ellery, striving to make the lie sound natural.

"I'm all right, thank you. Very well. I—" She paused; a spasm of lightning terror flashed over her features like the shadow of a hunted thing. Then it was gone. "Isn't Bill coming?"

"I'm sure he is. When did you see him last?"

"Yesterday." Her bloodless fingers gripped the steel mesh; behind it her face looked like a poor engraving made from an already engraved photograph, overlaid with a double screen. "Yesterday. He comes every day. Poor Bill. He looks so badly, Ellery. Can't you do anything with him? He really shouldn't worry so." Her voice drifted off. It was strange, as if everything she said were an afterthought, lying ready on the thin verge of her consciousness to be uttered as a defense against her real, her deeply hidden thoughts.

"You know how Bill is. If he hasn't something to fret about he's unhappy."

"Yes," said Lucy in a child's tone. The ghost of a smile was on her lips, as remote from her as her voice. "Bill always was that way. He's so strong. He always makes me feel"—the voice lifted, fell, lifted again as if in surprise at its own vitality—"good."

Andrea started to say something but stopped before it was uttered.

Her own gloved fingers were entwined in the mesh; Lucy's face was very near hers. Her fingers contracted on the steel suddenly. "How are they treating you?" she asked, in a rush. "I mean…"

Lucy's eyes sought hers slowly; deep eyes covered with glass, protected like her voice from the real, the free, the wide world. "Oh, quite well, thank you. I can't complain. They're very kind to me."

"You have enough to…" Andrea's cheeks began to burn. "I wonder if… Is there anything I can do for you, Mrs. Wilson? I mean, is there anything I can get for you, something you need, perhaps?"

Lucy looked surprised. "Need?" Her thick, vigorous, woman's brows contracted, as if she were thinking it over. "Why, no. No, thanks." Then, amazingly, she laughed. It was a pleasant little laugh, quite untouched by irony or scorn, naive and full-toned. "There's only one thing I want. But I'm afraid you couldn't get that for me."

"What?" pleaded Andrea. "Anything… Oh, I do want to help you. What is it you want, Mrs. Wilson?"

Lucy shook her head, smiling the faint, remote smile again. "My freedom." The quick terror flashed over her face again and was gone.

The burn left Andrea's cheeks; she felt Ellery's elbow dig into her ribs and mechanically she smiled in return, "Oh," she said. "I'm afraid—"

"I wonder where Bill is." Lucy's slow glance went to the visitors' door. Andrea closed her eyes, the corner of her mouth twitching. After a while Lucy said, "I've fixed my—I've fixed the cell up so nicely. Bill brought me some flowers and pictures and things. It's against the rules I guess, but he managed it. Bill's so good about managing things like that." She looked at them almost with anxiety. "Really, it's not so bad. And then it's only for a while, isn't it? Bill says he's sure that I'll get—get off when my appeal…"

"That's the spirit, Lucy," said Ellery. "Chin up." He tapped her dead fingers through the mesh. "Remember, you have friends who won't stop working for you—ever, Lucy. You'll remember that, won't you?"

"If I forgot it for even a second," she whispered, "I think I'd go mad."

"Mrs. Wilson," stammered Andrea. "Lucy—"

The black eyes went wistful. "How is it outside today? It looks so nice—from here." There was a window high up in the wall, its thick squat bars straining the sunlight like a sieve. The rectangle of sky was blue there.

"I think," said Andrea in a choking voice, "it's going to rain. It's really not—"

The Amazon leaning against the far stone wall said, without inflection, like an inhuman and detached metallic vocal chord, "Time's up."

The terror came again, but this time it did not go away. It made the muscles of Lucy's jaw quiver as if a blunt finger had poked a raw wound. The glass shivered away from her eyes, revealing the profound and liquid agony beneath. "Oh, so soon," she whispered, and tried to smile and then frowned and bit her lip and finally, without warning, with a devastating alteration of features, like the bursting of a dam, she began to weep.

"Lucy," muttered Ellery.

She cried, "Oh, thank you, thank you!", and her fingers came away from the steel screen crisscrossed with livid marks. And she turned and stumbled toward the yawning dim doorway with its grim bulk of sexless guard.

They heard her shoes scraping on the stone floor long after nothing was left behind the mesh but the woman's scent of her hanging in the still fetid air. There was a spot of bright blood on Andrea's lower lip.

"What the devil," demanded a harsh voice from the visitors' doorway, "are you doing here?"

Ellery came about like a startled cat. He had not wanted this. Bill Angell's big right hand was clenched about the paper-covered butt of a bouquet of flowers whose blossoms drooped toward the floor.

"Bill," he said swiftly. "We've come to—"

"Well," growled Bill; his eyes were fixed on Andrea with a remorseless glare. "How do you like it here? Swell, eh?"

Andrea groped for Ellery's arm; he felt her fingers tighten on his biceps. "Oh," she said faintly. "I—"

"It's a wonder to me you don't collapse of sheer shame. The damned brazenness of it!" The words were arrows, bitter to the mark. "Coming here! To gloat? Well, you've seen her. Do you think you'll sleep comfortably tonight?"

Ellery's biceps hurt. Her eyes were so wide they looked unnatural. Then she released him and ran toward Bill. Her stride broke as she reached him. Reluctantly he stepped aside, still glaring. She sped past with her head lowered.

"Bill," said Ellery quietly. Bill did not answer. He looked down at the flowers and deliberately turned his back on Ellery.

Andrea was waiting at the end of the corridor, leaning against the blank wall and sobbing. "All right, Andrea," said Ellery. "Stop that."

"Take me home," she choked. "Oh, take me away from this horrible place."

*

Ellery knocked at the door and Bill Angell's weary voice said: "Come on in." Ellery opened the door on one of the Astor's long, old-fashioned rooms to find Bill bent over the brass bed packing a bag.

"The prodigal returns," he said. "Hello, you fool." He closed the door and set his back against it. Bill's hair was tousled and there was a defiant jut to his chin. He continued packing as if no one had been there. "Don't be an ass, Bill. Stop fiddling with those socks and listen to me." Bill did not reply. "I've chased you over three States. What are you doing in New York?"

Bill straightened up then. "Isn't this a peculiar time to be showing an interest in my affairs?"

"My interest has never flagged, old boy."

Bill laughed. "Look here, Ellery. I don't want any trouble with you.

I don't blame you. Your life is your own; it certainly isn't mortgaged to me or Lucy. But since you've chosen to step out, please stay out. You'll oblige me by getting the hell out of here."

"Who says I've stepped out?"

"Don't think I'm blind to what's been going on. You've been rushing that Gimball girl ever since Lucy's conviction."

Ellery murmured, "Have you been spying on me, Bill?"

"Call it what you like." Bill flushed. "I think it's damned funny. I wouldn't think so if I thought you were working on her, if your interest was professional. But I never heard of a professional interest in a woman that manifests itself by taking her to clubs and dances and dives night after night for weeks. What do you think I am, anyway—a damned fool?"

"Yes."

Ellery pushed away from the door, tossed his hat and stick on the bed, and poked Bill so hard in the stomach that Bill gasped and fell back on the bed. "Now stay there and listen, you idiot."

Bill jumped up, his fists flailing. "Why—"

"Pistols at dawn, eh?" Bill flushed more deeply and sat down. "In the first place," continued Ellery calmly, lighting a cigaret, "you wouldn't be acting such a twerp if your brain were functioning normally. But it isn't, and so I forgive you. You're madly in love with that girl."

"Rot. You're crazy yourself."

"The mental battle to reconcile your passion with your conscience and sense of duty toward Lucy has addled your wits completely. Jealous of me! Bill, you ought to be ashamed of yourself."

"Jealous!" Bill laughed bitterly. "As for you, I don't mind giving you a bit of friendly advice. With all your self-confidence, you're still just a male. Watch yourself with that girl. She'll make as big a sucker of you as she made out of me."

"Emotionally, you've gone back to a vernal seventeen, my son. The trouble with you is that you can't recognize your own symptoms. Don't tell me you don't dream about her. You can't forget that moment in the dark when she kissed you. You're all tied up in knots and you're fighting yourself twenty-four hours a day. I've had my eye on you from afar since the trial. Bill, you're an ass."

"I don't know why I'm listening to you," said Bill savagely.

"It doesn't take a Freud to see what's making the wheels spin so crazily. And your analysis, therefore, of a 'professional interest' in Andrea is just as adolescent."

"In love. Why, I despise every inch of that—"

"Of course you do," grinned Ellery. "But I haven't come here to lecture on the intricacies of the tender passion. Let me explain matters and give you a chance to apologize."

"I've heard enough—"

"Sit down! When Lucy was convicted in Trenton one thing stood out so prominently as to overshadow everything else. That was Andrea's peculiar behavior—before, during, and after her session on the stand. It set me to thinking." Bill grunted derisively. "My thoughts led me to certain conclusions. My conclusions led me to cultivate the girl. There was nothing else I could do; all other leads had failed. I've checked and rechecked every angle of the case; I've found nothing suspicious anywhere, and everything's wound up at a blank wall."

Bill frowned. "What the devil could you hope to accomplish by taking her out? You can't blame me if I thought—"

"Ah, we're rational again. As a matter of fact, my assiduous devotion to the young lady has worried more than your own noble ego. Mrs. Gimball—I should say Jessica Borden—is on the verge of prostration, Senator Frueh is frothing at the mouth, and Finch is chewing his immaculate fingernails. As for young Jones, from last reports he's been trying to kill some of his polo ponies. Excellent! Exactly what I wanted. I've accomplished something."

Bill shook his head. "I'll be jiggered if I see what."

Ellery pulled a chair over to the bed, "Answer my questions first. What are you doing in New York?"

"Cleaning up." Bill lay back on the bed and stared at the ceiling. "Going through the motions. After the trial I made a demand payment of the National Life by filing the usual proof-of-death form. Just a gesture, of course. The National ignored the formal demand, refusing in effect to pay the face value of the policy on the ground that the beneficiary had been convicted of the murder of the insured."

"I see."

"The company notified Gimball's executor—some bigwig friend of the family—that they were prepared to pay over to him for the Gimball estate the cash-surrender value of the policy on release of all future claims. I understand that's already been done."

"The conviction invalidates the policy?"

"Oh, absolutely."

"And how's the appeal going?"

"We've forced New Jersey to finance it; I suppose you've read that in the papers. I've managed on various technical grounds to delay matters; it will be next year before final action is taken. Meanwhile," Bill's face darkened, "Lucy's in Trenton. Better than the Pen." He scowled at the ceiling. Then he said: "What was the idea of bringing her…?"

"Who?"

"The—damn it all, all right! Andrea!"

"Look here, Bill," said Ellery quietly. "Why was Andrea so terrified at the thought of going on the witness-stand?"

"Blessed if I know. Her testimony certainly didn't bring out anything of a damaging or significant nature."

"That's approximately true. It makes her reluctance even more astonishing. It couldn't have been, of course, that she was so averse to revealing that she had visited the scene of the crime. That aversion may have motivated her in keeping mum about the visit before we dug it out, but it wouldn't have when you asked her to testify. In fact, she had every reason to accede to your wishes."

Bill sneered. "Yes, she had!"

"Stop being a child. The girl likes you—I shan't sicken you by employing a stronger term." Bill colored. "She felt sorry for Lucy—"

"An act! She was playing me—"

"You're more sensible than that remark indicates, Bill. She's a fine lassie; there's good solid stuff in her that her environment hasn't been able to spoil. And she's not a hypocrite. Under normal circumstances she should have been glad, as I say, to help Lucy. Instead… well, you saw how she acted."

"She wouldn't do anything for us. She's on the other side of the fence. She's sore at both of us because of Gimball."

"Nonsense. She was the only one that night at the shack to show any sign of human sympathy toward Lucy."

Bill plucked at the white spread, pinching it, smoothing it down, pinching it again. "All right. What's the answer?"

Ellery went to the window. "What would you say has been her predominant emotion since the business of her visit to the shack came out?"

"Fear."

"Exactly. Fear of what?"

"I wish I knew," growled Bill.

Ellery came back and gripped the footrail of the bed. "Obviously, fear of telling her story. Now, why should she be afraid of that?" Bill shrugged; he was pinching the spread again. "Don't you see that it's fear not from inside that poor girl, but from outside? Fear under pressure? Fear induced by threats?"

"Threats?" Bill blinked.

"You've forgotten that charred cork."

"Threats!" Bill was on his feet; it was astonishing how his eyes had brightened with hope. "Good Lord, Ellery. I never—Poor kid!" He began to walk up and down before the bed, muttering to himself.

Ellery gave him a quizzical look. "L'affaire marche, I see. It's been evident to me for some time. It's the only theory that takes all the facts, physical and psychological, into consideration. She wanted to help you; yet

179

she couldn't bring herself to it. If you had seen that girl's face the night… Well, you didn't; you're blind as a bat, anyway. She's been through hell. Why should she submit herself to such torture unless it were an ulterior fear that kept her silent? It's fear clearly not for herself, you see."

"So that's why—"

"The problem admitted of a crude sort of analysis. If she had been threatened by someone—warned to keep her mouth shut—it was obvious that the threatener was afraid of something within her power to disclose. My course of action was therefore dictated to me. By monopolizing her time, I tended to accomplish two things: one, to play on her better nature so that she would finally disclose what she knew despite everything. Two," Ellery blew a quick puff of smoke, "to force the hand of the person who had threatened her!"

Bill said swiftly: "But, Ellery, that means—"

"That means," murmured Ellery, "that I've plunged Andrea into danger. Quite true."

"But you've no right to!"

"The tune changes. Up in arms in her defense already?" Ellery chuckled. "Well, we mustn't take personalities into account, Bill. Whoever's warned Andrea must know by this time that I've been cultivating her acquaintance. They know my interest in this case. They will be wondering what I've managed to accomplish with the girl. They'll be nervous. In a word, they'll take action."

"Well," roared Bill, "what the hell are we waiting for?"

Ellery smiled and jabbed his cigaret out against the tray. "In either event, I've managed matters so that we're on the road to a discovery. I took Andrea up to Trenton the other day to break down her last defense. I knew a sight of Lucy in her present condition and surroundings would do the trick. She cried all the way back to New York. I think today…"

But Bill was already in the corridor punching the elevator bell.

*

The fish-faced man frowned. "Miss Andrea is not at home." His tone suggested that Miss Andrea would never be at home as he stared at Bill.

"Come off it," said Bill curtly, pushing the man aside. They stepped into the duplex living-room of the Borden-Gimball apartment. Bill looked around quickly. "Well, where is she? We haven't all day!"

"I beg your pardon, sir?"

Bill put his hand on the narrow chest and pushed. The fish-faced man's nose came down and he staggered back with a look of fright. "Will you talk or do I have to shake it out of you?"

"I—I'm sorry, sir, but Miss Andrea isn't at home."

"Where is she?" snapped Ellery.

"She went out about an hour ago, sir, very suddenly."

"Didn't she say where she was going?"

"No, sir; she left no word."

"Who is home?" demanded Bill.

"Only Mr. Borden, sir; it's the nurse's afternoon off and he is asleep in his room. I'm sorry, sir, but in his condition he really shouldn't be disturbed."

"Where's Mrs. Gimball?"

The man looked distressed. "She's out, too, sir. She left for Mr. Borden's country estate on Oyster Bay."

"Alone?" asked Ellery queerly.

"Yes, sir, at noon. For a few days' rest, I believe, sir."

Ellery's face became very grave. Bill, looking at him, felt himself go suddenly cold. "Was Miss Andrea at home when her mother left?"

"No, sir."

"You say Miss Andrea went out without explanation an hour ago? Alone?"

"Yes, sir. You see, sir, she had received a telegram—"

Ellery said, "Good Lord, man."

"We're too late!" shouted Bill. "Now you've done it, damn you, Ellery. Why didn't you—"

"Now, Bill, this may be nothing at all. Where is this wire? Do you know? Hurry!"

The man's eyes stared wildly now. "I took it to her boudoir, sir. It must still be—"

"Show us to her room!"

The butler scuttled off toward the stairs, leading them up to the second floor of the apartment. He indicated a door and backed away, looking scared. Ellery opened the door; the room was empty. There were evidences of a hasty departure. In the cool green-and-white chamber the silence was, somehow, ominous.

Bill cried out and pounced on a crumpled yellow paper lying where it had been thrown on the rug. It was a telegram, and it said:

SOMETHING DREADFUL HAS HAPPENED COME AT ONCE ALONE SAY NOTHING TO ANYONE STOP AM AT NORTH SHORE INN BETWEEN ROSLYN AND OYSTER BAY ON MAIN ROAD HURRY… MOTHER

Ellery said slowly, "That's bad, Bill. The North Shore Inn is Ben Duffy's place—the orchestra-leader. It's been shut down for months."

Bill's face worked. Then without a word he flung the telegram on the floor and sprang through the doorway. Ellery stooped, picked up the yellow paper, hesitated, thrust it in his pocket, and followed. Bill was already downstairs. Ellery said to the butler, who seemed fixed to the spot, "Ware there any unusual callers today?"

"Callers, sir?"

"Yes, yes. Visitors. Speak up, man!"

"O-oh, yes, sir. A lady from the newspapers, sir. Some peculiar name. I think—"

Ellery blinked. "A Miss Ella Amity?"

"Yes, sir! That was her name."

"When? Whom did she see?"

"She was here early this morning, sir. I don't believe she saw any-one… Well, I don't know, sir. I was off duty—"

"Rats," said Ellery, and sped down the stairs.

*

The sun was low when Ellery's Duesenberg rolled into the driveway before the sprawling, garish structure whose rather streaky sign said NORTH SHORE INN. The place was boarded up. There was no sign of life.

They jumped out of the car and made for the entrance. Ominously, the door stood ajar. They plunged into a vast chamber, dusty and stripped, its bare tables piled high with gilt chairs. In the gloom they could make out no details. Bill swore; and Ellery put his hand out. "Whoa, Bucephalus. There's no sense in charging blindly into the unknown." He paused and muttered, "I didn't really believe… It does look as if we're too late. The damned cheek of that woman!"

Bill shook him off and lunged forward. He began running up the room, knocking chairs and tables aside and raising dry dust. Ellery stood still, frowning. Then he turned aside and went to a half-door with a ledge above which a sign said CHECK ROOM. He leaned over the edge, eyes narrowed. "Bill!" he called in a low voice, and then he vaulted the ledge. Bill came pounding back, his face frantic. He found Ellery kneeling inside the tiny room beside the crumpled figure of Andrea. She was sprawled on the dirty floor, her knees drawn up, her hat off and her hair tumbled about, and she was very still. In the gloom her face was ashen.

"Good God," whispered Bill. "She's—she's—"

"Nothing of the sort. Rustle a pail of water. There must be some sort of tap working in the kitchen. Where's your nose? She's been chloroformed!"

Bill swallowed hard and sped away. When he came back he found Ellery still on his knees, supporting the unconscious girl in a half sitting position and methodically slapping her cheeks. The imprints of his fingers were visible; but she was still as motionless as a corpse.

"No good," said Ellery quietly. "She got a real dose. Put that pail down, Bill, and find some towels, a tablecloth, napkins—anything in the line of linen. Don't be finicky about cleanliness. This is going to take heroic measures. Pick up a couple of chairs, too."

When Bill returned, staggering under two chairs and an armful of dusty linen Ellery was bent over the girl's torso, working swiftly. Bill's eyes widened with shock. "What the devil are you doing?" he shouted.

"Turn your eyes away if you can't bear the sight of female flesh. I'm exposing her chest, if you must know. What a moral young man! It's part of the treatment, idiot. But first put those chairs on the path outside—together. She needs fresh air most of all."

Bill gulped and hurried to the main door, yanked it open, looked back, gulped again, and disappeared. A moment later Ellery strode outside carrying Andrea's limp body. "Get the pail. Together, I said! Right. Now get the pail."

When Bill came back with the pail Andrea was lying face up on the two chairs, her head drooping far backward. Ellery had ripped open the waist under her sports suit, revealing her brassière. It was very pink and lacy.

Bill stood by, rather helplessly. Ellery worked in silence. He stuffed a tablecloth under the small of the girl's back; he flung the napkins into the pail of cold water. Then he fished one out, sopping as it was, and curled it about Andrea's pale face like a barber's hot towel, so that only the tip and nostrils of her nose showed.

"Don't stand there like a politician," growled Ellery. "Come around and pick up her legs. Hold 'em high—and don't let her drop off these chairs, either. What the deuce is the matter with you, Bill? Haven't you ever seen a girl's legs before?"

Bill stood there with his arms about Andrea's silk-sheathed legs, blushing like a boy and every once in a while plucking at her skirt to keep it decently covering her. Ellery soaked more napkins and applied them to her bare chest. He lifted them off and slapped them down again, sharply.

"What's the idea?" asked Bill from dry lips.

"Simple enough. Head low, feet high—get the blood rushing to the brain. Restore circulation. It's a method," grunted Ellery, "that I learned from a chap by the name of Holmes some years ago. Young surgeon. My father was the victim then—it was more of an emergency in that case, considering dad's age. The case of those Siamese twins, remember?"

Bill said in a strangled voice: "Oh, yes. Oh, yes." He kept looking at the darkening sky.

"Keep those legs of hers elevated! There... How's that, young lady? The position isn't especially recommended by Miss Agatha's Dancing School, but I believe you'll come around in a moment." Ellery changed napkins on her chest. "Hmm. There was something else. What in thunder was it, now? Yes! Artificial respiration. Blessed if it wasn't one of the most important parts of the treatment!" He thrust his hand under the napkin rolled about the girl's face and by main force opened her jaws. His hand knocked the napkin off, revealing a face already a little less pale, and dripping wet. "Pshaw! Well, it did its work; let it lie." With a grimace he pulled her tongue out. Then he stooped over her torso and began to pump her arms up and down.

Bill said with a feeble grin, "It's something out of Rube Goldberg."

And Andrea suddenly opened her eyes to the sky.

Bill stood there stupidly, still holding her legs high and gaping down at her. Ellery put his arm under her head and raised it. Her eyes, bewildered at first, rolled about and then fixed on Bill.

"There," said Ellery with satisfaction. "How's that for a perfect job by Dr Queen? It's all right, Andrea; you're with friends again."

Awareness rapidly filled her bloodshot eyes. Her cheeks stained with crimson. She gasped, "What are you doing?"

Bill still gaped. "For heaven's sake," snapped Ellery, "put her legs down, Bill! What do you think this is, anyway?" Bill dropped them as if they burned. They fell with a thud, and she winced at the shock.

"Oh, you fool!" groaned Ellery. "Fat lot of help you are. Take it easy, Andrea. Sit up, now… There! Feel better?"

"I'm so dizzy." She sat up, Ellery's arm still supporting her, and touched her forehead. "What happened? Oh, I'm filthy!" Her glance went from the pail to the unclean napkins strewn about the gravel, and then to herself. Her stockings were torn at the knees, her suit was plastered with wet dust, and her hands were smudged in a dozen places. Then she looked down at her chest.

"Oh," she gasped, and with a snatching gesture covered herself with the lapels of the suit. "I'm—you—did you—"

"You are, and we did," said Ellery cheerfully. "It's all right, Andrea; Bill didn't look, and I'm virtually sexless. The important thing is that we pulled you out of that stupor. How do you feel?"

She smiled wryly. "Rotten. Sick as the deuce. My stomach feels as if somebody had been punching it for an hour."

"That's the effect of the chloroform. It will pass soon."

She glanced, still blushing, at Bill. He had turned his broad back and was staring with remarkable interest at a weather-beaten and quite illegible billboard across the road. "Bill," she whispered. "Bill Angell."

His shoulders jerked. "I'm sorry about the other day," he said abruptly, without turning.

She sighed and leaned back against Ellery's arm. "That was the other day."

He swung about. "Andrea—"

"Don't talk, please." She closed her eyes. "Just let me—let me pull myself together. Everything's so mixed up now."

"Damn it, Andrea, I've been a fool."

The air chilled a little as dusk deepened. "You?" Andrea smiled rather bitterly. "If you've been a fool, Bill, what have I been?"

"I'm glad," remarked Ellery, "that you've both saved me the trouble of characterizing you."

"It was a trap." He felt her stiffen against his arm. "The wire—"

"We know all about the wire. What happened?"

She jumped up suddenly. "Mother! I must get to Mother—"

"There's nothing to be afraid of now, Andrea. The telegram was a hoax; it wasn't sent by your mother, obviously. It was meant to lure you here."

She shivered. "Take me to Mother, please."

"Didn't you drive down?"

"No. I came by train and walked from the station. Please."

"Surely," said Ellery, "you've something to tell us now, Andrea?"

Her hand went to her lips, leaving a smudge. "I—I'd rather think things over first."

Ellery stared at her. Then he said lightly, "My car's a two-seater, you know. Rumbleseat's working, though, if you—"

"I'll sit in the rumbleseat," said Bill thickly.

"I'm sure," said Andrea, "we can all three sit—"

"Would you rather sit on Bill's lap or mine?"

"I'll drive," said Bill.

"Not you," said Ellery. "Nobody drives this car but Dr. Queen. I'm afraid you're stuck, Andrea. I've been told by habitués that Bill's is the most uncomfortable lap in the world."

Bill strode off; his back was stiff. And Andrea plucked at her hair and said softly, "I'll take a chance."

Ellery drove with a negligent air, whistling. Bill sat like a lump beside him, his hands at his sides. Andrea was very quiet on Bill's lap. There was no conversation; only occasionally Andrea murmured a direction to Ellery. The car bounced around rather more than seemed necessary; for some reason Ellery seemed unable to resist the smallest bump in the road.

Andrea joined them in the sloping gardens within fifteen minutes of their arrival. She had changed from her dusty clothing into something cool and pastel, of indeterminate color in the dusk. She sat down in a basketwork chair and for a moment none of them said anything. The gardens still exuded a moist warmth, aftermath of the gardener's hose and the afternoon sun, soothing their tired skins as the scent of the flowerbeds about them filled their nostrils. Below and far away the waters of the Sound were deep blue velvet, gently restless. It was quiet and peaceful. Andrea leaned back and said, "Mother's not here. I'm glad."

"Not here?" Ellery frowned slightly over his pipe.

"She's off visiting the Carews, old friends. I've warned the servants not to say anything about... the way I came here. There's no point in alarming her."

"Of course not... You remind me of the heroine in one of those careless movies, Andrea. Finding a fresh wardrobe so conveniently!"

She smiled, too tired to answer. But Bill said in tones hardened by the tension of his throat, "Well?"

She did not reply at once, looking up into the cool heart of a tree. A catfooted man materialized among them balancing a tray on which were three tall frosty glasses. An assistant bore a table, linen. For a moment they were busy; then they were gone. Inexplicably Andrea sipped once, set her glass down, and rose to begin a drifting patrol before them, moving from bush to flower-cluster, her face always turned from them.

"Andrea," said Ellery patiently, "hasn't the time come?"

Bill sat forward gripping his glass; he did not stir thereafter. His eyes were magnetized by the languid course of the girl. Andrea's fingers jerked, snapping the long stem of a gladiolus. She whirled about, pressing her fingers to her temples. "Oh, I'm so tired of keeping it to myself!" she cried. "It's been such a nightmare. If I had to choke it back another day I think I'd go completely mad. You don't know, you can't know the torture I've been through. It wasn't fair; it isn't right!"

"Do you remember Browning's reference in The Ring and the Book," murmured Ellery, "to 'the great right of an excessive wrong'?"

She grew quiet at that, and moved over to finger a jonquil, and then sighed and sat down in the basketwork chair. "I think I see what you mean. Perhaps this wrong was right. I thought it was. I had to think so. Now," she whispered, "I don't know. I don't know anything surely any more. I'm dizzy with thinking about it. Now I'm just… afraid."

"Afraid?" asked Ellery quietly. "Yes, I should think you would be afraid, Andrea. Because of that fear, won't you understand that we want to help you, to help poor Lucy Wilson? Don't you see that with a united front we may palliate this fear of yours and fight off the danger?"

"You know?" she said in a panting voice.

"Not everything. Not half enough. I know that on the night you visited the shack near the Delaware something happened. Something happened to you. I think, Andrea, that those match-stubs and that charred cork were correctly evaluated during Lucy's trial. The murderess wrote a note using that cork as a pencil; the note is gone; but so were you, you see. The note, then, must have been meant for you. And your subsequent actions showed clearly that the note threatened you." His hand lifted and impatiently brushed away the drifting smoke from his pipe. "But these are conjectures. I want the facts, the truth, from you as the only person besides the murderess who can establish the truth."

"But it won't do you any good," she whispered across the barrier of dusk. "It can't possibly. Oh, don't you think I've been all through that with my conscience? Despite everything, don't you think I would have told if I'd thought it would help Lucy?"

"Why not let me be the judge of that, Andrea?"

Her sigh was surrender. "Most of what I told you before was true. Not all. But I did receive that telegram, and I did borrow Burke's roadster and drive out that Saturday afternoon to Trenton."

"Yes?" said Ellery.

"It was eight o'clock when I got there. I mean when I drove up. I honked the horn; no one came out. So I went in. The shack was empty. I saw the man's suits hanging on the wall, the table, everything—it struck me as terribly queer, and I began to feel… funny. Something told me that a dreadful thing had happened or was about to happen. I ran out, jumped into the car, and drove off toward Camden to think things out." She paused and they were silent. In the gathering darkness Bill strained his eyes to see her, a quiet, pale curve on a shadowy chair. His own face was as colorless as her gown.

"And then you returned," murmured Ellery. "And it wasn't at nine as you told us, was it, Andrea? It was considerably before nine."

"It was eight thirty-five by the clock on the dashboard."

Bill said hoarsely: "You're sure? God, Andrea, don't make a mistake this time! You're sure?"

"Oh, Bill," she wailed, and to their consternation she began to sob. Bill stiffened, then he kicked over his chair and bounded across the glade. "Andrea." The words tumbled out. "I don't care any more. About anything. Please don't cry. I've treated you so shabbily. Just don't cry. But I didn't know. You see that, don't you? I was frantic about my sister. If only—"

Her hand crept into his. He held it timidly, scarcely breathing, as if it were something incredibly precious. And he stood that way for ever so long, while she began to talk again. It was quite dark now and only the glow from Ellery's motionless pipe-bowl was visible. "When I'd come at eight," she said with a curious tremor in her voice, "the shack was rather dim inside. I'd turned on the lamp—the lamp on that table. When I returned at a little after eight-thirty the lamp was still burning. I saw the light shining through the front windows."

Abruptly, Ellery asked, "There was a Ford in that semicircular driveway when you got there the second time, wasn't there?"

"Yes. I parked just behind it. I remember wondering whose it was. It was an old Ford coupé and no one was in it. Later—" She bit her lip. "Later I knew it was Lucy's. But then I didn't know. I went into the shack, expecting to see Joe."

190

"Yes?" said Ellery. "Yes?"

She laughed, a bitter little laugh. "I was disturbed, but I never expected to see… what I saw. I pushed open the front door and stopped on the threshold. All I could see was that table, the plate on it, the glowing lamp. I think I was scared to death even then. Something told me—I took a few steps into the room, and then…"

"Andrea," muttered Bill. Her hand fluttered in his.

"I saw two legs on the floor behind the table. They were so still. I put my hand to my mouth—I couldn't think for a moment… Then everything exploded. Went absolutely black. All I was conscious of was a sharp pain at the back of my head, and that I was falling."

"She hit you?" shouted Bill.

The echo died away before anyone spoke. Then Ellery said: "Whoever it was who heard your car drive up knew someone was coming. She might have escaped by the side door, but she wanted to drive that Ford away; that was part of her plan to implicate Lucy. So she lay in wait behind the front door. When you came in she struck you on the back of the head. I should have seen that. The note… Go on, Andrea."

"I was lucky I was wearing a hat," replied Andrea with a half-hysterical giggle. "Or perhaps she—she didn't strike me hard. I came to at a few minute past nine; I remember looking at my wristwatch in a daze. The place was empty again. I thought it was empty, at first. I was on the floor in front of the table, where I'd been struck down. My head was aching hideously. My mouth felt like flannel. I got to my feet and leaned on the table, still weak and stunned. Then I became conscious that there was something in my hand…"

"Which hand?" asked Ellery quickly.

"The right. My gloved hand. It was a scrap of paper, wrapping-paper. Like the paper I'd seen on the mantelpiece above the fireplace. Ripped off."

"What a bungler I am! I should have examined that wrapping-paper more carefully. But it was so torn… I'm sorry, Andrea. Go on."

"Still dazed, I looked at it. It had marks on it. I was at the table, by the lamp. I read what was written on the note."

"Andrea," said Ellery softly. "If only… Where is that note? Lord, be good to us! Did you save that note, Andrea?"

He could not see in the dark. But Bill, still holding her hand as if it were a lifeline stretched wonderfully across an abyss, sensed her eagerness, the swiftness with which her other hand went to the bosom of her gown, vanished, and reappeared.

"I knew some day… Despite everything," she said simply, "I saved it."

"Bill!" snapped Ellery. He was out of his chair and before them so quickly that they drew back a little in alarm. "A light. Dig that box of matches out of my pocket. I must have a light. Heavens, man, you can do your hand-holding later! Give me light."

There was a confused scuffling; and after a while a match fizzed. Bill's cheeks were dark with blood. Andrea closed her eyes to the tiny blob of illumination. But Ellery was bent over the note, swallowing every mark, every letter, every word as if the torn and crumpled scrap of paper were an ancient and blessed holograph.

The match sputtered out. Bill struck another. And another. He used up most of the box before Ellery straightened, still studying the crudely printed capitals with a detached puzzlement, a frown, the faintest disappointment.

"Well?" said Bill, safe in darkness again. "What does it say?"

"Eh?" Ellery grunted and went back to his chair. "Not much, but what's here is to the point. I believe I'll keep this, Andrea, if you don't mind. It says, 'Say nothing about anything you have seen or heard tonight, if you value the life of your mother.' The word 'anything' is heavily underscored. I think, Bill, we both owe this young woman an apology de profundis."

"Andrea," said Bill in a pleading, humble voice. But he did not seem able to say anything more. Ellery heard Andrea sigh from across the glade; Bill felt the hand in his, recaptured, tighten a little.

"Interesting," continued Ellery in an absent tone. "Of course it's plain now, for one thing, Andrea, why you felt you had to keep quiet. Upon your silence, imposed by someone who had proved herself a murderess, depended your mother's life. It's so clear now, after the event." They heard him make an annoyed, clicking little sound. "I'm to be severely censured for my attack of stupidity. You didn't know when or where the blow would fall. Yes, yes, very interesting indeed. Your mother knows nothing of this, I take it?"

"Oh, no!"

"You've confided in no one at all until tonight?"

"How could I?" She shivered a little.

"That's a load," said Ellery grimly, "I shouldn't particularly care to carry about myself."

"But now—tonight. She must be frightened now. I mean this awful, awful person. It was I who was stupid, not you. I should have known better. But when the wire came this afternoon I was frantic. It took me in completely. I imagined all sorts of dreadful things. So I rushed out to that inn and… Whoever it was took no chances. I'd no sooner run into the lobby there—I had no time even to realize how I had been fooled—when a hand holding something soft and smelly pressed it to my nose and I passed out. The next thing I knew I woke up outside on those chairs with Bill—" She stopped, and Bill squirmed like a child.

"Didn't you see anything—the face, a hand, a scrap of garment?"

"Nothing."

"How did the hand feel?"

"I didn't feel the hand at all. I suppose it was a hand. Just that cloth—it must have been a handkerchief—saturated in chloroform."

"A warning. Again a warning. Remarkable!"

"What's remarkable about it?" demanded Bill.

"Forgive me; I was thinking aloud. Well, the warning didn't work, did it, Andrea? Instead of inducing you to clamp your lips tighter, it parted them completely."

"Don't you see?" cried Andrea. "As soon as you got me out of that stupor I saw it. The woman who attacked me this afternoon must have been the same woman who attacked me in the shack that day and put the note in my hand. I realized that at once. And so I was sure—sure at last."

"Of what?" asked Bill blankly.

"Sure that your sister hadn't been that woman, silly! I never really believed, Bill, that Lucy killed Joe and attacked me that day, but I didn't know. This afternoon I knew. Lucy's in prison; so she couldn't possibly have been—don't you see? That was one thing I was clear about at last. It made up my mind for me. It's still important to protect mother, more important than ever; but the terrible injustice to Lucy—I had to tell you my story."

"But your mother—"

"Do you think," she whispered, "that anyone…"

"No one knows we're here, Andrea," said Ellery gently. "And when your mother returns we'll see to it that she's well protected without her knowledge. This note, however… No salutation, no signature. That was to be expected. Can't get anything typical out of the phraseology, either. On the the other hand, the comparative length of the message was a little troublesome to the writer. The words 'of your mother'—the last phrase in the message—grew regularly fainter, with 'mother' virtually illegible. Of course the length of the note explains the many matches used. A singeing of cork carbonizes only the upper surface; a stroke or two and the carbon is gone, necessitating another application of fire. Andrea, when you went in—and before you were struck on the head—did you see the knife lying on the table with the cork imbedded on its point?"

"No. I mean it wasn't there then. I saw it only when I recovered from the blow."

"That's something. Before you were struck the knife therefore was in Gimball's heart. Between the time you were struck and the time you recovered the murderess withdrew the knife, stuck the cork on its tip, charred it, tore off a piece of the wrapping-paper, and wrote the note to you. Before you recovered she stuck the note in your hand and fled in Lucy's Ford. You didn't catch even a glimpse of the one who struck you, Andrea?"

"No."

"Not even her hand—anything?"

"It was a complete surprise."

"What happened when you recovered?"

"I read the note. I was really frightened then. And I looked over the table and saw Joe. He was lying on the floor with blood on his chest. He looked dead. When I recognized him I must have screamed."

"I've heard that scream of yours," muttered Bill, "a hundred times in my dreams."

"Poor Bill. I grabbed my bag and ran for the door. I saw a car's headlights on the main road nearby. I realized then what a dangerous position I was in—alone with a dead man, my stepfather. I jumped into the roadster and drove off, putting a handkerchief to my face as I passed the car. Of course I didn't know whose car it was, or who was in it. I left the main road going back and managed to reach the city by dodging in and out about eleven-thirty. I slipped into the apartment without being seen, changed into my evening things, and drove down to the Waldorf. I did say something to the others about having had a headache, or something; they didn't question me. The rest," she sighed with an infinitude of weariness, "you know."

"Have you had any further messages, Andrea?" asked Ellery absently.

"One. It came the day after the... you know. A wire. It merely said, 'Say nothing.'" "Where is it?"

"I destroyed it. I didn't think a wire—"

"What office was it sent from?"

"I don't believe I noticed. I was practically petrified." Her voice rose. "Oh, how could I say anything to you when I knew someone was watching from the dark, ready to—to harm Mother if I said a word?"

"Don't, Andrea," said Bill tenderly.

"But doesn't this story of mine change things for Lucy, Bill? You— you could see to it that Mother and I were both protected from now on. The attack on me today proves that Lucy couldn't have been the one who—"

"No, Andrea. From the legal standpoint it's no proof at all. Pollinger would say that the attack on you today was engineered by friends of Lucy's for the very purpose of making her appear innocent of the murder for which she's been convicted."

"I agree with Bill," said Ellery suddenly. "As a matter of fact, our plan from now on must be entirely different. Andrea, I shall give you what is popularly known as the air—a generous gift, under the circumstances. You will say nothing to anyone about the attack on you at the North Shore Inn today, not even to your mother. Your assailant, inferring that I have given you up as a bad job, that you took her warning to heart and said nothing, will feel more comfortable—ample protection, I believe, against further assaults. Whoever it was who chloroformed you, my dear, isn't bloodthirsty; you'll be safe enough."

"Whatever you think best," murmured Andrea.

"But, Ellery—" protested Bill.

"No, no, I'm sure there's no danger if we let matters rest, Bill." Ellery's chair scraped. 'I think we'd better be on our way, Bill. Andrea's mother will be along soon and there's no point in remaining for awkward explanations. Shall we see you—"

Someone was crashing through the underbrush. Ellery stopped talking. The sounds grew louder. It was as if a large animal, blind, were blundering toward them through the bushes and trees.

"Not a word, Bill," whispered Ellery. "Come out of that. Quickly! Andrea, sit tight. At the first sign of anything, run like the devil."

Bill stole toward him in the darkness. Ellery grasped his arm and squeezed. Across the glade Andrea was very still. A man's voice shouted, "Andrea!" with a queer thickness.

"Burke," whispered Andrea.

"Andrea!" It was an angry roar. "Where the hell are you? Can't see a thing in this blasted darkness."

They heard him thrash through the last barrier of undergrowth into the glade. His breath came in gusts, as if he had been running. "Here I am, Burke," said Andrea quietly from the basketwork chair.

Jones grunted; he was clearly groping about for her. Bill, crouching beside Ellery, was glaring toward the source of the noise. "Here you are," Jones's heavy laughter rolled out from the glade. "Dodging me, Andy? That's a hell of a way to treat your fiancé. Had to trail you, by God. Telephoned your apartment and some servant said you'd come out here with the old lady. How about a kiss? Come on—"

"Take your hands off me," said Andrea. "You're drunk as a swill-filled pig."

"What's a couple o' drinks between friends? Come on, now, Andy, gimme a kiss and make it hot."

The listening men heard a scuffling noise and then, sharp as a punctuation mark, a slap. "I said take your hands off me," said Andrea evenly. "I don't like drunks pawing me. Now get out, Burke."

"So that's the way it is, hey?" growled Jones. "All right, Andrea; you asked for it. What you need is a li'l old-fashioned lovin'. Now, now…"

"Stop that, you filthy—"

"Like that sheep-eyed Philadelphia lawyer better, don't you? Well, I don't want my fiancée playing around with other men, see? No, sir, not my fiancée. My property, Andy; t'have and t'hold. Now gimme that kiss and be quick about it!"

"Burke, we're through. Will you go now, please?"

"Through? Oh, no, we're not. What d'ye mean—through?"

"Washed up. I'm breaking our engagement. It was a mistake. You aren't yourself; you're tight, Burke. Go now, before you do something you'll be sorry for."

"What you need, li'l one, is a touch of the whip. Break 'em… You come here!"

They were struggling across the glade. Bill shook off Ellery's hand and silently streaked forward. Ellery hesitated, shrugged, and retreated more deeply into the protection of the tree above him. He heard a tearing sound, as if something had been ripped forcibly away. Jones grunted in pure surprise. "What the—"

"This is Angell speaking," said Bill grimly. "I can't see you, you swine, but I could smell you all the way across the glade. How's that flipper of yours?"

"Leggo my collar, damn you!"

"Arm healed yet?"

"Sure! You going to leggo, or do I have to—" A fist thudded against bone, and a body crashed to the grass.

"It's a shame to take advantage of a drunk," growled Bill from the darkness, "but you had it coming to you."

Jones scrambled to his feet. "Oh, it's little Bill, is it?" he snarled. "Arranging pretty rendezvous in the dark, hey?" He said something obscene very clearly, and struck out.

"Bill, don't!" cried Andrea.

Bill's fists played a momentary tattoo, and again Jones went down. "That will teach you to be a good little polo-player, Jones. Now are you going peacefully, or do I have to boot you out?"

"Bill!"

Jones was silent now; Ellery could almost see him crouching on the grass. Then he sprang again. For several seconds Ellery heard nothing but panting exhalations and the soggy sounds of fists striking flesh. Then someone fell again. Jones cursed; Ellery heard him pick himself up and stagger away. And after a while they heard the sound of a motor retreating in the distance. Ellery stepped into the glade again. "My hero," he said dryly. "Do you know what you are, Sir Galahad? You're a fool."

"Go sit on a tack," said Bill defiantly. "I itched to maul that egotistical pillar of society the first time I set eyes on his ugly map. And nobody talks to Andrea that way—"

"Where is Andrea? It's uncommonly quiet here."

"I'm here," murmured Andrea.

"Where?"

"The location," she said softly, "is somewhat private, sir."

Ellery threw up his hands. "I never knew an investigation that was materially assisted by the presence of little Eros. Disgusting! Well, there's nothing I can do about it. Bless you, my children. Shall we see you back to the house, Andrea?"

"I'll meet you at the car," said Bill in a rather dreamy voice. Ellery grinned under cover of the darkness. He heard them walking slowly away.

When Bill rejoined Ellery he was silent and his face was shining. Ellery glanced at him once in the light of the Duesenberg's dashboard, chuckled to himself, and drove off. Ellery parked the car on the main street of Roslyn, excused himself, and hurried into a drug-store. He was gone for a long time. When he came out he strode up the street toward a telegraph office and went in. Five minutes later he was back, looking thoughtful.

"What's the idea?" demanded Bill.

"A few chores. By telephone. One to Trenton."

"Trenton?"

"I wanted to speak to Ella Amity. But she hasn't been in her office at the newspaper all day. Off on some tangent of her own, no doubt. Brainy female. And then I spoke to Sergeant Velie."

"Oh, private business?" Bill slumped down as Ellery put the car into gear again, the dreamy look reappearing on his face.

"You might call it private," chuckled Ellery. "The Sergeant, you know, is a veritable rock of ages. I always lean on his brawny shoulders when I'm weary—he's my father's Man Friday, you know, and as tongueless as a mummified Pharaoh. Well, Velie knew a good agency and promised to set the hounds on the trail instanter."

Bill sat up abruptly. "Ellery! So you did—"

"Of course, you idiot. Your little attack of gallantry back there at Oyster Bay has made me change my plans. I deliberately concealed myself to keep him ignorant of my presence; but if he talks he may do damage nevertheless. Your having been there might strike a suspicious note in someone's mind."

"I couldn't let that bird—" began Bill doggedly.

"Yes, yes, Romeo, I quite understand. The way it's worked out there's an additional advantage. A guard is always more effective when the guardee is unaware of his presence. Velie's friends will watch Andrea and her mother closely enough, never fear. So we've given them protection under the best possible circumstances."

"But won't this blamed shadow of a murderess find out?"

Ellery looked hurt. "My dear Bill. If the arrangements give me a sense of security, they should satisfy you. I'm rather finicky in these delicate matters."

"All right, all right. But it would be hell if she did. She'd know that Andrea had spilled—"

"Spilled what?"

"What?"

"What did Andrea spill?" asked Ellery patiently.

"Why, she told us exactly what happened that night—"

"Yes, and does it mean anything?"

Bill scowled. "I don't get you."

Ellery drove silently for a long time. He murmured at last, "Don't you see, Bill, this criminal is deathly afraid of something connected with Andrea's presence on the scene of the crime that night? Well, you heard Andrea's story. Did it enlighten you? Did it point the road to the vital truth? Was there anything in it that struck you as damaging to an individual from the detective standpoint?"

"No," admitted Bill.

"But there should have been. If Andrea had caught a glimpse of the murderess, her face, figure, clothing, even her hand, it would be conceivable that this dancing shadow of ours might feel it necessary to warn Andrea to say nothing. But the killer must have known that Andrea saw nothing: she was struck from behind and fell unconscious instantly. Then what was it the killer was afraid of?"

"You tell me," said Bill gloomily.

Ellery said in a casual tone, "How about spending the night with me, Bill?" Then, as the Duesenberg howled under the impact of his foot on the accelerator, he muttered: "Perhaps I will, perhaps I will."

"What d'ye mean by that?"

"Oh, nothing."

"And why did you go into that telegraph office?"

"Oh! To check up on that wire sent to Andrea today that lured her out to the North Shore Inn"

"Well?"

"Nothing. The clerk doesn't remember who sent it."

*

The next morning the Inspector had left for Centre Street, and they were dawdling over their second cup of coffee in the Queens' living-room, when the doorbell rang. They heard Djuna, who had a mind of his own, sharply questioning someone in the little sitting-room into which the door opened. "Djuna!" called Ellery from the breakfast table. "Who is it?"

"A girl," said Djuna sulkily, appearing in the living-room doorway. Djuna, for all his tender years, was an incorruptible misogynist.

"Heavens!" said Andrea Gimball from behind him. "This young ogre almost snapped my head off. You don't receive females often, I gather… Oh."

Bill half rose, clutching the lapels of his borrowed dressing-gown over the russet and tan stripes of his borrowed pajamas; he glanced in panic at the bedroom door. He said, "Oh," too, and sank back with a foolish grin.

"A plethora of orotundities," observed Ellery with a smile. "So good of you, Andrea. You catch us literally with our… Well, never mind. Come in, Come in! And, Djuna, if ever you bark at this lady again I'll wring your blasted young neck."

Djuna scowled and departed for the kitchen. But he was back almost at once bearing the peace-offering of a clean cup and saucer, napkin, and spoon. "Coffee?" he growled, and vanished again.

"What a refreshing young person," laughed Andrea as Ellery poured. "I think I like him."

"He likes you. He reserves his sternest manner for those of whom he secretly approves."

"Bill Angell, you look positively embarrassed. I thought bachelors preserved their poise under all circumstances."

"It's the pajamas," said Bill, still grinning foolishly.

"They are weird. Yours, Mr. Queen? Thank you." She sipped the coffee. She looked fresh and almost happy, dressed in something gay and perky, and showing no evidences of the previous day's experience.

"It's my libido sneaking out," said Ellery. "Well, Andrea, you seem in better spirits this morning."

"I am. I had a sound night's sleep, a canter in the Park this morning, and here I am. And here you are, you two. Not dressed at ten-thirty!"

"Bill's fault. He snores, you know—quite adept at it; has a most amazing virtuosity. Kept me awake half the night." Bill blushed angrily.

"Bill!"

"It's not true. I never snored in my life!"

"Thank goodness. I don't think I could stand a man who—"

"Oh, couldn't you?" retorted Bill. "Well, I'll snore if I choose, and I'd like to see the woman—"

Andrea said maliciously, "Look, the little boy is angry. Oh, Bill, I do like you when your eyes get bright that way, and you make the funniest faces!"

"By the way," said Ellery hastily, "did everything go off all right, Andrea? I mean last night?"

"Oh, yes." Andrea sobered. "Mother came back just after you left. She was surprised to see me, of course, but I invented some excuse or other and persuaded her to return to the city."

"No trouble?" asked Bill rather anxiously.

"Not the least bit. Not what you would call trouble." Andrea's chin hardened a little. "When we got back I found a series of frantic messages from Burke's mother. I suppose you don't know Burke's mother?"

Bill grunted, looking glum, and Ellery said dryly, "Haven't had the pleasure. Is she horsy, too?"

"Worse than that. She has aviation on the brain, an acute case. Goes about flying, gets in everybody's hair. The professionals are afraid of her. Gray bobbed hair, a nose like Caesar's, and the riches of Midas. Well, dear Mrs. Jones wanted to know what in heaven's name had happened to her little Burkie boy."

"Oh," said Bill. He was scanning Andrea's face with renewed anxiety.

"It seems," murmured Andrea, "that he came home last night with a black eye, a smashed nose, and a front tooth missing. Burke's very proud of his appearance, you know, and this will keep him out of circulation for some time."

"Break for the horses," muttered Bill. "Did you—?"

"And of course," continued Andrea, "Mrs. Jones wanted to know why I broke off the engagement. Then Mother got in on it and we had a perfectly lovely time. I was afraid Mother would throw a fit right on my bedroom rug."

"Did you—?" began Bill again.

"Well, no, I didn't. I thought," Andrea looked at the floor, "one shock at a time was sufficient. Later…" Her voice was low. Then it lifted and she smiled again. "I suppose you're wondering why I'm here?"

"Sufficient unto the day is the fact thereof," said Ellery gallantly.

"No, but really. I awoke this morning remembering something that I'd completely forgotten last night. It's a small thing that can't be important, but you said you wanted to know everything."

"Andrea." Ellery rose, then he sat down again. "About that night in the shack?"

"Yes. Something I saw before I was struck by that fiendish woman."

"Something you saw?" Ellery's gravity was smothered in a rising tide of excitement. "What, Andrea? Don't worry about its unimportance; let me do the fretting. What was it?"

"The matches." Andrea shrugged. "Those yellow paper-matches on the plate. You see, I told you it was trivial. But they were different."

Bill jumped up and went to the window, as if a thought had suddenly struck him. Below, on Eighty-seventh Street, a black town-car shone opulently at the curb. A few yards behind was parked a nondescript sedan with a hard-faced individual smoking at the wheel. "Andrea! You shouldn't have come. Have you gone out of your mind? I just realized. That town-car downstairs simply shrieks. If that woman gets wind of this—"

Andrea went pale. But Ellery said impatiently: "There's no danger, Bill; don't be an old woman. Come, come, Andrea! What about those matches? In what way were they different?"

Her eyes were wide on Bill. "There weren't as many," she said in subdued tones.

"Not as many?" snapped Ellery. "When?"

"When I was standing in front of the table just before she hit me on the head. I saw the plate clearly. Everything was perfectly clear, like a photograph. It must have been my nerves. My nerves were on edge and my brain was racing—"

Ellery was leaning on the table now, his knuckles white. "Before she struck you the plate held fewer matches than—when?"

"Than when I came to and found the note in my hand and the woman gone and Joe on the floor."

Ellery pushed back from the table. "Now, look here, Andrea," he said softly. "Let's get this straight. You came in, advanced to the table, saw the plate, were hit on the head, and when you revived noticed that there were more matches on the plate than when you'd come in.

204

Is that right? Now, how many more were there?" his voice became urgent. "Think hard, please. I want the exact number."

Andrea was bewildered. "But what could it possibly—"

"Andrea, will you answer my question!"

She frowned dutifully. "I don't remember how many more there were when I revived. All I recall is how many there were on the plate when I came into the shack."

"That will do."

"There were six; I'm sure of the number. Six matches on the plate. I think subconsciously I counted them."

"Six. Six." Ellery began to pace up and down between Andrea and Bill. "Burnt, eh?"

"Oh, yes. Or rather half-burnt. You know."

"Yes. Six matches which had been struck and used." Ellery compressed his lips and continued to pace, his eyes abstracted.

"But, Ellery," said Bill wearily, "what difference can it make how many she saw?"

Ellery made an impatient gesture. Andrea and Bill looked at each other, first in perplexity and then, as Ellery flung himself into a chair and began telling something off on his fingers, with a half-glimpsed excitement. Then he stopped counting, his features perfectly at rest. "Andrea, what was the situation as regards that plate when you first looked into the shack?"

"You mean at eight o'clock?"

"Yes."

"Why, the plate was empty."

"Wunderlich! Andrea, this is vital news. Are you sure you haven't left anything out? There's one thing—if only…" He stopped again to remove his pince-nez and tap them against his lips.

Andrea looked blank. "Why, I don't think so. I think that's all."

"Please, Andrea. Concentrate. The table. Try to visualize the table as you saw it. What was on it at eight o'clock?"

"The empty plate. The lamp, unlit. I lit it then, as I think I told you. That's all."

"And at eight thirty-five, when you walked in—that is, just before you were assaulted?"

"The lamp, the plate with the six half-burnt match-stubs, and—oh!"

"Oh," said Ellery. "We've struck a mnemonic chord."

She said breathlessly, "There was something else; I remember it all now. There was a match-packet on the plate, too! Closed!"

"Ah," said Ellery, and he put the pince-nez back on his nose. "An interesting point." The way he said it, the way his eyes behind the rimless lenses glittered, made Bill glance at him sharply. "This packet of matches, Andrea—do you remember anything about it?"

"Why, no. Just that it was closed. It was a packet of paper-matches. You know. Those little things where the top fits into the piece where you strike the match—"

"Yes, yes. That's everything, Andrea? You're sure?"

"Really, I don't see… That's all."

His eyes flickered. "Well, that takes care of the period before your assault. Now what was on the table when you came to?"

"The plate with a great number of those burnt yellow match-stubs—you saw them yourself later that night—the lamp, and that horrible paper-cutter with the—the—blood and burnt cork on its tip."

"Nothing else?"

She thought for a moment. "No. Not a thing."

"Wasn't the match-packet still there?"

"No."

"Hmm." Ellery studied her for a moment rather queerly. Then he heaved himself out of his chair and said to Bill, "How would you like the job of sticking close to Andrea for a few days? I've changed my mind. I agree there may be some danger now—more than last night."

"I told you there would be!" raged Bill, waving his arms. "Andrea, that was childish—coming here so openly. What do you think I ought to do, Ellery?"

"Take Andrea home. And stay there. Be her shadow. That shouldn't be a specially onerous assignment."

"You really think—?" began Andrea faintly.

"It's safer, Andrea. Well, well, Bill, don't stand there like one of Madame Tussaud's exhibits!" Bill dashed off to the bedroom. He was back in an impossibly short time, fully dressed and flushed to the tips of his ears.

"Wait a minute," said Ellery; he vanished into the bedroom. When he came back he was thoughtfully hefting a .38 police revolver. "You might pack this piece of hardware. It's loaded; don't monkey with that safety. You know how to use a gun, of course?"

"I've handled 'em." Bill took it grimly.

"Lord, Andrea, don't look so apprehensive! This is just an extra safety measure. Now, off with you both. Take good care of her, Bill."

"We may have some trouble with Andrea's people," grinned Bill, waving the revolver. "Is that why you've given me this?"

"You might," said Ellery gravely, "use it on Fish-Face."

Bill seized Andrea's arm, still grinning, and hustled the bewildered girl out of the apartment. Ellery walked quickly to the window. He stood motionless until he saw Bill and Andrea running down the stone steps below, Bill's left hand gripping Andrea's arm and his right jammed into his pocket. They jumped into the town-car and were gone. The nondescript car parked down the street rolled off at once. Eyes gleaming, Ellery sprang for the telephone in the bedroom and called the Long Distance operator. While he waited his lips were screwed up in a most extraordinary expression. "Hello, De Jong... De Jong? This is Ellery Queen calling. Yes, from New York... Fine, thanks. I say, De Jong, what happened to the evidence in that Wilson case?"

"Cripes, you still harping on that?" growled De Jong. "What evidence?"

"Well, specifically, that chipped plate I saw you stow away the night of the murder. The plate with all those match-stubs on it."

"Oh, that's on file down here." A note of curiosity crept into the Trenton policeman's voice. "Why?"

"For excellent reasons immaterial at the moment. De Jong, do something for me. Dig out that plate with its contents and—" Ellery paused—"count the match-stubs."

"What?" He could almost see De Jong blinking. "You spoofing?"

"Never more serious in my life. Count the stubs. And call me back. I'll be waiting." He gave his number. De Jong grunted and hung up. While he waited Ellery paced again with lean and hungry strides. At last the telephone rang.

"Well?" he snapped.

"Twenty."

"Twenty," said Ellery slowly. "Well, well, what do you think of that? Thanks, De Jong. Thanks ever so much."

"But what the hell is the idea? Count the matches! I don't—"

Ellery smiled vaguely, murmured something, and hung up. He stood still for a moment, musing. Then he threw himself on the bed. After a while he got up to fish a cigaret out of his coat-pocket. While he smoked he examined his face absently in the mirror over his bureau. Then he went back to the bed again. Finally he flung his butt into an ashtray and went into the living-room. Djuna was clearing away the breakfast dishes, his dark gypsy face scowling at the cup Andrea had used.

He looked up briefly. "That his girl," he demanded, "that girl?"

"Eh? Oh, I shouldn't wonder."

Djuna looked relieved. "I guess she's all right," he said. "Pretty keen."

Ellery went to the window and clasped his hands behind his back. "Djuna, you always were a mathematics shark. How much is left when you subtract twenty from twenty?"

Djuna looked suspicious. "Any kid knows that. Nothing!"

"No," said Ellery without turning, "that's where you're wrong, my son. When you subtract twenty from twenty, oddly enough you have left… everything. Now isn't that curious, Djuna?"

Djuna snorted and went on with his work; he knew the uselessness of discussion at times like this. And after a moment Ellery said, with a sort of wonder in his voice, "Everything! Lord, the thing's as plain as a pikestaff now."

"Yah!" said Djuna derisively. Ellery went to the big armchair reserved for the Inspector and covered his face with his hands. "A what did you say?" frowned Djuna. But Ellery did not reply. So Djuna shrugged and sailed off to the kitchen with his tray.

"As plain as a pikestaff. Plainer." Ellery sprang out of the chair suddenly. "Yes, by thunder!" he shouted. And he made for the bedroom and the telephone with the swift determination of a man who sees clearly and grimly that there is work to be done.

THE READER IS CHALLENGED

"T HE PUBLIC," THOMAS De Quincey once wrote, "is a bad guesser." If hedonistic Tommy was right about the public of his own time, then man in the mass has changed remarkably during the past century. For any fashioner of crime tales these days will tell you that the modern public—at least, that part of the public which seeks its escape in detective fiction—is a very good guesser indeed; much too good, if you ask me. In fact, from the letters hurled at my poor head it would appear that the reader who is fooled is the exception rather than the rule.

But we have a sound defense. Guessing isn't fair. Although each writer is his own Hoyle in composing the rules of the game, we all manage to agree on that fundamental. Guessing isn't fair because the number of characters in any detective story is necessarily limited; and somewhere, at some stage of the tale, the reader is bound to suspect in his turn the character who ultimately is unmasked as the author of all the villainy.

For many years I have been a voice crying in the wilderness—I trust not vainly—beseeching readers to repress heroically their guessing proclivities and play the game scientifically. It's harder, but immeasurably more fun.

Why not begin with the problem of Joseph Kent Gimball's murder?

At this point in the story you are in possession of all the facts needed to build up a complete and logical solution of the crime. Your job is to spot the vital clues, assemble them in rational order, and from them deduce the one and only possible criminal. It can be done; it has been done, as you will see.

If you fail, of course, you can always fall back on the old reliable guesswork. If you succeed, let me know about it. As a matter of fact, that's hardly a necessary admonition. If you succeed, I will know about it. And, as Inspector Queen likes to point out, how!

Ellery Queen

V

THE TRUTH

"While we are examining into everything
we sometimes find truth
where we least expected it."

UNTIL THE DAY Andrea related her curious little story of the half dozen match-stubs, the riddle of Joseph Kent Gimball's death remained in a state of suspension, fixed there by the dark hands of fate. But when the story was told, animation superseded suspension, mystery became knowledge, suspicion turned into certainty. The case was snatched out of those dark hands by Mr. Ellery Queen, who directed its destiny thereafter with all the carefulness and cunning which years of experience as a diagnostician of crime had taught him.

Ellery was monstrously busy for days after the event. Whatever he was conniving, he meant it to be secret from most; his two hurried trips to Trenton were surreptitious, and no one knew of his dozens of telephone calls except those persons to whom they were addressed. He conferred privately with various hard-looking individuals; he sought the professional advice of Sergeant Velie; and, if the truth had been known, arranged a certain matter of unsuspected and illegal entry with a bland disregard of the civil rights of a free citizenry which would have made his father, the Inspector, shudder.

Then, his plans made, he came out into the open.

He began hostilities, strangely enough, on a Saturday. Whether this was a whim of chance of cynical design Ellery never explained, but mere fact served to heighten the tension. The persons concerned could not help but recall the bloody events of that other Saturday when Gimball felt the cold bite of metal in his heart; the memory was clearly reflected by their strained faces.

"I've called you ladies and gentlemen together," Ellery announced that afternoon in the Borden apartment on Park Avenue, "out of no idle desire to hear myself make a speech. There's magic in the wind, and time is crowding me. Some of you may have lulled yourselves into a state of lethargy, feeling secure in the monotony of the status quo ante. If that's so, it's unfortunate; before the day is over I promise to awaken you with what may prove considerable rudeness."

"What do you mean?" snapped Jessica. "Are we never to have any peace? And what right have you—?"

"None whatever, legally speaking. Nevertheless," sighed Ellery, "it would be wisdom to humor my little fancy. You see, the tragedy of Joseph Kent Gimball's death is about to be exhumed."

"You're reopening the case, Mr. Queen?" growled old Jasper Borden with a bitter half-twist of his lips. He had insisted upon being wheeled downstairs; he sat among them with the immobility of a corpse, only his one good eye alive.

"My dear sir, it has never been closed. Lucy Wilson of Philadelphia has been convicted of the crime, but her conviction did not solve it. Certain forces have been continuously at work since that grotesque débâcle in Trenton. They have never relaxed. I'm happy to announce," Ellery said dryly, "that their efforts have been rewarded."

"I can't see that that concerns these good people," said Senator Frueh sharply, playing with his beard, his shrewd little eyes intent on Ellery. "If you have new evidence take it to the prosecutor of Mercer County. Why continue to harass this group? If you want to make a fight of it," he added in a grim tone, "I'll be glad to oblige personally—I know the rules."

Ellery smiled. "Oddly enough, Senator, that reminds me of something that was said some time ago by our friend Marcus Valerius Martial. African lions, he pointed out, rush to attack bulls; they do not attack butterflies. As an epigram—"

The lawyer was purple. "You leave these people out of whatever devilry you're up to!" he shouted.

"Spare the rod?" sighed Ellery. "You wrong me, Senator. If I could, obviously I would. I'm afraid you'll have to endure the nausea of my company for just a while longer. After that… well, let's not discuss the future. I've found that the future generally gets where it's going despite every effort of mere Man to arrest its progress."

Jessica toyed with her handkerchief in an annoyed way, but she was stiff with enforced self-control. Grosvenor Finch stirred uneasily, watching her. Only Andrea, sitting quietly to one side, and Bill Angell, standing behind Andrea's chair, seemed unaffected. Both kept their eyes riveted on Ellery. "No further objections?" murmured Ellery. "Thank you." Glancing at his wristwatch, he said, "Then I think we had better be on our way."

"On our way?" Finch was puzzled. "Where are you taking us?"

Ellery picked up his hat. "To Trenton."

"Trenton!" gasped Andrea's mother.

"We are going to revisit the scene of the crime."

They all went pale at that, and for a moment were too startled to speak. Then Senator Frueh jumped up, brandishing a fat fist. "Now, that is going too far!" he roared. "You've no authority—I shall forbid my clients—"

"My dear Senator. Have you a personal objection to visiting the scene of the crime?"

"I've never been there!"

"You relieve me. Then that's settled. Shall we go?"

Nobody stirred but Bill. The old millionaire asked quietly, in his bass voice: "May I ask what you hope to achieve by this unusual procedure, Mr. Queen? I know you would not make such a painful request unless you felt it to be necessary to some end you have in mind."

"I had rather not explain my hopes, Mr. Borden. But the plan is simple. We are going to engage in a very dramatic undertaking. We shall re-enact the murder of Joseph Kent Gimball."

The eyelid drooped. "Is that essential?"

"It was necessity that mothered the invention, sir, but the demonstration will be art in imitation of nature. Now, please, ladies and gentlemen. I shall greatly dislike having to exert official pressure to compel your attendance."

"I shan't go," said Jessica Borden sullenly. "I've had enough. He's dead. That woman is—why don't you let us alone?"

"Jessica." The old invalid turned his good eye toward his daughter. "Get your things on."

The woman bit her thin lower lip. Then she said submissively, "Yes, Father," rose, and went upstairs to her bedroom.

No one said anything until Jasper Borden again broke the silence. "I believe," he said heavily, "that I shall go, too. Andrea, ring for the nurse."

Andrea was shocked out of her immobility. "But, Grandfather—I"

"Did you hear what I said, child?"

Ellery retired to the door to wait. They all rose now and began to scatter, moving slowly. The piscine butler appeared loaded with hats.

"Ellery," said Bill in a low voice.

"Hello, Bill. Well, how has your job worked out during the past few days? I don't see any scars or wounds."

215

Bill was grim. "It's been hell. The duchess is a demon on wheels. I haven't been able to get in here at all until today. But Andrea and I worked out a plan. I've been spending my days hanging around outside, watching. She agreed not to set foot from the apartment when I wasn't on duty. At other times, we've been out together."

"Promising start for a young couple with honorable intentions," grinned Ellery. "Any signs of trouble?"

"No."

Andrea came down, dressed for the street. She had a light coat on and her right hand was jammed into its pocket. It was almost as if within that pocket she were gripping a gun. Bill took a step toward her eagerly, but she shook her head, looked around, and signaled Ellery with her blue eyes. Ellery frowned, watching the pocket. Then his nod told Bill to wait where he was, and he stepped out into the corridor with Andrea.

She began in a swift whisper, "I had to talk to you before—," and stopped to look around again, apprehensively.

"Andrea, whatever is the matter?"

"This." The hand came out of the pocket. "This came in the mail this morning, wrapped in cheap paper, addressed to me."

Ellery did not take it. His eyes rested on it for a moment and then searched her face. The hand holding the object trembled. It was a cheap little plaster group of figures, colored a mottled red. The group represented three squatting monkeys on a pedestal. One had his paw on his mouth, one on his eyes, one had both paws on his ears. "Speak no evil, see no evil, hear no evil," said Andrea in the same whisper. "Or however it goes. Isn't it insane?" She laughed rather hysterically. "But it frightens me. It's—"

"Another warning." Ellery frowned. "Our quarry is growing nervous. Did you save the wrappings?"

"Oh! I threw them away. I'm sure you couldn't have got anything from them."

216

"Tush. You confident people. And you've messed that thing up so that even if there were fingerprints on it they're gone. Have you told Bill about this?"

"No. I didn't want to worry him. Poor Bill! He's been such a comfort these past few days—"

"Put it back in your pocket," said Ellery sharply. "Someone's coming." The elevator-door opened and a tall figure stepped out. "Ah, Jones! Good man. Nice of you to come," said Ellery.

Andrea blushed and fled into the apartment. Jones's surly, bloodshot eyes remained fixed on the open doorway through which she had vanished. "Got your message," he said thickly. He was apparently very drunk. "Don't know why I came. They don't want me here."

"Well," said Ellery cheerfully, "they don't want me here, either."

"What's up, Sherlock? More deep stuff?"

"I thought you might like to join us. We're bound for Trenton and an experiment."

Jones laughed. "Or for hell. It's all the same to me."

The sun was a sliver of orange arc over the trees beyond the Delaware when they reached the isolated shack near the Marine Terminal. Ellery, piloting his Duesenberg in the van of the fleet of cars, had led them by a circuitous route on the outskirts of Trenton to Lamberton Road with a caution that indicated his reluctance to attract the attention of some inquisitive reporter roving the city streets.

It had been a sultry day; the leaves of the trees surrounding the shack were motionless. The foliage was so still, stood up so woodenly, that there was something unreal about the scene, as if it were a crude and lifeless imitation of nature. Even the surface of the river, glimpsed beyond the wooded shore, was only a glassy representation of living water. In this solitude the shack stood silently, a poor daub on a brutal landscape.

There was no conversation as Ellery, with a quick glance about, led his unwilling guests into the shack. They were making stern efforts to

217

control themselves, all except Jasper Borden, whose grim eye in that iron face missed nothing. Finch and Bill Angell had some difficulty in maneuvering the old invalid's wheelchair, which had been carted along, into the house. But finally they were all inside, disposed along the walls, quiet as awed children, the lamp on the table lit against the dimness of dusk and Ellery holding the center of the stage.

For a time he said nothing at all, content to let them steep themselves in the atmosphere of the place. Nothing, apparently, had altered since that eventful night weeks ago except that the area beyond the table was clear, the suits of clothing on the wall-rack were gone, and the odor of death had dissipated. But as they stood and sat there, watching emptiness, it came back distilled by their imaginations until they could almost see the dead flesh of Gimball frozen in its agony on the floor between them.

"Now if you will excuse me," said Ellery suddenly, striding to the door, "I'll get the props. As long as we're staging a drama, we may as well use the technical terms. Please don't move, anyone."

He went out quickly, shutting the door behind him; and Bill moved over and set his back against it. The side door was shut. But suddenly, in the deep and awkward silence, it made a noise; and their eyes flew about in something like panic. It was open. The tall willowy figure of Ella Amity stood framed in the doorway.

"Hullo," she said slowly, looking around. She wore no hat. Her red hair against the light of outdoors was a flaming and untidy nimbus about her hair. "It's little Ella, folks. May I come in?" She calmly moved forward, closed the door, and stood there with roving, gleaming eyes. After a moment they looked away. The newspaper-woman's nostrils began to quiver.

"So this is the dump where he got it, eh?" muttered young Jones, staring at the floor beyond the table with his blood-streaked eyes.

"Shut up, Burke," said Finch irritably. Senator Frueh's hand paused in its restless stroking of his beard, then resumed with a queer energy.

Andrea sat in the armchair Lucy Wilson had occupied on the night of the murder. She was very still and seemed asleep. Bill's head swiveled from side to side carelessly; there was a febrile flush on his tan cheeks.

The front door opened, and they started again, but it was only Ellery, lugging a large suitcase. He shut the door and turned. "Ella Amity," he murmured. "Well, well, Ella. Where did you come from?" He seemed in a strange and secret way disturbed.

"A birdie whispered to me today," the red-headed woman said lightly. "Told me something was going to pop around here. So here I am. I think you're a heel for not letting me know."

"How did you get here?"

"Walked. Good for the figure. Don't worry, darling, I've nothing up my sleeve, and my record's clean. I've been out back mooning at the river. Or is it sunning? Well, no matter. What's going on here?"

"Keep quiet and perhaps you'll find out." Ellery went abruptly to the table, slung the suitcase on it. "Bill. I want you to run into town for me on an errand."

Bill growled: "What—"

But Ellery pounced on him and spoke for some time in an urgent sotto voce. Bill nodded. Then, with a glance about that was oddly savage, Bill shoved the door open and disappeared. Ellery, who seemed especially solicitous about the door, closed it again. Without a word he went back to the table, opened the suitcase, began pulling things out of it. They were realistic stage properties, the actual articles removed by Chief De Jong from the scene of the crime after the initial investigation. As he worked in silence, they heard the sound of a motor outside. The curtains had been drawn at the windows, so they could not see what was going on, but they knew it was Bill Angell leaving for Trenton on his mysterious errand, and they glanced uneasily at one another. Bill seemed to be having difficulty in getting started. His car made a good deal of noise as he raced the engine. The racket was so loud that when Ellery began to speak they had to lean forward to hear.

By this time they were grateful for the light of the lamp; darkness had fallen unexpectedly outside.

"There," said Ellery, depositing the last article in its proper place and returning to the table to stand tall and motionless in the lamp's radiance. "The stage is set. You will observe that Gimball's clothes are now back on the wall-rack; that the wrapped package containing his birthday gift of a desk-set to Bill Angell is again on the mantel above the fireplace; that the clean, empty plate is once more on the table near the lamp. The only thing that's missing is the body of the victim. But that, I feel sure, will be supplied by your own imaginations."

He flicked one hand over his shoulder. Their eyes went obediently to the spot on the floor indicated, and although it was still a bare patch of fawn rug, it was dreadfully easy to visualize the sprawled body that was no longer lying there.

"Now let me retrace for you," continued Ellery in a brisk tone, his eyes glittering in the lamplight, "the antecedent events of that day, June the first. A recapitulation will help you understand what happened subsequently. I've compiled a timetable which may not be completely accurate, but it gives the relative times involved closely enough to serve our purpose."

Senator Frueh tried to interrupt, but he had to pause and lick his dry lips first. "Whatever that purpose is. I think this is the most preposterous—"

"The gentleman from Eighty-seventh Street," said Ellery, "has the floor, Senator. I will be grateful for your absolute silence, as well as the silence of everyone else here. You will have unfettered opportunity later to talk to your hearts' content."

"Keep quiet, Simon," said Jasper Borden out of the side of his mouth.

"Thank you, Mr. Borden." Ellery waved a finger. "Observe. This is the afternoon of Saturday, June first. It is raining outside—raining hard. The rain is lashing at the windows. There is no one here. It is still light, the lamp is unlit, the package is not on the mantelpiece. The doors are closed."

Someone drew a tremulous breath. Ellery went on in a swift, merciless voice. "It is five o'clock. Joseph Kent Gimball is in New York, at his office. He has come in from Philadelphia in the old Packard, probably not stopping here on his way in, otherwise he would have left the Packard here and taken his Lincoln to New York. The fact that the Packard was found parked in the side driveway indicates that that was the last car he used.

"Now. He has already sent two telegrams, one to Bill Angell, one to Andrea, both worded identically and asking the addressees to meet him in this place at nine tonight and giving minute instructions about how to find it. In the afternoon he has supplemented his telegram to Bill by telephoning Bill at his Philadelphia office, again urging him to be present at the rendezvous tonight.

"What does he do at five? He leaves his office, goes down to where he has parked the Packard near his New York office, and drives off to the Holland Tunnel bound for Trenton. In the car he has the dummy sample-case of his Wilson personality and the wrapped birthday gift he has purchased in Wanamaker's Philadelphia yesterday intended for his brother-in-law. He reaches this shack at seven o'clock, runs up the side drive. It is still raining. A little later the rain stops. Meanwhile, the rain has washed away all traces of former footprints and tire marks, leaving, as it were, virgin ground."

Senator Frueh muttered something that sounded like "tiresome old wives' tale," but promptly stopped as the old millionaire glared at him.

"Pipe down, Senator," snapped Ella Amity. "This isn't Congress, you know. Go on, Ellery. You fascinate me."

"Gimball is in this room," said Ellery coolly, as if there had been no interruption. "He wanders about, puts the gift on the mantel, pauses at the window to scan the sky. He sees the sky has cleared. It is still early; he is restless, worried; he needs something to take his mind off the ordeal of confession to come. So he goes out by the side door and trudges down the path to the boathouse, leaving his footprints in the hardening mud. He hauls out his sailboat and scuds off down the Delaware to quiet his nerves. It is seven-fifteen."

They were sitting forward gripping the arms of their chairs, those who sat, and those who stood clutched the backs of the chairs. "To this point I have described what probably occured," Ellery went on, "because the description concerned itself with a man dead and buried. But now we come to the living. Andrea, I shall need your assistance. It is eight o'clock. You have just driven up to the shack and parked the Cadillac roadster you borrowed from Mr. Jones, parked it in the main driveway facing toward Camden. Will you re-enact what you did?"

Andrea rose without a word and went to the door. She was pale now with a cold pallor that made her fresh young face ghastly. "Shall I… go outside?"

"No, no. You've just opened the door, let us say. Pretend that it's open."

"The lamp," she whispered, "was off."

Ellery moved. The room went black. From the darkness his voice came, disembodied, sending a chill up their spines. "It was not so dark as this. There was still some light outdoors. Go on, Andrea!"

They heard her moving slowly forward toward the table. "I—I looked in. The room was empty. Of course, I could see, although it was getting dark here. I went to the table and switched on the lamp—this way."

The light clicked on; they saw her standing by the table, face averted, hand on the chain under the cheap shade. Then her hand fell. She stepped back, looked around at the fireplace, the clothes-rack, the dingy crumbling walls. She glanced at her wrist. Then she turned and went to the door again. "That's all I did—then," she said, again in a whisper.

"End of Scene I. Thank you; you may sit down now." She obeyed. "Andrea realizes that she is an hour early; she goes out, gets into the roadster, drives off toward Camden, probably onto Duck Island, for what she has testified was an hour's spin. The criminal," said Ellery curtly, "arrives at eight-fifteen." He paused, and the silence was unbearable. Their features might have been carved out of the living rock of an age-old convulsion of nature. The night, the sullen lowly room, the grisly whispers of outdoors, were twisted about their consciousness, not to be shaken off.

"The criminal has driven up at eight-fifteen from the direction of Camden in the Ford coupe she has stolen from Lucy Wilson's garage in Fairmount Park—no matter when. She is outside now. She steps carefully onto the stone ledge outside the door. She opens it, comes in swiftly, closes it again, whirls about, prepared for—"

He was at the door now, acting out his recital. They followed him, fascinated. "She sees the place is empty, however. She relaxes, pushes back her veil. For a moment she is puzzled; she has expected to find her victim here. Then she realizes that he has gone off somewhere, but that he has been here: the Packard is outside, the lamp inside is lit; Gimball must be nearby. She will wait. She expects no interference; this is an isolated spot and she believes that no one in the world except herself and Gimball are aware of its relationship to Gimball. She prowls, restless. She sees the package on the mantelpiece." He strode to the fireplace, reached up, tore away the wrappings of the package ruthlessly. The gift-set lay revealed. Ellery took the bundle to the table, bent over it. "Needless to say," he murmured, "she wore protecting gloves." He lifted out the still bloodstained paper-cutter, the little card, stained now by the many fingers that had handled it.

"Observe what chance has thrown into the path of this woman," he said sharply, straightening up. "She finds the card, indicating that the desk-set is a gift from Lucy Wilson and Joseph Wilson. She has stolen Lucy Wilson's car to frame her for the crime, but here, at hand, is something even better: a weapon identifiable with Lucy Wilson! Whatever weapon the criminal has intended to use, she discards it at once. She will use the paper-cutter. It will be another and stronger link to Lucy Wilson. She does not know, of course, how fortunate she is, for it is quite impossible that she should have known that Lucy Wilson's fingerprints were on the knife. At any rate, she puts the package back on the mantel. But the knife is not with it; the knife is in her hand."

The society woman made a moaning sound through stiff lips. She was evidently unconscious of what she had done, for she continued to glare at Ellery with an unwavering glassiness. Ellery grasped the bloody knife firmly, stole toward the side door. "She hears footsteps, coming from the river-side. It must be her victim. She stands behind this door, knife raised. The door opens, concealing her figure. Joseph Kent Gimball stands there, back from his sail on the river; he scrapes the mud off his shoes on the doorsill; he closes the door and walks in, unconscious of the menace at his back. The time is a little past eight-thirty, a matter of seconds or minutes." Ellery suddenly lunged. "She makes a sound in moving. Gimball, behind the table, whirls. For an instant they see each other; she has turned down her veil again, but he sees her figure, her clothes. Then the knife plunges into his heart and he falls—apparently dead."

Amazingly, Andrea's mother began to sob. Still glaring at Ellery. The tears rolled slowly down her faintly lined cheeks. She sobbed almost indignantly.

"What happens?" Ellery whispered. "The knife is in Gimball's heart. Only flight is necessary to complete the crime. Then—"

"I came back," said Andrea in a low voice.

"Good God," croaked Finch. "I thought you said, Andrea—"

"Please!" snapped Ellery. "Never mind what you thought. There has been a great deal of misrepresentation going on through which we've had to stumble to reach the truth. Andrea! Go through it for us."

He ran toward the front door, took up his stand beside it.

"The criminal hears the sound of the returning car. Someone is coming. A miscalculation! She hopes the car will pass; instead, it stops outside door. She still has time to escape by way of the side door. But she wants to drive that Ford back to Philadelphia. She can handle herself. She crouches behind the door…"

Andrea was at the door now. She moved like a somnambulist, slowly, across the fawn rug toward the table, eyes fixed on the patch of rug behind it.

"Only the legs are visible," said Ellery softly.

Andrea stopped by the table, looked at it, hesitated. Then Ellery sprang at her and his arm descended toward her head. Andrea drew in her breath.

"The criminal attacks Andrea from behind, knocks her unconscious. Andrea slips to the floor. The woman works swiftly. She sees now whom she has assaulted. It is necessary to leave a note of warning. She has no writing implements herself; she searches Andrea's bag; none there. She searches the house; no pen or pencil. The pen on Gimball's body has run dry. There is no ink in the desk-set. What to do?

"Then she sees the cork which came from the tip of the paper-knife, has an inspiration. She tears off a piece of wrapping-paper, goes to the table with the cork, takes the knife out of the dead man's body, sticks the cork on its tip again, begins to char the cork with paper-matches. She chars, writes, chars, writes, dropping the burnt matches on the plate. Finally the note is finished—a warning to Andrea to say nothing whatever about what she has seen this night, or her mother's life will be forfeit."

"Andrea. Darling," moaned Jessica feebly.

Ellery gestured with one hand. "The woman thrusts the note into Andrea's limp hand. She drops the knife with the burnt cork on it on the table. She leaves, drives off in the Ford. Andrea comes to about nine. She reads the note, sees the body, recognizes her stepfather, thinks he is dead, screams, and flees. Then Bill Angell arrives, talks to the dying man. That," said Ellery with a peculiar intonation, "is the script as it has been related to me."

Again the dreaded silence fell. Then Senator Frueh said slowly, quite without anger or rancor, "What do you mean, Queen?"

"I mean," said Ellery in a cold voice, "that a page of the script is missing. Something has been omitted. Andrea!"

She raised her eyes. There was something very strange in the air. She was wary, tense, sitting forward. "Yes?"

"What did you see when you came in here the second time, before you were struck on the head? What did you see on this table?"

She moistened her lips. "The lamp. The plate. With—with—"

"Yes?"

"With six match-stubs on it."

"How interesting." Ellery leaned toward them, his eyes narrow and completely dangerous. "Did you hear that? Six match-stubs. Well, let me go into this a little more scientifically. Andrea says that before she was struck, while the murderess was still here, she saw six half-burnt match-stubs on the plate. An obviously significant fact. It changes everything, doesn't it?" There was such an odd quality in his tone that they searched one another's faces for a confirmation of their own confused, timid, and terrible thought. His voice pulled them up again. "But this was before the cork was charred. Therefore those six matches had not been used for charring the cork, the deduction I made when I thought that all twenty matches had been ignited after the crime. No, no, six of them were used for a different purpose altogether. Well, if they weren't employed in charring the cork, why were they struck?"

"Why?" asked Ella Amity swiftly. "Why?"

"Simple—so simple. Too simple! Why are matches struck, generally speaking? Well, for conflagration? But nothing was consumed by fire— there was no debris or ashes anywhere on the premises, inside or out, as I've once before explained; nor to char the cork, for the knife was still in the body when Andrea says she saw the six stubs. So conflagration is out.

"For light, to find a way in the dark? The light was on in here, and outside there were no footprints except Gimball's. But Gimball would have needed no illumination outside; it was still daylight when he returned to get a knife in his chest. For heating? No ashes in the fireplace grate, and the broken-down old coal-stove is utterly useless. And there is no gas. For—improbably—torture? Logically, it is possible; this was a violent crime, and conceivably the victim might have been tortured to give information. But I once asked the coroner to discover if there were signs of burnt flesh on the victim. No, there were none. Then what the devil were those six matches used for?"

"It sounds screwy to me," muttered Jones.

"It would be," retorted Ellery, "if there weren't still one more possible use. It's the only one left. They were used for smoking."

"Smoking!" Ella Amity's lips parted. "But you said at the trial that they couldn't have been used for smoking!"

Ellery's eyes flickered. "I didn't know then that Andrea had seen six matches before the cork was charred. Let's leave that now. Andrea?"

"Yes?" Again the wariness, the stolidity, so alien to her.

Ellery snatched an envelope out of the discarded suitcase. He shook its contents onto the plate on the table. Half-burnt matchsticks poured out. They watched him, puzzled. He put all but six back in the envelope. "Come here, please."

Andrea rose wearily, trudged toward him with stiff limbs. "Yes?" she said again.

"It works out so neatly, doesn't it?" Ellery murmured with a trace of irony in his voice. "All right. You're back here at eight thirty-five that night, at the table, about to be hit on the head. Here are the six matches on the plate."

"Well?" Even her voice was tired, strangely old, as if in the midst of youth she had come to the end of the road.

"Look at this table, Andrea." At the steel in his tone she seemed surprised out of her stolidity, for she took a backward step, looked down, looked up at the table. "The lamp. The plate with the six matches. Was that all?"

"All?"

"Wasn't there something else? Think, Andrea! Think and look and tell the truth." He added in a merciless voice: "I want the truth, Andrea, this time."

Something in the way he said it touched a live nerve somewhere in her; she glanced about at the intent, stupid faces wildly. "I—" And then the most incredible thing happened. Her glance returned to the table, to the plate with the matches. It remained there for an instant and slowly, as if impelled by a force against which resistance was futile, moved to a spot three inches beyond the plate. A bare spot; there was nothing there. But Andrea saw something there; her face said so, her eyes, the clenching of her hands, the quick breath. Knowledge flooded through her like liquid through a blotter; it was as plain to those who watched as the distress, the indecision, the agony on her face. "Oh," she whispered. "Oh, dear—"

"What lie," and Ellery's voice cracked like a whip, "are you going to tell me now, Andrea?"

Her mother jumped up, stopped. Grosvenor Finch said something inarticulate. Senator Frueh was white. Burke Jones was gaping. Only the old man in the wheelchair sat unmoved, a corpse among living, fluttering beings.

"Lie—?" choked Andrea. "What do you mean? I was just going to tell you—"

"Another lie," Ellery said with terrible softness. "Spare us the pain of listening. I know now, young woman. I've known for some time. Lies, all lies. Lies about the six matches. Lies about being struck over the head. Lies about the 'warnings' you received. Lies about everything! Shall I tell you why you lied? Shall I tell you what factor you represent in this bloody equation? Shall I tell you—?"

"Good merciful God," said Andrea's mother hoarsely. On the right half of old Jasper Borden's blue lips there was a blind and groping protest. The others sat so still...

In the light of the lamp Andrea stood fast, cemented to the floor by what was so horribly evident to them all: her guilt. Her lips moved, like her grandfather's, but they made no sound. Then, with a swiftness that caught them—already steeped in horror—by complete surprise, Andrea streaked toward the side door and was gone.

It happened so suddenly that until the cough of an automobile engine came muffled to their ears they were too stupefied to stir. Even Ellery stood rooted to the spot. Then the motor roared and they heard a car thunder away, receding with incredible swiftness.

Senator Frueh screamed, "What's she done, damn her?" and scrambled toward the door. His cry snapped the spell; they awoke and boiled in a mass after him. In a moment the shack was empty except for the old man in the wheelchair. He sat alone, staring sightlessly with his one good eye at the open doorway.

Outside they stumbled over one another in their haste. In the darkness that tail-light of a car was rapidly diminishing on Lamberton Road in the direction of Duck Island. Everybody ran for a car. A voice shouted: "My car—it won't go!"

Other shouts arose. "Mine, too! What—?"

"The gas. Smell the gas," muttered Ellery. "Someone's drained the tanks…"

"That damned Angell!" There was a blistering oath. "He's in cahoots with her! The two of them—!"

And then someone else yelled: "Mine—there's still some…" They heard a flywheel turn over. A car shot out of the driveway and careened on two wheels into Lamberton Road. It was soon lost to sight behind the first car.

They grouped themselves in the road, straining into the darkness. Everything was unreal. Nothing seemed possible in this night, on this road, by this house, under this sky. They could only stare and breathe, stupidly, like animals.

Then Ellery said, "She can't get far. There must be some gas left in each tank. We'll pool the dregs and follow!"

The occupant of the second car, nerves singing, drove recklessly, intent on the speck of crimson light far ahead. The road was pitch-dark; they were somewhere on Duck Island already. The night, the sky, the road, seemed interminable. Crazily, that red speck in the distance danced, bobbed, fell, stopped. It grew larger and larger as the second car hurtled toward it. Something had happened. In Andrea's condition—panic-stricken, blind, driven by fear—it was a wonder she had managed to control the car at all.

The brakes of the second car squealed, the car staggered, stopped dead, throwing its driver against the wheel. Across the road Andrea's face, behind her wheel, was a cerulean smudge; she was slumped in the seat, staring hopelessly into the sea of the night. She had taken a huge sedan in her flight; it had run slightly off the road and smashed into a tree. The only light came from the stars, and they were far away.

"Andrea!" She did not seem to hear; her right hand stole to her throat and pressed. "Andrea, why did you run away?"

She was afraid now, very plainly afraid. Her head turned slowly, pivoted by her terror. In the faint light her eyes glowed with it. The pursuer stood calmly in the road between the two cars, hands hanging loosely. "Andrea, my dear. You needn't be afraid of me. God knows I'm tired of it all. I wouldn't harm you. If you only knew." The dim face between the two cars stirred, settled, was still. "They'll be along soon. Andrea, you did remember seeing, on the table that night, the…?"

Andrea's lips moved soundlessly, as if even her vocal cords had been paralyzed by the pressure of her fear.

Far up the road a car was coming, swimming in dark dust. Its headlights, stuck on the tips of the tubular beams like the antennæ of an insect, probed the darkness, lightened the sky a little.

"Before they come." The speaker stopped, sighed with a childlike weariness. "I wanted you to know I never intended you any harm. I mean, after you walked in on me that night so unexpectedly. I didn't know it was you when I struck. Then, when you fell... I couldn't kill you, Andrea. That would have been insane. I killed Joe Gimball because he was no longer fit to live. Only death could wipe out what he had done, and someone had to send him along. Why not I? Well, it's done. It's over. This man thinks you killed Joe, ran away because you are guilty. I know why you ran away, Andrea—because just now you remembered what it was you saw on the table that night.

"Of course I can't permit you to keep quiet any longer when you yourself are suspected. I thought I could be clever; I didn't see why I should sacrifice my life in taking a life which had to be taken. I see now that I should have done it simply, without plan, and then given myself up. It would have been—well, cleaner." There was a wry smile on that steady face hanging in the road. Andrea cried out suddenly, a sobbing cry torn from her throat not by horror but by pity.

Something flashed in the hand so near her. There was a lightning movement from inside the sedan, simultaneous with the calm words, "Goodbye, Andrea. Remember me—well, remember me. I hope... she will remember me." The hand flashed again, upward this time.

Andrea screamed, "Oh, don't!"

Bill Angell roared from the back of the second car: "Andrea, for God's sake! Down!"

Men were spewed forth from the side of the road behind the sedan, guns in their hands. The rear door of the sedan swished open; Bill Angell sprang down to the road.

The face of the pursuer on the road convulsed; a finger tightened, there was a stunning report, smoke, a flash of fire. But the figure merely staggered, it did not fall; an expression of immense surprise came over that handsome face, to be replaced instantly by bitterness and then determination. "Sold out!" It was a mutter.

Then the figure leaped forward, dropping the useless revolver, and grappled with Bill, groping fiercely for the weapon in Bill's hand. They

231

struggled all over the road, brilliantly illuminated by the headlights of the third car, just roaring up. The men who had materialized from the side of the road were upon them like ants, swarming, clutching, shouting.

There was another report; as if it were a signal, the struggle ceased, the men fell away. There was silence under the dark sky. The people pouring out of the third car stopped in their tracks. This time there was no surprise on the face of the executioner of Joseph Kent Gimball; only peace. The figure lay peacefully in the road, relaxed in death, asleep forever.

Andrea said stiffly: "Bill. Oh, Bill. You've killed—"

Bill was panting, drawing huge gulps of the night air into his lungs. As his chest heaved he looked down at the quiet figure. Bill's revolver was still clutched in its fingers. "Suicide. Fought me for the gun. I couldn't prevent it. Dead?"

Chief De Jong was squatting in the road, listening with his head on the motionless chest. Then he rose, looking grave. "Dead, all right. Mr. Queen?"

Ellery ran up. He demanded abruptly, "Are you all right, Andrea?"

"All right." Her voice was muffled. Suddenly she fumbled with the front door of the sedan, slipped down, stumbled weeping into Bill's arms.

"Mr. Queen?" said Chief De Jong again; he seemed embarrassed. "We got it all down—stenographer took it from the side of the road. It's a confession, all right, and you've prevented… well, I guess Pollinger and I owe you an apology."

"The one to be congratulated," said Ellery, "is this young woman." He pressed the cold fingers clasped about Bill's neck. "That was well done, Andrea; well done, my dear. The only thing I was doubtful about was our friend's reaction to your flight. It might have ended in tragedy for you. I prevented that by sending some friends of mine to the right place well in advance, for a little job of substituting blank cartridges for lethal ones. Well done, Andrea; you followed my instructions to the letter."

The group at the third car said nothing, did nothing, nothing at all. They just stared at the body lying in the road.

*

"Naturally," said Ellery on Monday morning, "although I'm a busy man I wouldn't have missed this for the world."

They were in Judge Ira V. Menander's private chambers at the Mercer County Court House. Certain formalities had prevented the release of Lucy the previous day, Sunday. But this morning Bill had made a motion before Judge Menander for a new trial on the ground of "new evidence" in which Prosecutor Pollinger had automatically joined. The judge had thereupon set aside the old conviction of Lucy Wilson, Pollinger had moved to discontinue the indictment, the motion had been granted, and Bill with Andrea clinging to him had hurried across the Bridge of Sighs into the adjoining prison with an official order to the warden for Lucy's release.

Now they were back at the old jurist's request, Lucy quite bewildered at the suddenness of her freedom, dumb and flushed with happiness. Paul Pollinger was with them, looking sheepish.

"I have been told, Mr. Queen," remarked Judge Menander after he had made his apologies to Lucy for the ordeal she had gone through, "that there is an extraordinary story connected with your solution of this case. I confess I'm a little curious. Yours seems to be a strange destiny, young man. I've heard tales about you. What magic did you perform this time?"

"Magic," muttered Pollinger. "That's what it was, all right."

Ellery glanced at Bill, Lucy, Andrea; they sat on the Judge's leather sofa with their hands joined, like three children. "Magic? For old hands, gentlemen, that's naive. The ancient formula: pick out the facts and put them together. Mix thoroughly with plenty of logic. Add a dash of imagination. Presto!"

"It sounds delicious," said Judge Menander dryly, "but not very informative."

"By the way," said Pollinger, "how much of that little scene Saturday night was planned? I'm still sore at the way you and De Jong ignored me."

"All of it. It was our job, anyway, Pollinger. When Andrea told me the story of the six matches, I saw through the whole fantastic business. I could develop a logical case, but none that would satisfy your damned courts of law. So it was necessary to be subtle. My criminal had to be trapped. It had been evident to me all along that one of the most curious characteristics of this criminal had been a really remarkable solicitude for Andrea. Now, if Andrea possessed knowledge dangerous to the criminal on the night of the crime due to something she saw on that table, why didn't the criminal take her life as well as Gimball's? Then the 'warnings', the dainty chloroforming! Another killer would have resorted at the last to really desperate measures against Andrea; this one was content with mere admonitions, threats made empty by the lack of force employed. So, I reasoned, if the criminal was solicitous of Andrea's welfare, my logical plan was to put Andrea in danger.

"The best way to do this was to make it seem that I thought her guilty of the crime. The criminal could do only one of two things after this: kill Andrea to prevent her from finally disclosing the dangerous knowledge she had; or confessing to the crime to save Andrea from further complicity, which was—under the circumstances—the more plausible possibility. I didn't believe the criminal would attempt her life because of past performances; however, I took no chances and had the teeth drawn from the criminal's weapon. And, of course, I had De Jong and his men waiting at the place planned for the 'breakdown' of the 'escape' car, and Bill here waiting outside the shack in the car itself, hidden from sight and armed. He didn't go to Trenton; that was just an excuse to get him out of the shack; he raced his motor while some of De Jong's men emptied the necessary gasoline tanks and then left for the rendezvous. I had instructed Andrea beforehand in her role; told her just what to do in the shack and when to do it; arranged for Andrea's and the criminal's car to be let alone while the others were tampered with; and thereby insured the criminal's following Andrea a little in advance of the others and providing an opportunity for the confession to Andrea."

"Then you knew in advance who was the guilty party?" asked the prosecutor.

"Certainly. The plan could not have been concocted without that vital knowledge to build on. How would I have known whose car to let alone if I hadn't known who killed Gimball?"

"It seems like a nightmare now," sighed Andrea. Bill said something to her and she laid her head on his shoulder.

"Well, Mr. Queen," said the Judge, "when am I going to hear that story?"

"If Your Honor please, right now. Where was I?" Ellery repeated for the benefit of the old gentleman and the prosecutor the reasoning he had gone through in the shack on Saturday night. "So, you see, it was evident that the six burnt matches Andrea saw before the criminal charred the cork had been used for smoking. The logical question, then, was: By whom had those six matches been used for smoking?

"On Andrea's first visit to the shack at eight o'clock that night, there was no one in the place, and the plate on the table, she said, was quite clean and empty. At that time Gimball's car was parked on the side driveway. When Andrea returned at eight thirty-five, the car was still there, and another car stood before the house, on the main driveway. And inside the shack the plate contained the six burnt match-stubs.

"Clearly, then, those six matches were burned in Andrea's absence, between eight and eight thirty-five. Who was in the house during Andrea's absence? Gimball, of course, returned to be knifed. And the evidence of the tire tracks established that the other car, the Ford, was the only car to come while Andrea was away. No one came on foot: for there were no footprints in the mud except Gimball's. Therefore, since Gimball was killed in the interim between Andrea's two visits, and only one car arrived in that interim, and no one came on foot, the criminal must have come in that one car. Therefore, the only ones who could have burned those six matches were Gimball and his killer.

"Now, if the six matches had been used for smoking, I could eliminate Gimball at once. He never smoked—scads of testimony and evidence to that effect. That left only the criminal.

"Theoretically, of course, it was possible that Andrea had used the six matches herself, despite what she told us to the contrary. But it was she who found the match-stubs and it was upon her story that the entire logical structure of my solution rested. If I doubted the veracity of her story I simply could not proceed. So, working on the assumption that she was telling the truth, I eliminated her. Obviously, if she came in and found those matches, then it wasn't she who had used them."

The old jurist's eyes narrowed. "But, my dear Mr. Queen—"

"Yes, yes, I know," said Ellery hastily. "Trust the judiciary to put a finger on the weakness. But it isn't a weakness, as I shall demonstrate later. Let me go on. I knew now that the criminal had smoked in that shack before Andrea's arrival at eight thirty-five, and had used six matches in the process. Well, what had the criminal smoked? I saw at once how important and at the same time arresting the question was."

"Important," smiled the judge, "but to me baffling."

"Had the criminal smoked cigarets? Quite impossible."

"How the deuce," demanded Pollinger, "do you arrive at that?"

Ellery sighed. "Six half-burnt matches meant as many as six cigaret butts; cigarets scarcely ever require more than a single match. Six matches, well burnt down as they were, surely implied a multiplicity of cigarets, if cigarets were smoked. Very well. What had the smoker done with those butts? Where had they been ground out? We know that the criminal used the plate as an ashtray, for Andrea found the six burnt matches there. Wouldn't the criminal have ground cigaret butts out in the plate as well? But Andrea saw no butts or ashes in that plate at a time when the killer could not have anticipated being interrupted and therefore would have had no reason to hide the butts elsewhere.

"If the killer had been smoking cigarets before Andrea's arrival, the butts and ashes should have been either in the plate on the table, on the rug, in the fireplace, or under the windows outside the shack. But they weren't in the plate or on the table; there wasn't a trace of even a single butt or the slightest speck of ash on the rug or anywhere inside the shack—not a shred of tobacco or anything else, for that matter. There were no burns on the carpet, such as might have been made by a foot grinding out a cigaret; and such burns would have been left even if the criminal had ground the cigarets out on the rug and then taken away the ashes and butts so ground. As for the area beneath the windows outside the shack, none were found in the muddy earth or I should have been informed, and I was definitely told that there were no footprints anywhere outside the shack except Gimball's, indicating that the murderer had not thrown butts or ashes through a window and then retrieved them before fleeing from the scene.

"And so it was quite clear, after this analysis, that although the criminal had smoked before Andrea's arrival, it had not been cigarets. That left," continued Ellery with a shrug, "only a cigar or a pipe as possibilities."

"How did you eliminate?" asked Pollinger curiously.

"Well, obviously a cigar would have left ashes, too, although not necessarily a butt. The same analysis that eliminated ashes in the case of cigarets would eliminate ashes in the case of a cigar. On the other hand, a pipe would leave no ashes at all, unless it were knocked out to dispose of the dottle, which wasn't necessary; and besides the use of six matches was consistent with the theory of a pipe. Pipes are always going out and having to be relit. It wasn't essential for me, however, to pin it down specifically to either a pipe or a cigar. The true significance arose from the mere elimination of cigarets, per se."

Pollinger frowned. "Yes, yes, of course. I see that now."

"It's obvious, certainly. If the criminal smoked a cigar or a pipe, then the criminal was a man!"

"Beautiful." Judge Menander nodded enthusiastically. "Quite so. A woman would naturally be ruled out by that line of reasoning. But all the evidence indicated that the criminal was a woman."

"Then all the evidence," retorted Ellery, "was wrong. If you rely on logic, you must stick by it or fall back on mere guesswork. The deduction pointed indisputably to a man; the evidence indicated a woman; the evidence, then, must have been either misleading or false. The evidence said a heavily veiled woman committed the crime; the deduction said; no, it was a man; therefore it was a man dressed as a woman, and the veil becomes important and significant as the essential cloak to a man's undisguisable features.

"As a matter of fact, the more I thought over this deduction the more convinced I became of its truth. There was at least one psychological confirmation of the sex of the criminal—a small point, but it is on small points that the world's most startling discoveries are built."

"What was that?" demanded the judge.

"It was the curious phenomenon of the lipstick that wasn't used," smiled Ellery.

They were puzzled. Pollinger scrubbed his chin and said: "The lipstick that wasn't used? By George, Queen, that sounds like something out of Doyle."

"A handsome compliment. Surely it's evident? We knew that the criminal, who at the time we supposed to be a woman, found it necessary in an emergency to write a note to Andrea. We knew that there were no ordinary writing implements available—I'll take that up later—and that 'she' was forced to char a cork in order to write. A laborious process, eh? Well, didn't it occur to you that every woman, almost without exception, carries with her a natural writing instrument? A lipstick? Why go through the slow and unsatisfactory process of charring a cork when all she had to do was open her bag, take out her lipstick, and write? The answer was, psychologically, that she had no lipstick. This in itself pointed to the fact that the 'woman' wasn't a woman at all, but a man."

"Well, suppose by chance this was really a woman and she didn't carry a lipstick?" argued Judge Menander. "It's possible."

"Very well, it's possible. But there was Andrea lying on the floor, unconscious! Didn't Andrea have a bag? Didn't Andrea, a woman, carry a woman's natural weapon, a lipstick? Of course she did; it was unnecessary to mention it. Then why didn't this 'woman' open Andrea's bag and borrow Andrea's lipstick to write with? The answer again was that 'she' didn't think of it. But a woman would have thought of it, being a woman. Again a psychological indication of a man."

"But lipsticks in these modern days of scientific criminology," objected Pollinger, "can be traced by the chemical formula."

"Can they? How nice. But then why didn't the criminal use Andrea's lipstick? Even if it were traced, it would be traced back to Andrea, not the criminal. No, no, no matter how you look at it, there is still psychological confirmation in this point that the criminal was a man masquerading as a woman. We now have, in fact, two points of description in the murderer's portrait: he is a man, and he smokes most probably a pipe."

"Beautiful, beautiful," said the Judge again.

"Now," said Ellery briskly. "The use of paper-matches inevitably suggested a match-packet. I asked Andrea specifically if she couldn't remember having seen anything else on the table—with a packet in mind. Of course, the criminal might have put the packet away in his pocket, but then again he might not have done so. Remember again that Andrea's appearance that night was unexpected and came directly after the crime when the murderer was still not finished with the bloody work at hand. Yes, said Andrea, she did remember that when she saw the six matches in the plate there was also a closed paper match-packet on the table near it. Perfect! It gave me the last clue."

"I confess," said the Judge ruefully, "that I don't see how."

"Well, perhaps you aren't aware of a further fact which also came out in Andrea's story the other day. That was that when she recovered consciousness, the packet was gone. Now, if it was gone, the criminal had taken it away. Why?"

A little flicker of interest disturbed the beatific expression on Bill's face. "Why not, El? Smokers do that all the time. Especially pipe-smokers; they're always running short of matches. They use the packet and put it right back in their pockets."

"Touché," murmured Ellery, "but not in a vital spot, my son. Putting it back in your pocket implies that there are still matches left in the packet, n'est-ce pas?"

"Of course!"

"But you see," said Ellery gently, "there couldn't have been any matches left in the packet the criminal first used."

"Hold on, young man," said the Judge in haste. "This seems to be the magic I referred to. How do you arrive at that remarkable conclusion?"

"By a simple process. How many matches were found in the plate— all the matches, those used for smoking and those used for charring the cork?"

"Twenty, I believe."

"How many matches are there in these cheap, common, universal match-packets?"

"Twenty."

"Precisely. What does that mean? That means that at least one packet of matches was fully depleted by the criminal in the shack that night. Even if the criminal didn't start with a full, fresh packet but with, say, a packet already started and having only ten matches left,

240

and then pulled out another packet to complete the total of twenty found, the first packet would have been emptied in the process.

"Well, there we were with one empty packet. Yet the criminal took it away with him. Why? People don't do that, you know. When you use up a packet, you throw it away."

"Ordinary people, perhaps," retorted Pollinger, "but you're forgetting that this man was a murderer on the scene of his crime, Queen. He might have taken his packet away out of sheer caution—not to leave a clue."

"Aptly phrased," murmured Ellery with a sly grin. "Not to leave a clue. But how would an ordinary packet of matches leave a clue, Pollinger? These things are used for advertising anything and everything under the sun. You may say that the product or place advertised on the cover has an address which the murderer might feel would leave a trail to his place of origin or recent movements. Indefensible; you can't base a single conclusion on the address of a match-packet advertisement. In New York you may be handed a packet originating in Akron, Tampa, or Evansville. I've been given packets with my purchases of cigarets and tobacco emanating from as far away as San Francisco. No, no, it wasn't the address or the advertisement on the packet that forced the murderer to take it away." Ellery paused. "Yet take it away he did. Why? What other kind of clue was he afraid the leaving of the packet might give? Obviously a clue, direct or indirect, that would lead to himself—a clue to his identity." The two men nodded soberly; the three on the sofa sat forward.

"Now, remember this. From the beginning the murderer was afraid that Andrea had seen something damning on the scene of the crime. It couldn't have been his face or figure; he had struck her from behind and she had never had an opportunity to glimpse the person who assaulted her. Yet he must have considered what Andrea saw of terrible importance: he took time out on the scene of his crime, still smoking with the blood of the victim, to go through that slow and difficult process of writing the note; he wired her another warning the day after the crime; he sent her a more subtle warning only last Saturday when he felt the trail getting hot. These things were fraught with peril for him, even though he negotiated them without detection. Nevertheless, he persisted in warning Andrea to keep quiet. Why? Why? What had she seen, or what did he fear she had seen, that made him so apprehensive? It could only have been that match-packet which he had taken away and which she had observed on the table with the six match-stubs just before she was struck on the head.

"But we're looking for a reason for his having taken the packet away. There's only one feasible reason. The packet was closed. He knew that; it was lying on the table in full view. Whatever it was that worried him about that packet, it was something simple, direct, seen at once, understood in a flash, and connected with the outside of the packet. Was he afraid she had recognized it as belonging to him? Implausible; people don't ordinarily 'recognize' match-packets, and even if they do anyone else might be using an identical one. So it could only have been that there was an insignia, a monogram perhaps, some simple inscription on the cover of that packet which Andrea could identify at once with a specific individual."

"It's so funny, all this," said Andrea with a catch in her throat. "To think—"

"The irony of it," said Ellery grimly, "was that Andrea didn't remember anything special about the cover of that packet. She saw it, but it didn't register in her mind, upset and scared as she was at the time. It was the other day, while I was planning our little drama for Saturday night, that I recalled it to her mind by a direct question after I'd deduced the answer; and then, for the first time, she remembered. But the criminal couldn't take the chance that she hadn't seen. After all, he had observed her staring directly at it. He never doubted for an instant that she had read what was on it and knew his identity as the murderer. And so I now had another element in the description of the murderer. He was a man. He smoked a pipe. He used match-packets with some sort of identifying inscription on their covers."

"Remarkable," muttered Judge Menander, when Ellery paused to light a cigaret. "But surely that isn't all? I still don't see—"

"All? Scarcely. It was merely the first link in the chain. The second was forged by that charred cork. I've demonstrated in the past that if the criminal used the cork as a writing instrument, then clearly there was no more practical writing instrument at hand that he thought of. I add this last, of course, because of the lipstick which he didn't think of using, being a man. This meant that he himself carried no pen or pencil on his person at the time—remember, the necessity for writing the note arose unexpectedly—or, if he did have a pen or pencil, there was something about it that made him unwilling to use it." Ellery paused again. "Pollinger, do you recall my little extemporaneous effusion shortly after the crime, when I pointed out that you could not say who had been killed, Gimball or Wilson?"

Pollinger made a wry face. "I do. I remember you said it would prove important in the solution."

"How important even I didn't grasp at the time. It's proved incalculably vital in the solution. Without this knowledge—in which personality the man was killed—no final logical elimination could have been made. For this knowledge led to the most revealing characteristic of the murderer. The picture of the murderer would have been vague and meaningless lacking the answer to this question. I can't stress too much the totality of the point."

"You make it sound portentous," observed the Judge.

"It has proved portentous to the murderer," replied Ellery dryly. "Now. In what personality had our victim been killed: as Gimball or as Wilson? I was now in a position to answer the question.

"Follow me: Since the murderer had killed his victim and framed Lucy Wilson for the murder, then he must have known that Lucy Wilson would be believed by the police to possess a powerful motive for the crime. For no one frames an innocent person without knowing that that person has a conceivable and credible motive. The mere fact that

Lucy was the wife of the victim didn't make her in any sense a logical victim of the frame-up. Well, what were Lucy Wilson's 'motives'? What motives, in fact, were actually ascribed to her during her trial? It was pointed out by our clever friend here that: one, she could have learned just before the crime that Joseph Wilson was really Joseph Kent Gimball, having deceived her about his true identity and other life for ten years, and that this knowledge would turn her love to hatred; two, that by his death she stood to gain a million dollars. These, it was said, were Lucy Wilson's motives—there were no others, for she and Wilson had led an ideal domestic existence. But for the murderer to have visualized these motives for Lucy Wilson meant that the murderer was aware of them. He knew, then, that Joseph Wilson was really Joseph Kent Gimball; he knew, then, that at the death of Joseph Wilson, Lucy Wilson would be paid the million dollars of Joseph Kent Gimball's insurance. To know these two facts the murderer therefore must have learned somehow that his intended victim was both Gimball and Wilson, that the man had been leading a double life for many years.

"But if the murderer knew his intended victim was leading a double life, he also knew that he was killing not Joseph Kent Gimball alone, not Joseph Wilson alone, but both. The man was murdered, then, in neither personality exclusively, but in the two collectively; and how important this is I leave you to judge."

"I'm afraid I'll have to leave it to you," grinned Pollinger.

"Pshaw! If the murderer killed Gimball-Wilson, the man of two lives, knowing that he was killing Gimball-Wilson, the inevitable question was: How had the murderer learned of those two lives? How did he know that Gimball of New York, the society man, was also Wilson of Philadelphia, the itinerant peddler? For years Gimball had taken every precaution to keep his double life a dead secret; for years no one suspected; for years apparently Gimball made no mistake and went unsuspected; and Wilson kept his Gimball identity equally secret for the same length of time. He had told Bill here in so many words, according to the story Bill told De Jong and me on the night of the crime, that no one he knew was aware of the existence of the shack. Yet the murderer chose Halfway House for the scene of the crime. True, Gimball meant to reveal his secret to Bill and Andrea that night, but he was murdered before he could carry out his intention. Had he meant to tell a third person, he would have certainly told that third person no earlier than the night of the murder. Yet the murderer knew the whole story. How, then, had the murderer learned it?"

"That was the logical question, of course," nodded the Judge.

"And there was a logical answer to it," drawled Ellery.

"But couldn't he have learned the story," demanded Bill from the sofa, "by sheer accident?"

"Possibly, of course, but very unlikely. Gimball, we know on good authority, never relaxed his vigilance. The two telegrams, had they fallen into the hands of the murderer, would have revealed nothing but the location of Halfway House—I love that phrase! But if the location of the place had been the only thing the murderer learned, it would not have been enough. The murderer must have known well in advance of the day Gimball sent the telegrams—the day he died—all about the Gimball personalities. He had to know not only the location of Halfway House but the identity of Gimball's real wife, where she lived, something of her character and background. He had to have time to plan the crime, to find out about Lucy's car, to learn her Saturday-night movie habit so that he could depend on her probable lack of an alibi, and so on. All this would have taken time. Not a day—perhaps more than a week, if the man were investigating surreptitiously as he must have. No, Bill, hardly an accidental discovery."

"Then how?" cried Pollinger.

"How? There was one means by which the murderer could have learned which was so plain I couldn't ignore it. While it's impossible by pure logic to eliminate beyond doubt the murderer's accidental discovery of Gimball's dual-life background, we can discard the unlikely accident-theory for a positive indication, which clearly exists. Gimball was slain very shortly after he decided to make a clean breast of his predicament and tell the story of his double life to representatives of both his families. When you consider that his first step along the road to confession was to change his insurance-policy beneficiary from his false wife Jessica to his true wife Lucy, the fact becomes too overwhelming to be coincidence. Don't you see? At last there was a record of his double life—nine records, so to speak: the name and address of the new beneficiary on the original application and on the eight revised policies! And then, on the heels of these records, he was murdered. How could I doubt that it was by this means that the murderer had learned that Gimball was Wilson and Wilson Gimball? Anyone who learned of this change, or had access to the policies, could have investigated; learned the secret from the name and address; followed Gimball on one of his stopovers at Halfway House; and in two weeks discovered all that was necessary to plan the murder and implicate Lucy as the murderess."

Lucy was crying softly; Andrea sat up and put her arm around the weeping woman. At the spectacle Bill began to smile rather fatuously, like a proud parent watching the antics of his two children.

"And so," said Ellery, "I now had a complete portrait of the criminal. I'll give the characteristics numerically.

"1. The criminal was a man.

"2. The criminal was a smoker, probably a pipe-smoker, certainly heavily addicted to the weed, for only one chronically in the grip of tobacco would have resorted to it on the scene of an intended crime while waiting for his victim.

"3. At the time of the murder the criminal carried a monogrammed or similarly identifiable match-packet.

"4. The criminal had motive against both Gimball and Mrs. Wilson.

"5. The criminal had no writing implement on his person, or the one he did have he preferred not to use because its use might in some way be traceable to him.

"6. The criminal came most probably from the Gimball side of the fence—his deliberate framing of Lucy implied that.

"7. The criminal had a tender feeling for Andrea, indicated by the mildness of his attacks despite great provocation. The criminal had an even tenderer feeling for Andrea's mother, for he didn't once attempt to carry out his threat to harm her—an attempt which, had it been made even as a feint, would have very effectually sealed Andrea's mouth forever.

"8. The blow which killed Gimball, said the coroner, was delivered with a right hand. So the criminal used his right hand.

"9. The criminal knew that Gimball had changed the beneficiary of his policy."

Ellery smiled. "In mathematics, you know, you can do a lot of tricks with the number nine. Now let me show you a little trick I was able to do in a murder-case with the same number. With nine definite characteristics of the murderer, the analysis became child's-play. All I had to do was to go through my list of suspects and test each one against the nine characteristics."

"Fascinating," beamed Judge Menander. "Do you mean to say that by this method you can reach a definite conclusion?"

"By this method," retorted Ellery, "I can eliminate every suspect but one. I'll discuss them one by one.

"In the first place, of course, point number one eliminates in a single swoop all women. The criminal had to be a man. Who are the men? Well, old Jasper Borden first…"

"Oh!" gasped Andrea. "You horrid thing! Do you mean to say that you suspected Grandfather for a single instant?"

Ellery grinned. "My dear child, everyone is suspect in an objective analysis; we can't afford to be sentimental because one person is old and decrepit and another young and beautiful. As I say, Jasper Borden. Well, you say, he's an invalid; he never leaves his house; this was the crime of an active man; and all that is quite true. But let's pretend that this is a detective story where Mr. Borden would probably have been shamming and slipping out of his Park Avenue apartment quite spryly at ungodly hours and doing all sorts of dreadful things under cover of the night. How do we stand, logically speaking, on Jasper Borden? Well, he is eliminated on point two completely: he does not smoke any more, as he told me before a witness—his grim nurse, who certainly was in a position to deny this if it hadn't been true. Besides, since this isn't a detective story, we know that Mr. Borden is a semi-paralytic and could not possibly have committed the crime."

"Next, Bill Angell."

Bill half rose from the sofa. "Why, you damned Judas!" he grinned. "You don't mean to tell me you actually considered me a possibility?"

"Of course I did," said Ellery calmly. "What did I know about you, Bill? I hadn't seen you for over ten years—you might have become a hardened criminal in the interval, you know. But seriously, you were eliminated on several counts: points four, five, and six. That is, while you might have had motive against Gimball, you certainly had no motive against Lucy, your own sister, whom the criminal framed. Five, the criminal had no usable writing implement on his person. Ah! but you did!"

"How on earth," said Bill, astonished, "do you know that?"

"You gullible people," sighed Ellery. "By the simplest method in the world—I saw them. Remember? I even mentioned in our little chat in the taproom of the Stacy-Trent that, from the pocketful of nicely sharpened pencils I saw, you must be a busy man. Well, that was only a matter of minutes after the crime. If you had a pocketful of pencils and were the criminal, you would certainly have used one in writing the note to Andrea. Pencils, with all our science, are untraceable. And point six, the criminal came from the Gimball side of the fence. Obviously you didn't. So you were eliminated logically."

"Well, I'll be damned," said Bill feebly.

"Now, our pompous friend Senator Frueh. But what have we? An amazing thing! Senator Frueh, I find to my astonishment, fits all the characteristics! I mean, conceivably. But in his case alone one fact is sufficient to eliminate him which doesn't even appear on the list of characteristics, although I might have included it, at that. He wears a beard. Nothing phony about that brush! It's been his pride and joy for years; it has decorated newspapers for a generation. But no man with a beard as long as his—it reaches to his chest, remember—could possibly have concealed it, even with a veil. There was one witness who saw the veiled 'woman' quite clearly: the garageman. He could not have avoided noticing a beard if the 'woman' wore one. The veil didn't reach below the chin; the beard would have shown. Besides, the 'woman', said the witness, was husky and large; Frueh is short and fat. And even if Frueh had shaved off his beard for the crime, he exhibited one afterward. Was it false? Most improbable, with all the worrying he does to it. If there's still any doubt in your mind, the next time you see it just pull it.

"Now friend Burke Jones. Eliminated at once on point eight. There could have been no chicanery in the report that he had suffered a broken arm in a game of polo—it was reported in the papers and obviously had been witnessed by hundreds of people. But it was Jones's right arm that was broken. The criminal delivered the lethal blow with his right arm. Jones couldn't physically, therefore, have committed the crime.

"The portrait was complete," said Ellery quietly, "and so was the process of elimination. I had painted the picture of only one person, who fitted all nine characteristics so perfectly that there could be no doubt whatever. That person, of course, was Grosvenor Finch."

There was a long interlude, during which the only sound was Lucy's tired and curiously happy sobbing.

"Remarkable," said Judge Menander again, clearing his throat.

"Not at all. Sheer common sense. How did Finch fit?

"1. He was a man.

"2. He was addicted to smoking, and a pipe at that; the day I visited his office his secretary, Miss Zachary, offered me some of his personal pipe-tobacco, blended for him by a famous tobacconist. Now only a

249

hopelessly incorrigible pipe-smoker goes to the length of having his tobacco specially blended for him.

"3. He possessed match-packets even more distinctive than logic had indicated! For his secretary that same day, when I approved vocally of Finch's tobacco, promised to have the tobacconist Finch patronized send me some—with, she took the liberty of adding, Finch's compliments! The tobacconist, Pierre of Fifth Avenue, eventually delivered a pound; and with it came a box of match-packets with my name printed on each one! Pierre was even kind enough to add in his note that this was his usual custom. If he sent match-packets with all deliveries of tobacco to his customers, and mine had come with my name printed on the covers of the packets, and this was Pierre's usual procedure, then obviously Finch possessed numerous match-packets with his name on them! Not a monogram, not an insignia, but his name in full. No wonder he was worried. No wonder he snatched that empty packet away. He had every reason to believe that Andrea had seen the name Grosvenor Finch on its cover."

"Good Lord," exclaimed Pollinger; he threw up his hands.

"4. The criminal had motive against both Gimball and Mrs. Wilson. This followed as a result of the criminal's learning about Gimball's double life, which I shall come to in a moment. But, knowing this, it is clear that anyone from the Gimball side of the fence would have reason to wish the death of Gimball, the author of Jessica's shame, and might seek to revenge himself on Lucy, the living symbol of Gimball's double life. And Finch was very close to Jessica.

"5. The writing implement? Curious note. The same day I visited Finch's office he offered me a cheque as a retainer for investigating the crime for the National Life. Before my eyes he wrote on that cheque with a fountain-pen I saw him take from his pocket. When he showed me the cheque the only thing in script was his signature written in green ink. Green ink! Distinctive; not at all usual. He could not afford to take the chance of writing the note on the scene of the crime in that ink.

So, he had to use other means. Unquestionably, he had the pen with him. Now that he's dead, we shall never know the exact truth about how he was dressed that night, but the probabilities are that he rolled his trousers up and slipped a woman's dress over himself as he was, fully dressed. The coat he put on would conceal the neckline. That's how he came to have matches and his pipe with him—they must have been in the pocket of the male clothing beneath the feminine outer attire.

"6. Certainly he came from the Gimball side of the fence. He had known both the Gimball and Borden families intimately for years.

"7. That he had a tender feeling for Andrea is unquestionable— we've had repeated evidences of it from his actions. As for Andrea's mother, well, there are no specific facts to base the opinion on, but his solicitude for her, his constant attendance on her since Gimball's death, were clear enough implications of a fondness that may have been even more."

"That's true, I think," said Andrea in a low voice. "I'm sure he—he was in love with her. From 'way back. He was a bachelor, of course. Mother's often told me that he never married because she married my father—my real father, Richard Paine Monstelle. And when father died and mother married Joe…"

"Love for your mother was the only plausible reason I could ascribe to Finch as the murderer of your stepfather, Andrea. Discovering that Gimball had betrayed your mother into an illegal marriage, that he was spending most of his time with another woman in another city, that his own sacrifice had been in vain, Finch decided to kill your mother's betrayer.

"8. The criminal was right-handed, or at least used his right hand in striking the lethal blow. This was rather indeterminate in adapting Finch to the complete portrait, but in the light of the overwhelming evidence of the other eight points, it was unimportant. At least it was possible for Finch to have used his right hand.

"9. The last point and in many ways the most important. That Finch knew of the change of beneficiary of the million-dollar policy.

The point was simply resolved. Who knew of this change of beneficiary? Two persons. One was Gimball himself. But Gimball had told no one; I've been over that ground already. The other was Finch. Finch, and Finch alone of the possible murderers, had known of the beneficiary change before the crime."

Ellery smoked thoughtfully. "You know, this last point wasn't all plain sailing. It presented certain difficulties of theory. Access to the application and the policies was the only way in which someone could have discovered the clue to Gimball's double life. But from the time of the change until Gimball deposited the sealed envelope with Bill, only the insurance companies involved had access to the policies. We can eliminate the insurance-company employees who performed the clerical work involved on the ground of sheer improbability. But we cannot eliminate Finch, who on his own confession was aware of the change, having been notified by his company in his capacity as personal 'broker' for Gimball that an application for change-of-beneficiary had been received.

"The problem that naturally arises is: Despite Finch's protestations to the contrary, did he really tell someone else of the change of beneficiary, thus placing another person in possession of the vital clue? I will ignore the fact that Finch, in insisting that he did not, made the most damaging statement possible under the circumstances, since he was virtually naming himself, and himself alone, as the sole possessor of the vital knowledge. Had he been conscious of the implications, he certainly would have managed to tell someone else, just to spread the possibilities of guilt.

"But even if you choose not to believe him, whom could he theoretically have told? A woman? Mrs. Gimball—the then Mrs. Gimball, for ex ample? But as a woman she is eliminated from suspicion; the criminal was a man. Had she told another woman in turn, this other woman would be eliminated for the same reason. Had she told another man, or had Finch told another man directly, then we merely have to see if that man, or any man involved in the case, fits the characteristics of the criminal as we have now developed them. Well, what happens? There is no man except Finch who fits those characteristics completely. So, by a circuitous route, we arrive at the conclusion that Finch told no one; or if he did, his telling had no bearing on the murder as it subsequently developed.

"What followed I have already reconstructed: his suspicions, his probable secret visit to Philadelphia, his discovery of the background, his discovery of Halfway House, his plan for the crime and frame-up, and so on."

"The masquerade, of course," muttered Pollinger, "was necessary."

"Oh, yes. If Lucy was to seem to have committed the crime, there must be evidence that a woman drove her coupe. The veil, of course, he had to use to mask his masculine features, and naturally he couldn't speak to the garageman that evening because his voice would have given the masquerade away. As I pointed out once before, he deliberately stopped for gas there to leave an open trail to Lucy! Not being a lawyer, he didn't realize how flimsily circumstantial a case he was weaving about her; if he hadn't luckily found that paper-cutter and Lucy hadn't handled it the night before in her home I don't doubt that she would have been acquitted."

"Without the fingerprint evidence I should have thrown the case out at the first motion for dismissal by defense counsel," said the Judge, shaking his head. "As a matter of fact, even with that evidence the case was weak—I beg your pardon, Paul, but I think you realize that, too. It was a poor jury, I'm afraid. It all came down to a matter of believing Mrs. Wilson, and why they didn't believe her story I don't know to this day."

"The stout lady," said Ellery darkly. "Well, that may be as it may be, but there's the story. No magic now, eh, Your Honor? Just common sense. I shouldn't explain how I do these things; it disillusions people."

The two New Jersey lawyers laughed; but Bill was suddenly very serious. He gulped twice and then said in a formal voice, "Judge Menander, sir—"

"One moment, Mr. Angell." The old jurist leaned forward. "It seems to me, Mr. Queen, you've left something out. How about explaining away that weakness I pointed out some time ago? You worked on the 'assumption', you said, that Miss—may I call you Andrea, my dear?—that Andrea had told you the truth about the matches and so on. What right," he asked severely, "did you have to assume any such thing? I thought you work strictly by rule of established fact. If the young woman had told a lie, the entire structure of your solution would have collapsed."

"The legal mind," chuckled Ellery. "How I enjoy discussing these things with lawyers! Perfectly true, Judge. It would have collapsed. But it didn't, because Andrea told the truth. I knew she had told the truth when I reached the end of my mental journey."

"That's a bit over my head," said Pollinger, "How the devil could you have known that?"

Ellery patiently lit another cigaret. "Why should Andrea have lied? It could only have been because she herself had killed Gimball and meant to confuse the trail." He waved the fuming cigaret about. "But what did her lie, if it was a lie, lead to? It led to the guilt of Grosvenor Finch. How silly! For if she were the real criminal, she had originally framed Lucy Wilson for the crime! And where was Lucy Wilson? In prison, convicted of the crime. The frame-up of Lucy, then, had been successful from Andrea's point of view if Andrea were herself the criminal. Now when did she tell her lie which led me to the guilt of Finch? After Lucy Wilson's conviction! So I say: would she invalidate her successful frame-up of one person by then framing another person entirely? Unthinkable, of course. And even if in telling the lie she didn't know where it would lead, why should she lie at all if she had killed Gimball and framed Lucy? Her crime was safely committed; her victim, her living victim, was safely convicted. There would be utterly no point in a further confusion of the trial. So I knew that Andrea was telling the truth."

"I'll bet," said Andrea, "that you'd suspect your own father!"

"That was meant," grinned Ellery, "as a spiteful remark, but it turns out to be a shrewd guess. As a matter of fact, I investigated a crime some time ago in which that very thing happened: all the logic pointed to my father, Inspector Queen, as the criminal! Well, I had a time of it, you may be sure."

"What happened?" asked Judge Menander eagerly.

"That," said Ellery, "is another story."

"You're not finished with this one yet," said Pollinger with a certain humorous grimness. "I don't like to appear pernickety, but it seems to me if the fact that Finch knew about the insurance change was so vital to your solution, you haven't exactly shone, Queen. After all, you knew that Finch knew that from the very beginning of the case."

"Oh, Lord," groaned Ellery. "Why did I ever choose lawyers as an audience? Clever, Pollinger, very astute indeed. But you've missed the point. Finch's knowledge of the change of beneficiary had utterly no significance until the case with its various deductions had been completely developed. The fact meant nothing to me until I proved by logic that the criminal had to know of the beneficiary change. I couldn't know that the criminal had to know until I'd made all the preliminary deductions. The thing that told me that the criminal had to know of the beneficiary change was that the criminal knew of Gimball's double life. The thing that told me that the criminal knew of Gimball's double life was that he had deliberately framed Mrs. Wilson. The thing that told me that the criminal had framed Mrs. Wilson was that Mrs. Wilson was innocent because the criminal was a man. Without all those steps the final fact would have meant nothing."

"QED," said Bill hastily. "Swell. Great. Bravo. Judge Menander—?"

"What is it, young man?" said the old gentleman a little testily. "If you're worried about that insurance, I can promise you there will be no hitch in the proceedings. Your sister will be paid the full amount of the policy."

"No, no. Judge," stammered Bill, "It's not—"

"I don't want that money," said Lucy simply; she had stopped crying. "I wouldn't touch it for…" She shuddered.

"But, my dear child," protested Judge Menander, "you must take it. It's yours. It was the will of the deceased that you should have it."

Lucy's black eyes, shadowed and tired as they were, managed a sudden smile. "You mean it's mine—to do with as I wish?"

"Of course," he said gently.

"Then I give it," said Lucy, putting her arm about Andrea's slim shoulders, "to someone who, I think, is going to be related to me very soon… Will you accept it, Andrea, as a gift from me and… Joe?"

"Oh, Lucy!" cried Andrea, and then she began to weep.

"That's what I wanted to speak to you about, Judge," said Bill hastily; his cheeks were fiery. "I mean, Lucy's feeling that Andrea—you see, well, last week Andrea and I drove out one day to—well, sir," he managed to blurt at last as he took something out of his pocket, "here's the license. Will you please marry us?"

The Judge laughed. "I should be delighted to."

"Trite, trite," said Ellery gloomily. "Very unimaginative, Bill. That's what always happens. The hero marries the heroine and they live happily ever after. Do you know what marriage means? It means mortgages and warming bottles at two o'clock in the morning and commuting and all sorts of dreadful things that the author wisely neglects to mention."

"Nevertheless," said Bill with a nervous grin, "I'd like you to be my best man, Ellery. Andrea, too!"

"Ah," said Ellery. "Now that's different." He walked over to the leather sofa and stooped and raised Andrea's tearful face and kissed her resoundingly. "There! Isn't that the prerogative of best men? At least," he chuckled, dabbing tenderly at his lips with a handkerchief, "I've had my reward!"

ABOUT THE AUTHOR

ELLERY QUEEN was both a famous fictional detective and the pen name of two cousins born in Brooklyn in 1905. Created by Manfred B. Lee and Frederic Dannay as an entry in a mystery-writing contest, Ellery Queen is regarded by many as the definitive American whodunit celebrity. When their first novel, *The Roman Hat Mystery* (1929), became an immediate success, the cousins gave up their business careers and took to writing dozens of novels, hundreds of radio scripts and countless short stories about the gentleman detective and writer who shared an apartment on West 87th Street with his father, Inspector Queen of the NYPD. Dannay was said to have largely produced detailed outlines of the plots, clues and characters while Lee did most of the writing. As the success of Ellery Queen grew, the character's legacy continued through radio, television and film. In 1941, the cousins founded Ellery Queen's Mystery Magazine. Edited by Queen for more than forty years, the periodical is still considered one of the most influential crime fiction magazines in American history. Additionally, Queen edited a number of collections and anthologies, and his critical writings are the major works on the detective short story. Under their collective pseudonym, the cousins were given several Edgar awards by the Mystery Writers of America, including the 1960 Grand Master Award. Their novels are examples of the classic 'fair play' whodunit mystery of the Golden Age, where plot is always paramount. Manfred B. Lee, born Manford Lepofsky, died in 1971. Frederic Dannay, born Daniel Nathan, died in 1982.

CAN YOU SOLVE THESE OTHER MYSTERIES BEFORE ELLERY QUEEN DOES?

ELLERY QUEEN
There Was an Old Woman

ELLERY QUEEN
the Scarlet Letters

ELLERY QUEEN
the Murderer is a Fox

ELLERY QUEEN
the Four of Hearts

ELLERY QUEEN
the Finishing Stroke

ELLERY QUEEN
the Door Between

ELLERY QUEEN
the Devil to Pay

ELLERY QUEEN
Halfway House

ELLERY QUEEN
Face to Face

FOR NEWS ABOUT JABBERWOCKY BOOKS AND AUTHORS

Sign up for our newsletter*: http://eepurl.com/b84tDz
visit our website: awfulagent.com/ebooks
or follow us on twitter: @awfulagent

THANKS FOR READING!

Made in United States
Orlando, FL
25 August 2024

50724489R00161